AF491335

Copyright © 2020 Abby McCarthy

---

1.   http://www.byhangle.com/

Dedication:

For Katie,

I'm so glad you've fallen.

THE LAST GOODBYE

PROLOGUE

"There's still a chance. My lawyer says it's slim, but he thinks we have a shot." Even as he said the words, I didn't think he fully believed them. It was a fucking Hail Mary, and he knew it.

"I warned you, Linc. I told you, nothing good would come from you going with Alex."

"Lols, he's my brother. I couldn't let him go in there alone." His words rang hollow. I'd heard this before.

"Yes! Yes, you could have. Or you could've talked him out of it. You could've walked away. I told you it was stupid, and you shouldn't risk it. You could've done a lot of things. But you didn't. You put him first in front of our life together. Always. Everyone else always seems to come first."

"Lols. Love..." He looked heartbroken. He could see he was losing me.

"Don't." He put his hand up to the glass, and desperation filled his features. He could see my light dimming. He knew that this was real, that I was done. He couldn't make this right. It was too late.

If he could've touched me, I would've faltered. But the glass that separated us was a barrier he couldn't break. And for the first time, I was glad that he wasn't able to.

He watched as I clutched the phone to my chest. I was struggling. I wanted to break down and cry, but I was trying to be strong.

I took a deep breath, trying to prevent the quiver in my lip. I thought we had our whole lives together.

He gave me this look that willed me to put the phone back to my ear. I took a couple deep breaths and let a mask slip over my features. My chin no longer quivered. My eyes were suddenly reserved as I held the phone to my ear.

"Lola." Using my name, he begged me to forgive him, pleading with me to wait. My name on his lips implored that we were forever. It asked me to wait. It asked me to stay. It asked the impossible.

I cut him off, "Lincoln, I'm done. I can't. No—I just... I won't do this anymore." I hung the phone up, and like so many times when he'd said goodbye in the past, I said those same words back to him. "Goodbye, Linc."

"Lola, no. Don't do this," he yelled. I couldn't hear him through the thick plated glass, but I watched his lips move, and I couldn't bear the anguish. I had to turn and walk away for the last time. I couldn't watch the guards escort him away.

If I turned, he would see how completely gutted I was. He would see how badly I wanted to stay. But I was done letting my heart win out over my head. I hadn't gotten very far letting that lead. It was time to use my head. It was time to let go.

Chapter One

It was early. Too early for my alarm clock. The incessant buzzing wouldn't stop. Why, oh, why did they make these things start your day off with the most annoying sound? I slapped it lazily and did a roll/fall out of bed—the bed that's been empty for two years, nine months, and six days. Not that I'd been counting the days that Lincoln was gone, but today was the day that the manilla envelope sitting on the mantel explained that Lincoln was up for parole. Most wives in my situation would be happy that their husbands had a chance at parole. Then again, most wives would have visited their husbands in jail.

I untangled myself from my sheets that were still stuck around my ankles, just as Isabelle, purring loudly, rubbed against them. It was the only time of the day the cat was nice to me. She only ever warmed up to Linc.

"All right, Iz. I hear you."

I moved to the kitchen and sleepily grabbed a can of cat food from the cupboard. The coffee maker on an automatic timer went off, and my favorite drug, caffeine, began filling the small space with a rich aroma.

I filled the cat bowl and watched as Isabelle left my side and strutted straight to her bowl, forgetting I existed.

That figured.

I shook my head and grabbed my coffee mug from the metal dish strainer next to the sink. Sure, I had a dishwasher, but it was just me now. What did I need a big ole dishwasher for? After pouring my coffee, I grabbed my French vanilla flavored creamer and poured a healthy amount into my cup. It tasted divine. I inhaled the aroma like it was a drug, and it woke me up instantly.

I spent the next forty minutes getting ready for work. My hair was blown out. It was big, the way I liked it. The long thick black strands reached the middle of my back. My light hazel eyes were rimmed with black, and my eyeshadow was light, appropriate for office wear. I wore a subtle sheer lip gloss and used a bronzer, blush, and highlighter to contour my face. I dressed in a white blouse, a high-waisted black pencil skirt, and black pumps. This was my everyday polished look for work.

I moved to my jewelry box and grabbed a small pair of gold hoop earrings. My eyes briefly landed on my wedding ring. The pear-shaped diamond glinted against my jewelry, standing out as the nicest piece. I tried to keep my mind from going to Lincoln, but knowing what today was, it was hard.

What if he was released? How would I cope with that?

I shook my head and tried to rid the thoughts, reminding myself that he didn't have my phone number anymore. He didn't know where I lived. The only place he'd know to find me would be at my work, and there was a security guard at the door.

I took one final look in the mirror, accepting how put together I looked. I've always been grateful for my Spanish-Italian heritage. It gives me almost an exotic look, but today I thought about how my looks were what drew Lincoln to me. If I'd never met him...

No.

I needed to stop those thoughts and not continue to let my mind go there.

I threw on a thin black coat that cinched at the waist, grabbed my handbag, and keys, then locked the door behind me. Seconds later, I was on the elevator heading down to the first floor of my apartment and taking off down the street. The street was busy, as usual. People were too distracted on their phones to notice anyone around them. Not me. I was afraid of my phone today. I knew how resourceful he could be.

I boarded the L Train taking it to downtown Chicago. It's a twenty-minute ride from here and was always crowded. There were four seats open, so I hurriedly sat down in an empty one.

"Is this seat taken?" I looked up from my seat and saw an attractive hipster. He had a neatly trimmed beard, attractive glasses, and a tight man-bun. Even from down here, I could see how long his lashes were and the subtle pout to his lips.

"All yours," I replied, standing up so he could get to the window seat. There was no way I wanted to feel trapped with him on one side of me and the window on the other. That was the worst.

He sat down, and I did my best to not making eye contact. I didn't feel like talking. It seemed that these hipster types were always so friendly. I just wasn't up for it.

"So, are you on your way to work? That was a dumb question. Of course, you are. I mean, it's eight-fifteen on a Friday. Where else would you be going dressed like that?" He rambled.

"Mm-hmm," I answer non-committedly, hoping he'd get the hint.

My phone vibrated, making me jump and accidentally dropping it on the dirty train floor. I reached down to grab it and smacked my head right into the hipster.

"Ouch,'" I said at the same time he said, "Ow."

I sat up and rubbed my temple.

He handed me my phone, and for the second time, I thought that he was really attractive, almost pretty.

My phone vibrated again, and I looked down, seeing Ty flash across the screen. I let out a sigh. Ty is Lincoln's brother, whom I swore to secrecy with my phone number and address. He was the only person from my life with Lincoln that I continued to stay in contact with. No one else understood why I had to let Linc go. I couldn't handle the judgment. As if me finally being finished with my con of a husband was so absurd.

I looked over at the man next to me. It was rude taking a call on the train, but I answered anyway.

"Hey, Ty."

"Hi, Honey. You doing okay?"

"Yeah, I'm all right. Trying to keep my mind off things."

"I talked to Ma. She thinks it's going to happen. Said there's no reason he won't get released."

I nodded and foolishly realized that he couldn't see me. "Remember, you promised, Ty."

"Are you sure this is what you really want? He loves you."

I could feel my throat getting tight. I'd done so well by not crying in so long.

"Ty," I sighed out his name.

"All right, I just think..."

"I'm hanging up now," I said, almost croaking that out.

"Okay. Listen, I'll text you when I know for sure."

"Bye, Ty." I tapped end without waiting for a response. It all felt too overwhelming.

I slid my phone into my purse and glanced at the man next to me. His eyes met mine, "Was that your boyfriend?"

It was a little presumptuous for him to ask the question, but I shook my head no.

"I'm sorry, it just sounds like you're having a rough morning?"

"You have no idea," I responded.

"Look on the bright side. The sun's shining."

I looked out the window and noted it was going to be a beautiful day. "You're right, and it's a nice day."

"Sorry, I don't know you. You don't know me. Maybe you think all this stranger talking to you business is a bit much, but I can't really help it, see my mom's a hippie."

I wondered briefly what in the world he was going on about.

"Anyway, she taught me that when things seem bad, look around you for the good. The sun shining is always good."

I didn't know this man, but I admired the way he openly shared.

"What's your name?" I asked, which I never do.

His face softened, and there were small creases around his mouth as he smiled. "My name is Jet. What's yours?"

The smallest amount of guilt passed through me, and I pushed it aside. "Jet?" I asked because it was a peculiar name.

"Like I said, mom was a hippie, and Dad, well, Dad did the seventies. You know, I usually save this story for the first date." He said with levity to his voice, then studied me for a second. "What do you say?"

He talked rapidly, leaving me confused about what he was asking. My name, right? "Oh, sorry. I'm Lola."

"Well, Lola, what do you say? Can I tell you all about how a hippie and a Travolta-wannabe made a Jet?"

"Oh," I said, shocked. I was not picking up on the fact he was flirting at all. I rubbed my ring finger where my ring used to be, unsure of how I was feeling.

"Not the dreaded, 'oh.'"

"I'm sorry, Jet. You seem like a really nice guy, but I'm—well—I'm complicated."

"I'll tell you what? When you un-complicate things, call me."

He handed me his card, and it surprised me to see he was an audio engineer for Sound Machine Recording Studio.

"Sound Machine, huh? I'm in accounting at Black Label." I worked for a music label and often paid invoices from Sound Machine.

"Small world. See how much we already have in common?" Gosh, he was charming. Something about his carefree nature put me at ease.

The train stopped, and we all moved slightly forward as it lost momentum. "Well, this is me. I hope you'll call me when life gets less complicated." He tilted his head to the side, pondering his next words as I stood to let him out. "Come on, Lola, one date."

I had the smallest flutter low in my belly at Jet, saying my name. I shook my head, "We'll see. Nice to meet you. Oh, and Jet, you enjoy that sunshine."

"The sunshine's not what brightened my day." He left, and I found myself smiling. I usually shot men down right away, but something about how he shared so freely left me feeling intrigued. I could feel the lingering guilt that wanted to return full-force. It would consume my thoughts if I let it, and I couldn't do that. It had been years; long, hard years. I briefly wondered what it had been like for Lincoln, and I hated that my mind traveled there *again*. I usually did a good job of keeping my mind off of him, but today it seemed impossible. I tried to think of Jet and his carefree demeanor, but it was useless. No matter where I told my thoughts to go, they eventually led directly to Lincoln.

I got off at Union Station, and the bustle of people, like always, astounded me. I placed Jet's card in my purse and headed to the office, which was on the forty-seventh floor of the Hancock Building. The street seemed busier than usual at this hour. I walked down Michigan Ave, and once I got to the Hancock Building, I greeted Richard, the middle-aged but handsome doorman.

He had a few specks of grey in his hair but looked polished. He was clean-shaven, had great lips, and an even better smile. I wasn't interested in him, but I could appreciate his attractiveness.

"Morning, Mrs. Paige."

"Hey, Richard. How's Sam doing?" Sam was Richard's wife, who just pushed out an eleven-pound baby.

"She's doing great, exhausted but good. She's hardly sleeping because Logan seems to be up every hour to eat, but besides that, she's great. You should come by to meet him. I'm sure Sam would love that."

I'd only met Sam a few times, but every time I did, I thought she seemed incredibly kind and welcoming. One thing I noticed immediately was the way she loved her husband. It was evident in every single look she gave him. I knew that look. It was how I looked at Linc.

"I think that's a great idea, but I'll give her a little more time. I'm betting if I just pushed out a three-month-old sized baby I'd want to wait until I had a handle on everything before I had a ton of visitors."

"Good point," he said with a smile. "I'll tell her you asked about her. You have a great day."

"Thanks, you too."

Using my key card, I headed up the elevator, past Tiffany, our receptionist, and to my small office. I did this with a smile on my face thinking the second I had a little bit of extra money, I would buy Logan some super cute boy clothes.

The sun was shining so brightly into my office that I needed to close the blinds. I'd never be able to get any work done if I didn't. As I moved to do so, I noticed the tumultuous waves on Lake Michigan today. *Tumultuous*, now there's a feeling I could relate to.

My workday passed like every other day. I was at my computer, with the occasional phone call asking for receipts and invoices. It flew by, like usual, and I was completely immersed in work all day.

On the way home, I thought about my encounter with Jet. He seemed so much easier going than Linc. What would it be like to date someone as carefree as him? I waited for guilt to course through me, but it didn't. Instead, I realized that I hadn't checked my phone all day. How could I not check? It was probably my mind's way of trying to protect me.

Sitting on the L Train, I pulled out my phone. I needed to know one way or another if Lincoln was getting out. I closed my eyes before looking and took a deep breath. *Come on, Lola. You can do this. Once you find out the hearing results, today will be no different from any other day. He won't know where *you live. It'll be okay.* I told myself this lie because I wanted to believe it. Lincoln was and always would be resourceful. I hit the circle with Ty's face on it.

Ty: Call me!

Ty: Don't ignore me, girl!

Ty: All right, I get it. You don't want to talk.

Ty: They paroled him.

Ty: Did you read this yet?

Ty: I said Lincoln's free.

There it was, in bold letters.

He's free.

Chapter Two Past

I watched as Ellie chatted with Camille and Erin. Ellie wanted to be a part of their clique for as long as I could remember. I never cared the way she did. I looked at Camille with her blonde highlights and shorts that were way too short. She wore a green shirt with cap sleeves and buttons down the middle, stopping mid-belly and tying neatly in a little bow. Erin dressed a little more modest in a jean skirt with jewels on the back pockets and a black tank top. Ellie tried to dress like them and fit in, but she never quite hit the same mark of desperation. She was dressed similarly, but it didn't quite look like she was trying as hard to fit in.

We were at a home football game. There was no need to go all out. We've seen these kids practically our entire lives. I frankly couldn't care less about the boys in our school. They're all the same. They eat, sleep, and breathe football. It's not that I'm not interested in boys or anything. It's just that the ones at my school annoy the hell out of me.

I was not dressed like I was trying to pick up a boy. I was dressed the way I wanted to be: comfortably me. I was wearing my favorite Green Day tee, cut-off jean shorts, and my Chuck Taylors. Everything about my outfit screamed Lola.

I listened as Camille went on and on about how Braxton Tillerson was so hot and how she was going to wait for him after the game was over. I wanted to bang my head against the wall.

"Hey, Ellie. I'm going to go to the concession stand. Do you want anything?" I asked, not wanting to stand there a moment longer.

"You're going to eat?" Camille asked before I got a chance to hear if Ellie wanted anything.

"Well, yeah," I responded, but felt like saying, 'duh.'

"What if you get food on you or a hot guy sees you?"

"Um, since when is it uncool to eat?" I questioned.

"Hello, we're at a football game! This is prime guy-time." Camille looked at me like she couldn't believe what I was saying.

I looked at Ellie, who gave me a sympathetic look.

"I'll find you," I said to Ellie.

"Thanks," she responded with a guilty look in her eyes. She knew that these girls were superficial, but she also knew that they were high on the social food chain. Every teenage girl knew that you needed to be "in" with the popular crowd if you wanted to be popular. This was one place, Ellie and I differed.

I left the group, relieved to be away from them, and walked over to our concession stand. There were so many people in line that I couldn't see the front of it. It was too crowded. Across the field, the away team's concession stand looked far less crowded, as it should be since they had fewer people in the stands.

Not giving a crap about any of that, I decided to cross into enemy territory and walked halfway around the field to the not-as-popular stand. The thinning crowds were a welcome reprieve. There were only two people ahead of me. I waited patiently, thinking about how stupid it was to give a crap about eating here.

"Damn," I heard a guy say behind me, drawing out the words.

I chanced a look, ready to glare and saw another guy smack who, I was guessing, was the 'damn' upside the head, then murmured, "Shut up."

"Sorry about that," the smacker said. I sucked in a breath. Everything I had felt about boys and football games went out the window. My eyes raked over him. He was wearing black running shoes, black sweats, and a black fitted tank top. He was built—not like a high schooler—but like he'd been out of school for a while, and he was more man than boy. I had to look up to fully take him in. He was huge. His jaw was angular, bottom lip fuller than the top, and his eyes were dark. He was wearing a Cubs hat, so I couldn't quite make out his hair color. He was gorgeous. Suddenly, I felt like Camille and her posse, wanting to pant after a boy. But that wasn't exactly right. I didn't think anyone could describe him as a boy.

I attempted to say something but snapped my mouth shut then turned back around. *God, kill me now!* He was so hot. I felt tongue-tied, which wasn't like me at all.

I waited patiently to be the next in line when I saw Mr. Morris working the counter. All throughout high school, his son and I were in each other's homeroom, and our lockers were next to each other.

"Hey, Lola."

"Hey, Mr. Morris. How are you doing tonight? Busy?"

"I'm good. Be better if my boy wasn't sitting on the sidelines while North hands it to us." I looked back at the scoreboard and meant to check the score but became caught in the hot guy's gaze. I looked away again, wondering why this boy who was so freaking hot, was checking me out.

"Wow, we're losing badly," I said to Mr. Morris.

With an annoyed head nod, he asked, "What can I get for you, Honey?"

"I'll have a soft pretzel, a sprite, and some skittles."

"Cheese or mustard?"

"Cheese, please."

"Be back in a sec." He smiled at me, then turned and went about getting my food.

"Hey," the tall guy stood next to me and leaned against the counter.

I sucked in a deep breath. He was that beautiful.

"Hi," I managed to respond.

"Sorry about a second ago. Alex can be a jackass."

"Hey," the boy I now knew as Alex said.

"Ignore him. He's my younger brother, and sometimes he has no manners."

I looked back at Alex and was surprised that they we're brothers because Alex was black, and this guy wasn't.

"You're brothers?" I asked, surprised I could form a coherent question.

"Well, we're not from the same womb or anything, but yeah."

"Well, nice to meet you," I looked away from him and to my purse to take out money to pay.

"Lincoln," the guy standing next to me said.

"Pardon?"

"My name's Lincoln, and you're Lola?"

"I'm Lola," I confirmed.

Mr. Morris returned with my goodies. "That'll be six-fifty."

I moved to hand Mr. Morris, the twenty I dugout. "Here, let me." Lincoln handed Mr. Morris money before I got a chance to.

"I can't let you do that."

"You can. Think of it like I'm investing."

Mr. Morris gave Lincoln his change, while I grabbed my food and moved away from the window so Alex and Lincoln could order.

"Grab me a Coke, would you?" Lincoln asked Alex, moving closer to me.

"All right, Lincoln, how do you figure buying me snacks is investing?" I finally asked.

"Well, for starters, it wouldn't be as good of a how-we-met-story if I just eavesdropped your name and let you walk away. See, I'm hoping since I bought your goodies, I can bribe you into letting me get to know you."

I smiled shyly and was not even sure what to say. I never got stupid around guys. Never.

Alex walked over to where we were standing and handed Lincoln his Coke. "Thanks. I'll catch up with you in a bit, yeah?" Lincoln lifted his head to Alex.

"Yeah, bro," Alex said and ran to catch up with a group of guys.

"Do you want to sit for a few? So you can eat," Lincoln asked.

"All right." I followed him to a grassy area against the fence, a neutral territory. A few future football players, who may have been around the age of five, if I had to guess, were tossing a ball back and forth and doing it rather clumsily.

I noticed how long Lincoln's legs were next to mine, and wondered if they were muscular. Geez, who had I suddenly been replaced with? Sure, I'd been attracted to boys before, but not like this. I surely hadn't wondered what their legs were like. *Oh, I bet his calves were thick and muscular. I bet his chest was...* Oh, my God, I had to stop. I picked a piece of my pretzel off and wondered if I should eat it.

Holy fuck, what was happening to me? Were my palms sweating? Do palms sweat? Stop. Be calm. Say something.

"Um, so Lincoln. Do you go to North?" I asked because I didn't recognize him.

"Guilty. I'm a senior. What about you?"

"I'm a sophomore." I took a bite of my pretzel but not before dipping it into cheese.

"Sixteen yet?"

"Not until the Summer. I'm one of the youngest in my grade. I hate it. I think everyone will be driving before me."

"Fifteen." I watched as he shook his head in disbelief. "I'm the opposite of you. I turned eighteen right before school started."

"Do you have plans, for you know, after?" I asked, and a thrill chased up my spine because his leg brushed against mine.

"Going to be Army proud. Already signed the papers."

"Oh." I didn't know why I felt so let down by that. Maybe it was because I already figured out that he was a lot older than me and now knew he'd be leaving.

"How about you? What do you like?"

"I like music and numbers."

"Numbers, huh?"

"Math geek," I admitted. I made sure he knew exactly who I was. I might've been nervous, but I would never pretend to be someone I wasn't.

"There's nothing geeky about you, babe."

My heart fluttered. *He called me babe.* I took another bite of my pretzel, too nervous to do much else. I wanted to pretend that he didn't affect me. I was trying to play it cool.

"Not into the game?" he asked.

"Not really. I came with my best friend," I answered once I cleared the pretzel from my mouth. I was beginning to see Camille's logic in not eating. Ugh!

"Where's she?"

"I left her to get snacks. She's with a group of girls that are just, I don't know, *not me.*" I shrugged then continued. "You're not watching the game either," I accused.

"My brother, Trey, is the quarterback."

"So, he's the one who is basically demolishing us."

"That'd be him."

"Isn't he going to be mad if he looks up and you're not there?"

"I'll watch in a few, but we're winning forty-two zip. They'll probably take him out and let some other guys get a chance to whoop you."

"Gee, thanks."

"Sorry, not really a stretch there."

We chatted back and forth for a few more minutes, and the most obvious question came out. "So, Lola, are you dating anyone?"

Gosh, maybe this was why I didn't really talk to guys. I felt dumb when he asked me this. "My Dad is super strict. He doesn't want me to date until I'm sixteen." There it was out there.

"How about you? Do you have a girlfriend?" *Kill me now.*

"You think I'd be sitting here talking to the prettiest girl between both damn schools if I had a girlfriend?"

Oh, my God.

"I'd hope not." It felt intense. He felt intense. More so than I was used to. I liked it, though.

"Do you always do what your dad says?"

"Not always," I said even though that wasn't entirely true. My extent of not doing what he said was staying up late and using the phone secretly so I could talk to Ellie.

I watched as he licked his lips after taking a sip of his coke. Was it getting hotter outside?

"What's your dad like?"

That question made me pause. Well, either he was trying to get to know me or trying to find out what he could get away with.

"He's the best. His parents immigrated here from Spain, and I think since they did, he's sometimes old school."

"What's he do for a living?"

All right, I kind of loved that he seemed genuinely interested in my family.

"My Dad's a carpenter. He has his own business. He works a lot, and so my mom stays home."

"Any brothers or sisters?"

"Nope, I'm an only child."

"So, you have two brothers?" I asked, taking the attention from me.

"Three, actually. Do you speak Spanish at all?" He brought the conversation right back to me, and I got the feeling that he wasn't one hundred percent comfortable talking about himself.

"Kind of. I also speak a little Italian. My mom's a hundred percent Italian. I have so many cousins you wouldn't believe what Christmas Eve is like. My aunt Connie has five boys ranging from nine to nineteen. They all speak Italian. I think since my aunt also married Italian, they ingrain it into them. My parents don't really do that. I've just picked some up here and there."

"Say something to me in Italian."

"Qualcosa."

"What's that mean?"

"Something." I laughed and smiled when he laughed too. God, the way his face lit up. I watched as his face turned from smiling to something more. His eyes seem to change, and the playful look transformed in a way I wasn't sure I'd ever been looked at before.

"You're really beautiful. Especially when you laugh."

I stupidly asked, "I am?"

His eyes squinted on me, "You really don't know?"

"Penso che to sia anche bello."

"What's that mean?" he asked.

I looked at him shyly and wouldn't admit what it meant, even though it meant: 'I think you're beautiful too.'

He bumped me with his knee. "Tell me."

I fake zip-seal my lips shut just as I heard my name called.

"Lola!" Ellie called my name a second time as she approached us. "Hey, I was looking for you. Where have you been? Who's he?" Ellie fired question after question.

"Sorry, Elle. I guess I got distracted." I smiled at Lincoln conspiratorially, like we were in on some giant secret that only the two of us knew about. "This is my," I paused, unsure of what to call him, a friend just didn't seem right, "Lincoln." It just slipped out that way.

"That's right. I'm her Lincoln, and you are?" he asked cheekily.

"This is my best friend, Ellie. Ellie, meet Lincoln."

"Um, hey," Ellie answered in a way that was marred with confusion. "How long were you gone? Yeesh," she mumbled. "I saved you a spot on the bleachers. Are you coming?"

I shot Ellie a look, communicating that I really didn't want to.

"Camille and Erin are waiting on us." God, I couldn't stand those girls, but I really shouldn't leave Ellie all by herself.

I stood, and Lincoln followed suit. I watched Ellie's eyes as they lit up when she finally noticed all that was Lincoln.

"I should get going," I said to Lincoln even though it was the last thing I really wanted to do.

I could tell he read my indecision on what to do and saved me by saying, "Yeah, I better go too. If I leave Alex on his own for too long, he's bound to get into trouble. I need your number, though."

"Your dad," Ellie hissed like she thought she needed to remind me.

I was embarrassed, and I watched Lincoln's face change again. "Give me yours," I quickly added.

"Shit, I don't have anything to write with."

"I have a cell," Ellie interrupted, "You can give it to me, and she'll get it as soon as we have something to write with."

He rattled off his number to Ellie then turned to me. "I probably won't be available until after eleven. I have to drive the guys around after the game. Do you think you can call me after he's asleep?" He asked hopefully.

I nodded my head enthusiastically, all while feeling Ellie's astonished gaze at my back. Lincoln did something else that completely shocked me. He leaned down and cupped the side of my face. I felt like he was going to kiss me. He was so close, just staring or memorizing, I wasn't quite sure.

"So damn beautiful," he whispered. He meant for only me to hear, but Ellie heard it too and let out a soft gasp. He turned and jogged to a group of guys, and I watched after him as he did. Somehow, the last several minutes felt life altering, and I knew I'd never be the same.

Chapter Three Past

"I wanted to kiss you."

"I wanted you to." I couldn't believe I just admitted that. I was finishing a two-hour conversation with Lincoln. It was almost two in the morning, and I had Confirmation classes in the morning. Over the last few weeks, nearly every night, I'd been sneaking calls in with Lincoln.

"God," he groaned, "I wish you were older. I wish I could show up tomorrow and take you out."

"I do too."

"Will you call me tomorrow night?" he asked.

"I will."

"I'll be waiting. Goodnight, beautiful."

"Night, Linc."

I sleepily hung up and snuck the cordless phone back into the cradle. Some of my friends had cell phones, but my parents would never go for it. I laid down on my bed and looked at my room. My walls were a light shade of purple that Dad painted a few years ago. I had covered up a lot of the floral border with music posters, making my room feel like I was not quite old enough to date yet. It felt like I was in an in-between stage. I didn't want to be in-between any longer.

After my phone call with Lincoln, I didn't feel like my room was me anymore. I mean, it was, but somehow I felt different. I didn't feel like a kid at all. I felt like I was becoming a woman, one who was completely taken with Lincoln. After every call, I felt a little changed, a little less like I was, and a little more like the me I was becoming. I felt my self-confidence rising, and I wanted nothing more than to spend time with him.

In the morning, I went to my class with sleep-deprived bleary eyes. When I came home, I worked on my room. I wanted it to reflect me. I asked my Mom how to take off the wallpaper, and she helped me remove the border.

"What made you decide to do this?" Mom asked as we stared at my torn up wall. Small pieces of paper were still lying on my hardwood floor. We somehow managed to get a few strips on my yellow and white plush carpet that my canopy bed sat on top of.

"I feel like I really want my room to reflect me. I'm not really into flowers any longer if you know what I mean."

"I do. Your bed and dresser are antiques, though, so I don't want you to change them but think about the color you want for your walls, and I'll talk Dad into painting it. I'm not sure he'll go for new bedding yet, but maybe I can talk him into an early Christmas present from Santa."

I hugged Mom tightly. Her dark curls with wiry silver strands throughout brushed against my face. "I'd love that, Mom."

"I know you want to grow up, but don't do it too fast." Mom kissed me on my forehead then left me to finish cleaning up the mess. I wanted to call Lincoln and tell him what Mom and I did. I was excited, and I wanted to share it with him. I didn't do it, though. Instead, I called my BFF.

"Ellie, Hey!" I said as soon as she picked up.

"So, did you guys talk again last night? What happened?" She quickly rushed out before saying hello back. I recounted the parts of our conversation I was willing to share with Ellie. She was our cheerleader.

There were also parts I wouldn't share. I didn't tell Ellie how Lincoln became a foster child. I didn't tell her that he had three brothers he considered family even though they were also foster kids. I didn't tell her how he shared that his life had been pretty messed up until he was placed with Marlene. I also kept it to myself that he shared he started lifting weights to defend himself and his brothers. What I did tell her was that he admitted he wanted to kiss me, and I told him I wanted him to.

"Oh my gosh!" She exclaimed at this news. "You so like him, like a ton."

"I do. I don't know what it is about him. I swear he's all I ever think about."

"You mean besides the fact that he's hot!"

"It's different. It's the way he talks to me. I feel like he wants to know everything about me."

"Well, yeah. You're awesome."

"Ellie. I've seen him once. Already it feels like he's so..." I paused, trying to come up with the right word for how I'd describe how he feels to me.

"Go on." Ellie urged.

"He's so everything."

Ellie sighed. "We have to find a way for you two to meet up. Do you think your dad will let you go to the mall if I can get my Mom to drive us?"

"Maybe? Mom and I just took my border down in my room. I can tell her I want to window shop for bedroom ideas."

Ellie began squealing. "Why didn't you tell me you were working on your room? You know I love decorating. Can I help please?"

I laughed, "Of course."

"Okay, hang on. Let me ask my Mom. Mom!" I heard her yell for Mrs. Frank. "Can you bring Lola and me to the mall if Lola's parents say it's okay?"

I couldn't hear the rest of the exchange between Mrs. Frank and Ellie. A minute later, Ellie got on the line. "Yes! Mom said, okay!"

"I'll talk to them and call you right back." I hung up with Ellie, and with the phone cradled in my hand, I moved to the kitchen where dad was just coming in from what I presumed was a side job. He was wearing overalls and had a tape measure attached to the front, and he smelled like sawdust. Mom was pouring a cup of coffee. She usually drank several pots a day. "Hey, Daddy." I approached, reached up, and kissed him on the cheek.

"Lola, how was Confirmation Class?"

"Awesome," I joked, "I feel very prepared to be Confirmed."

Dad gave me a look. You know the look, the kind that says: I'm not amused.

"I just got off the phone with Ellie, and her Mom offered to bring us to the mall. Can I go?" My eyes screamed, 'please.'

"Did you finish cleaning up in your room?" Mom asked, referring to the tiny pieces of wallpaper.

"Almost, but I can do it in seconds."

"Get that done, and as long as your father says all right, I don't see why not," Mom answered.

Dad fished out his wallet from his back pocket, opened it, and pulled out a ten-dollar bill handing it to me. I quickly snatched it up, squealed out a thank you, and ran back upstairs with the phone clutched to my chest.

I called Ellie, and she was so excited, but we were quick on the phone, so I could call Lincoln.

It rang three times, and there was a sweet woman's voice on the other end, "Hello."

"Hi, is Lincoln there."

"Who's calling?" She was rather abrupt with the way she asked. It intimidated me.

"Um, it's Lola."

"The one he's staying up all hours of the night talking to?"

"I guess I'm guilty of that."

"Girl, Alex cannot stop teasing him about you," she sighed, "The boys are in the basement working out. Hang on."

I waited, and a few minutes later, Lincoln answered, "Lola?"

"Hey, I don't have much time, but Ellie and I are going to the mall, and I wondered if you could meet us there."

"When are you going?" His voice, even though it had only been hours since I heard it last, sent shivers down my spine.

"We'll probably be there in like a half an hour."

"Meet me by Angelo's in the food court."

"I'll see you soon." I nearly whispered.

"Yeah," he answered, and I was so excited I nearly forgot to say goodbye as I raced around my room to clean up so I could go.

HE WAS RELAXING BACK in a chair, his long legs were stretched out, as we approached. Various smells of all different food types wafted through the air. I smelled Chinese, Italian, Subway, and Taco Bell. The mix of scents, which generally was gross to me, faded away as I took him in. He seemed even more attractive today.

"Damn," Ellie whispered.

"I know," I muttered under my breath.

When he noticed me, his body language changed. He shifted in his seat, and it appeared that at the last second, he decided to stand.

"Lola, hey."

"Hi, Lincoln. Do you remember my friend Ellie?"

"'Sup," he said with a chin lift. Typical male. "So, do you ladies want to eat something first, or do you have major shopping to do?"

Ellie answered before I got a chance to, "Why don't you two get something to eat. I have a bedroom to start pre-decorating?"

"Pre?" I asked.

"Well, I'm not buying anything today. I'm mentally planning."

"Thanks, Elle." My girl! Making it so I could have a date with Lincoln.

"Cool of you." Lincoln grabbed my hand and threaded our fingers together as Ellie waved goodbye. His touch sent tingles through my body, making my heart beat wildly.

"Meet me by the water fountain in an hour and a half, okay?" Ellie called, walking backward.

I looked at my watch, "I'll see you then."

"So, are you hungry?" Lincoln asked.

"Not really. You?"

"I just worked out. I can always eat. But I don't have that much time with you, so how about I eat later?"

"All right, so what do you want to do then?" I was more nervous than I should be.

Picking up on my nervousness, Lincoln suggested, "How about we each pick a store that will let the other know something about them."

"I like that. And I know the exact store to show you."

I led Lincoln away from the food court and brought him into Sam Goody's. I headed straight to my favorite CD's. I handed him The Clash, then moved to The Ramones and, more recently, Green Day and Beastie Boys. He grabbed the Beastie Boys cd from me, "I know this one, but you'll have to teach me the rest."

"How about you? What do you like?"

"I like a little of everything." He grabbed Eminem, then Usher.

"Really?" I was surprised our music tastes were so off.

"How about this one?" He handed me Linkin Park.

I smiled, "I think we can agree on Linkin Park."

"Linkin Park is good, but Usher is sexy. Your music is not sexy. *You got it, you got it bad.*" he sang and moved his body in a way that I could only describe as pure sex.

My eyes became hooded just as Nine Inch Nails' Closer began to play on the store's speakers.

"My music can be sexy too. Just listen to this song," I said.

Lincoln moved behind me and wrapped his arms around me. His body was close, but he left an acceptable distance as he softly sang the lyrics in my ear, "*Help me, I broke apart my insides. Help me, I've got no soul to sell. Help me, the only thing that works for me. Help me get away from myself.*" He stopped singing, and although the next line that Trent Reznor sang was far dirtier, even if it was the censored version, what Lincoln sang did far more for me. I felt high off of his words.

He held me while the rest of the song played, and the entire time, I thought about what it would be like if he just turned and kissed me right there in the aisle.

We left the store, and he stopped me in front of the closed Army recruiter's office. Signs that read, '*Be all that you can be*' were displayed all over the windows.

It reminded me that he would be leaving. It also made me think of 9/11 and all our country endured in the short year since it happened.

"Where were you when it happened?" I asked, and he knew what I was talking about. Everyone knew.

"I'd like to say I was in class, but I wasn't. I'd been picked up by the cops. I was in a shit foster home. The old man tried to put his hands on me, so I fought back and took off. I'd only been on the streets for a day before I got picked up. When 9/11 happened, I was in a holding cell. What about you?"

"Well, nothing like that at all. I was at home, lying in bed with horrible cramps." I felt my face turn red from embarrassment.

"None of that. You don't ever need to be embarrassed with me." Lincoln gave me a gentle shove teasing me.

"So, the Army." I stopped talking, unsure of what to say next.

"I was in that cell and kept thinking I was trapped, and there was real shit going on. My whole life, I'd felt trapped. I just wanted to do the right thing and be the man I wanted to be, but I kept feeling like life's B.S. was getting in my way. Seeing the destruction of those planes crashing into buildings, I felt like there was something worth fighting for. All those lives lost for no good reason made me want to do something. Something real that if I made it through high school, I could join and make a difference. Does that make sense to you?"

"Yeah, it does," I paused, thinking how amazing he was. He was so young and had been through so much, yet he was thinking about others and how he could help. I then asked a question that was plaguing me, "Lincoln?"

"Yeah?"

"What are we starting here? Because it feels like we're starting something and it won't last."

"You're right. It feels big. It feels like we can't let anything get in our way."

"Yes." The word slipped past my lips. I know he didn't ask a question, but everything about what he said felt right. His words ran a pitter-patter all over my already rapidly beating heart.

Lincoln grabbed my hand and led me down an adjoining hallway. He pressed me against the concrete wall. For a moment, he stared into my eyes, reminding me of the way he looked at me at the football game. I felt the power behind it. It felt like he was searing me to the spot and looking into my soul. I almost wanted to look away because it was filled with so much. Never in my life had someone said so much to me without saying a thing.

His lips brushed mine, feeling soft and tender. It was an innocent and sweet kiss. He began to pull away, then gently sucked my top lip into his mouth. It wasn't lust-filled. It was something different. It was the perfect start to something bigger than the both of us.

Chapter Four

I held the phone to my ear, "Come, on Ty. Pick up." It had been two days, and I hadn't heard from him. He ignored my text yesterday, which wasn't like him at all, and he didn't call me last night like he usually did.

His voicemail picked up.

Dammit.

I hung up the phone and redialed. "You can't ignore me, Ty." All right, again, I was talking to a ringing phone, but he couldn't ignore me forever. I knew it was only eight-fifteen in the morning, and he was probably still sleeping, but I needed to know.

"Shit, Lola?" Ty's sleepy voice finally answered.

"I need to see you. Can we meet?"

"Hold on." I heard a door open, then close.

"Iz, leave me alone. Shoo." I tried to bat away the cat from hell, which was no use. She began standing up against my legs. I shoved her away. "Go play with something else. I'm not your toy. Shoo!" She swiped my toes as I tried to walk away from her. "Ouch, you little fucker." Iz continued her assault. I heard Ty's laughter on the other end of the phone.

"Don't laugh. I hate this thing."

"It's not a thing Lola, it's a cat." Ty's hushed voice held amusement, and only then did I realize that he was speaking in a hushed tone.

"Where have you been? Why haven't you called me?"

"Why do you think?" Ty answered.

"Is he there now?" I asked in a rush. I didn't think he'd be at Ty's house. I figured he'd be at Marlene's, not Ty's.

"Yes, he's on my couch, and I wouldn't be surprised if he's up now, seeing as you wouldn't quit ringing me."

"Well, I wouldn't have kept *ringing* you if you'd picked up the phone and actually called me." I released a breath in a huff. "How is he?" I told myself I didn't care, but I needed to know. He was my life for so long. I just needed to know.

"Look, Lola, you know how he is. He's heartbroken that you weren't there. So, he's on my couch sleeping, trying to figure out if there's a way to fix this. He wants to see you."

God, that hurt. It hurt to know he was in pain, but I had to be strong. I'd done a well enough job staying away while he was incarcerated. But knowing he was twenty minutes away on Ty's couch felt like a stab to the gut. The urge to go to him was strong, and I gripped the counter to hold myself in place.

"You know, I can't do that."

"Yeah, well, I never signed on to be the guy in between the two of you."

"You promised you wouldn't tell him where I moved." I rushed out in desperation.

"And I'll keep that promise, but you know Lincoln. The man's resourceful. Nothing ever stops him."

I closed my eyes for a brief moment, thinking of how resourceful he was. "Yes, Ty. Part of that is why he got himself into this mess."

"You know it's more than that. He did that for Alex. Not saying I agree with how he went about it, but the man is loyal."

"What about his loyalty to me?" I caught myself getting angry. "You know what, never mind. Just don't tell him where I am. I'm sorry I called. I was just..." before I got a chance to say 'worried,' a few tears I held back slipped free, and the burn in the back of my throat escaped, letting out a muffled sob.

"Shit, Darling. No, don't cry. I'm sorry. I should've found the time to call you. You have nothing to apologize for."

"I'm going to go, Ty."

"Sweetie," he said gently.

"No, it's okay. I should've waited for you to call. God, I can't believe after this long I still get tore up."

"It's because you love him, and he loves you."

"It doesn't mean we should be together."

I hung up before I admitted anything else. It felt like I betrayed myself somehow and that I wasn't as strong as I should've been.

I needed the day to slip by, so I logged onto my computer and got lost in a project I'd been working on in my spare time for work. It was a good distraction. I was always grateful for the way numbers could suck me in. I needed to keep my mind occupied. When I wasn't busy, my mind would move to Lincoln, and I needed that to be a Lincoln free-zone.

Who was I fooling? That didn't seem possible.

Chapter Five Past

"What are we doing here?" I asked, staring at the empty beach parking lot. It was an unseasonably warm day, but it had been cold lately. Too cold for the beach, that was for sure.

"You'll see. You sure don't have a ton of patience," Lincoln laughed. "Come on."

He opened his door, and I sat and waited for him to come around to open mine.

Grabbing my hand, he walked me down a path in a small wooded area headed towards Lake Michigan. I smelled damp soil as we walked past a large oak tree. I heard seagulls in the distance, which made me think the lake would be just ahead. I'd been to this park dozens of times, but as we traveled on, I marveled at how different this path was to others. Since this park was one of the largest parks along the beach, most of the paths were paved or wide and worn from overuse. This path was narrowing more and more, and the weeds and grass were so high it would often hit my jean covered knees. We came to a few boulders about four or five feet tall and stacked on one another.

"Do you want me to go up first, or do you want me to stay behind and spot you?" He asked as we stood in front of the boulders deciding on the best course of action.

"This isn't the rope in gym class. I'll be fine."

"Okay, then." Linc quickly went up the first two boulders with ease. He was also way taller than me, so it was much easier for him. It took a few tries, but I managed to climb it by grabbing hold of a crack on the boulder on top, then pulled myself up.

"Good. The next few are easier."

He was right. I was able to climb the next few boulders without any real issues. Finally, we reached the end, and I was mesmerized. A small blanket and picnic basket was set out on the large stone boulder that had the best darn view of Lake Michigan I had ever seen. I hadn't even realized we were up this high. We must have been about fifteen feet above the water. The stone we were on was actually two large pieces next to each other, so it was about ten feet wide.

"This is amazing," I said, stepping a little closer to the edge to get a better look. From here, it seemed like the lake was all around us. We could see the deep blue meeting the horizon. There were a few boats in the distance, but the lake was calm today. My dad would call it a glass lake. There were hardly any ripples or waves. It felt serene and peaceful. Aside from the random seagulls that were squawking, I could hear the gentle lapping of the water against the earth below.

Linc's arms came up behind me. "I'd heard about this place from a couple of friends, so me and the guys decided to check it out. It's not widely known, so mum's the word."

I pretended to zip my lips closed in response.

He held me in his arms for a few minutes. "Are you hungry?"

I looked up at him, noticing the small amount of stubble on his chin. I pressed up on my tiptoes so I could kiss the side of his jaw. "I could eat," I responded after kissing him briefly.

"C'mon," he said, leading me to the blanket. We sat down, and I watched as he opened the picnic basket. Inside, there were a couple of cans of pop. "Pepsi or Sprite?" he asked, showing me the bottles.

"I'll take Pepsi," I replied.

"It's nothing fancy, just a couple of subs Alex threw together for us."

"I like subs."

"See, that's one of the things I love about you; you're so easy to please."

Love about me?

Oh, my God! Did he just say that?

I looked at Lincoln with wide eyes, and he just smirked at me. The corner of those beautiful full lips lifted ever so slightly.

He handed me a paper plate with my sub on it then asked, "Do you want Italian dressing or mayo?" He held up a few packets, and it was like he knew I was still dumbfounded over what he just said.

"Um, Italian?"

"Is that a question Lols, or is that what you want?"

I felt like he was teasing me. "Give me the damn, Italian," I said, lightly smacking his arm.

He chuckled and handed me the packet.

"What time is your dad expecting you home?"

"He thinks I'm at Ellie's studying, so I need to be home by nine-thirty."

"That gives us some time, then. The sun sets around seven, so we'll have more than enough time."

I looked for the sun in the sky, and I'd seen enough sunsets that I figured we still had about forty-five minutes until the sun sets.

"I hate that you have to lie to him. I'd like to meet him one day, so it does not seem like I've been sneaking around behind his back."

"I know, me too. But he's old-school, and he's protective."

"I don't blame him. When we have a daughter, if she's half as beautiful as you, and she will be, because our babies will be gorgeous, then I'd probably want to kill any guy that came near her."

"Are you planning our future kids, Lincoln Paige?" I joked.

"Damn straight I am. I'm planning it all. Kids, a house, a future."

His voice was light-hearted as he said this, but I could tell he was serious, and I couldn't eat. Butterflies had taken flight in my stomach.

"Linc," I said breathlessly. Where had my ability to talk around him gone?

He took the plate from my hand and set it beside me.

"God, the way you say my name."

"How do I say it?" I whispered, feeling so much intensity.

"You say it like I'm it for you too."

I blinked up at him. Could this beautiful guy feel the same way about me as I was rapidly feeling about him? I knew it was too soon. We'd only been dating for a short amount of time, but it was intense from nearly the first moment we met.

"I brought you up here because I wanted to tell you something, and I wanted to do it somewhere beautiful, in a way that will stick with you."

My throat suddenly became dry, and I could swear I was getting warm all over.

"What did you want to tell me?" I croaked out.

He leaned closer to me and put his forehead against mine. There were a few seconds of him just staring into my eyes. I stared at his too and loved how dark they were, but with the sky turning slightly orange, I could see more browns in them than normal.

"I wanted to tell you that I'm falling completely in love with you." His voice was so confident when he said those words to me. He was completely sure of himself and what he said, and I knew it before he said it, but that confidence he held was one of the reasons I'd already fallen in love with him too.

I closed my eyes, wanting to take in his words and savor them. When I opened them again, he was searching my face, trying to gauge how I felt. I was only fifteen, but it didn't stop me from knowing my heart down to my very soul. So I said my truth because he deserved to hear it without any pretenses, "I've already fallen."

Then he was kissing me. It was soft and sweet and oh so gentle. There was no rush to the way his lips pressed against mine. He took his time, and it felt more about memorizing our love for one another than anything else. I felt every ounce of love he felt with the way his lips pressed against mine.

Once it started to get heated, Linc pulled away.

"Let's eat before the sun is gone."

Eating was the last thing I really wanted to do. I wanted more of him. I wanted him to touch me, and I felt an ache between my legs that I'd never felt before. I blew out a large puff of air, knowing he was right, we needed to cool it down.

He handed me my plate, and I cracked open my pop, trying to calm my nerves. After taking a sip, I looked at him again. The sun was much lower now, and hues of oranges, pinks, and purples covered the sky, but it was nothing compared to how beautiful he looked right then. He had the biggest smile on his face that I'd ever seen. It was almost like he was a different guy, lighter in some way.

"You're in love with me?" he asked, biting his lip.

"Yep, I love you, Linc. And you love me."

"Damn straight."

We finished our food as we watched the rest of the sunset. It was a calm and peaceful evening after that. We didn't talk much, just basked in how happily in love we were. That spot became a place for us, where we could just shut out the rest of the world, and it was just the two of us. And he was right, it was perfect, and I'd never forget it for as long as I lived.

"I HAVE TO STOP AT THE house real quick. I forgot towels," Lincoln said from beside me.

"You mean Alex forgot the towels," Ty grumbled from the back seat.

"It was an accident," Alex defended.

"You had one job," Trey bit out.

I noticed a small amount of tension coming off of Trey and tried to calm him down. "It's not a big deal. I don't mind us taking a detour."

"Marlene's home, so you'll finally get to meet her," Lincoln added.

I turned, looking wide-eyed at the boys. Alex chuckled. Ty lifted his chin then said, "She'll love you," and Trey nodded his head in agreement.

I nervously checked myself in the mirror and pulled my shorts down to cover more of my legs.

"Ty's right. She'll love you. Just be yourself." Lincoln reached for my hand and twined our fingers. I couldn't help feeling nervous. I'd heard so much about Marlene from all the boys. When I talked to her on the phone, she intimidated me, but they all loved her so much.

"Lols, does your dad know you're with us or are we on some covert mission again?" Alex asked. Lincoln squeezed my hand.

"He knows I'm going to the beach with some friends. That counts, right?"

"What if you run into someone who knows you and they see you with a bunch of brothers?" Trey asked.

"Well, I'd be in trouble for being with any guys. He wouldn't care that you're black," I defended.

"Sweetheart," Ty's voice gentled, "Are you sure about that?"

"He wouldn't,." I defended, then wondered, "Does that happen to you a lot?"

They all nodded, and I got another finger squeeze from Linc.

"I won't date white chicks," Trey said, "It's too much of a hassle."

"Not me!" Alex exclaimed, "I think of it as an adventure."

"You like running buck naked from Laura Smith's daddy?" Ty questioned.

Alex shrugged.

"That happened?" I asked with wide eyes.

"Last week," Lincoln confirmed as we pulled into his driveway. "Are you guys staying here while I introduce Lola to Marlene? I'll leave the car running."

"No way am I missing this." Alex began trying to squeeze past his brothers.

Ty pushed him back. "We'll all go." Ty opened his door, and Linc shut off the car.

His house was a modest house with a plain flat front painted a light shade of blue. It looked like it had been years since it was painted last. The yard was freshly cut, and there were a few unruly rose bushes against the front of the house. No sooner than we got out of the car, a short, slightly rounded waist, African American woman stepped outside. Her black hair was chin-length, shiny and smooth. She wore jeans and a t-shirt with a bulldog on the top corner of it.

"Marlene, this is Lola," Linc introduced us.

"So you're the one that's got these boys all smitten." She looked me over, and I wasn't sure what to make of her. I just knew that Lincoln, Ty, Trey, and Alex would all be in a very different place in their lives without her.

"These boys?" I questioned because Linc and I were definitely a thing, but I didn't know what she meant about the rest of them.

"Hmpf. Like you don't know that you have them all wrapped around that pretty little finger of yours." She moved around me like she was inspecting me, then stopped in front of me. I suddenly felt self-conscious wearing a baggy tank over my bikini that I had to hide from Dad. "Does your Daddy know you're going to the beach with these boys?"

I looked to Lincoln for help, but he was staring at Marlene and offered me none. I decided I'd be honest. "No, ma'am. He doesn't."

"Don't get my boys in trouble. You hear me?"

I nodded fervently.

Marlene turned to Lincoln. "You were right. She sure is pretty. Protect that one. Careful with her heart. You get me?"

"Already am, Marlene."

"Marlene, you got any Pepsi?" Alex asked.

"Do you have any Pepsi?" she corrected.

"Sorry, do you have any Pepsi?"

"There's a few cans left in the fridge. I have half a sub left too if you want it."

"Hell yeah." Alex moved to go inside.

"Grab the towels, will you?" Lincoln shouted after him.

"Got it."

"That boy is the smallest of all of them, but he would eat me out of my kitchen if I let him. I swear he eats double what Trey does. Trey was the biggest of all of them." I stared at Trey in mild shock.

"It's true," he shrugged.

I grinned.

"Think fast," Trey shouted, throwing a football past my head. Lincoln's hand shot up and grabbed it from the air.

"Come on. You guys ready?"

"Yeah. It was nice to meet you, Marlene."

"You too. Sweetie. You keep these boys in line." I smiled and turned to walk away when I heard, "Oh, and Lola."

"Yeah?" I asked, turning back.

"If I had a little girl and found out that she was lying to me and sneaking around and had a boyfriend I didn't know about," she shook her head, "I think I'd be more pissed than if I found out she had a boyfriend. You think on that, and you think about how your daddy would react."

Guilt coursed through me. I nodded. "I will."

"You do that," She said, then turned and yelled at Alex for grabbing the entire case of Pepsi.

I WIPED THE SWEAT FROM my brow and danced from foot to foot. My feet burned, but I ignored it because Lincoln was playing volleyball with his brothers. They were playing against some guys they knew from school. Watching Lincoln play was, by far, the sexiest thing I'd ever witnessed. He had no shirt on, and every time he jumped up and stretched to hit the ball, his muscles pulled in a way that seemed to make my entire body quiver.

They were beating the other team by a lot. After a while, Alex started goofing off. In retaliation, Trey threw the ball at his head, making Alex goofily scream, "Ow." He was pretending to be more injured than he was, causing me to crack a smile.

A group of guys I didn't recognize approached and began to heckle the other team. At first, it seemed like it was all in fun, and I heard one of them say, "Look at Ashton getting his ass handed to him by a bunch of shines."

I turned and glared. "You did not just say that." I hissed.

"What's it to you? You like fucking those black boys?"

"You motherfuc…" I lifted my hand to slap him when suddenly Lincoln was beside me, grabbing my hand and cutting me off.

"We got a problem?" Lincoln asked as his brothers surrounded him. "What'd they say to you?" he asked me.

"Called them shines and asked if I liked fucking black boys."

The opposing team and who must've been Ashton approached. "Lay the fuck off, Matt," one of the other teammates said.

"Fuck you," the guy responded, and a second later, Trey took the guy over his shoulder then pummeled him into the ground. Lincoln pulled me back away from the guys as Alex threw a wild punch at one of them.

"Stay back, Lola," Lincoln shouted, pulling the guy off of Alex, who grabbed him and hit him so hard in the face he started screaming about his nose.

Ty yelled, "Trey, stop." I realized then that Trey was grasping the man's throat. Lincoln grabbed Trey's arm. "Stop, Brother."

He loosened his grip and pulled him up. "Apologize."

"Jesus man, you're fucking nuts," one of the guys said.

"Apologize," Trey repeated.

The man he held up stuttered, "all right, man. I'm sorry. Okay."

"Cops," Alex shouted.

"C'mon." Lincoln grabbed my hand, and we all ran. We finally got far enough away and were in a less populated area of the beach when we stopped gasping for breath.

"That was fucking awesome," Alex shouted. "Did you see that punch? I beat that fucker's ass."

Ignoring Alex, Lincoln pulled me in his arms. "Lols, are you good?"

I nodded my head.

"You're shaking, Lola. Guys, give us a minute."

"I need a swim anyway," Trey said, puffing out his chest. Ty agreed and looked back at me with sympathetic eyes as Alex bounced on his heels, jumping around and reenacting the fight. Lincoln shot Alex a glare, and then they left us alone.

Adrenaline coursed through my body, and I didn't know what to say. I'd never witnessed a fight so brutal before, but more than that, I'd never been exposed to such blatant racism.

"Lols?" Linc questioned, "What's going through your mind? Are you okay? That was intense."

I thought about my words for a moment. I couldn't adequately grasp my anger, so I just gave it to him. "Does that crap happen a lot?"

"We don't fight like that..."

"No, I'm glad you kicked their asses. I mean, random entitled assholes who come up and spew such garbage? Who does that? What pricks. We were enjoying ourselves. Everything was good. And what, they thought they should just come up and show their ignorance? I'm beyond pissed. Linc, let's go back. I want a shot at them. I mean, who do think they are? Those ignorant pompous..."

A hand was thrown over my mouth, "Calm down, Lola. They're assholes, but we shouldn't have gotten physical. Trey has a scholarship to consider. I have the Army. We can't mess it up, and as pissed as they made me, we shouldn't have taken it there. We shouldn't have put you in a position like that either. What if they got near you? What if we got arrested? This shit is whacked. But yeah... fuck those dudes."

Somehow he managed to calm me down. "How do you deal with that?" I asked.

"As you can see, we don't always deal with it well. We should've walked away. This isn't the first time I've had to see my brothers deal with this kind of shit. It happens all the time, and I try not to let other people's ignorance affect me because it will eat at you if you let it. There is so much ignorance in the world. I've been angry in my life so often because of other people. I just don't want to give them that power, ya know? Letting other people's ignorance into my headspace isn't good for anyone. Sometimes it's harder than other times to let it go, though. Especially when it's towards my brothers. I know they can handle their own, but they shouldn't have to."

I nodded, hearing his words and trying to take it all in. I wasn't sure how I would feel if racism was constantly being thrown in my face. I wasn't sure if I could let it go.

He held me for several minutes, and eventually, I relaxed, then Alex barreled toward us. "Hey, let's get slushies. I could use a slushie. Slushies are so good. Lols, do you like red or blue?" And just like that, the tension was cut. We moved on like it didn't happen, but later that night, I wondered how that kind of constant ignorance would have its toll on them. And it made me love all four of them even more. They had already overcome so much, and life kept being difficult just because of their skin color. It wasn't right. But what I loved was the way they cared about each other and the way they all brought me into the fold, like I was one of them and part of their unique little family.

Chapter Six Past

"D on't peek. Promise?"

"I promise," I said, giggling behind Lincoln's hands. Lincoln's breath hit the back of my neck, making tiny goosebumps erupt over my skin.

He removed his hand, and we were cloaked in darkness in Marlene's backyard.

"Ready?" he called out. I assumed it was to one of his brothers.

His backyard that was once covered in bike parts and other tools was lit up with tiny white twinkling lights. The debris was gone. Shrubs covered the back fence, and fresh flower beds were filled with newly planted blue and white flowers. There was a small table covered with white linen. On it laid small tea light candles flickering inside a fishbowl. Mazzy Star's *Fade Into You* began playing.

Suddenly, I wished I was wearing more than just jean shorts and a t-shirt. I wished I'd dressed up, and that I had worn heels. I wished I was all the woman he made me feel like.

"Dance with me," he ordered quietly with a slight tremble to his voice.

I nodded, just as nervous as he was, which was silly. We were together. We had nothing to be worried about, but the atmosphere, so rich with love, made us that way. He grabbed my hand and pulled me close to him. I pressed my face against his dark blue t-shirt and listened to his racing heartbeat.

"This is beautiful," I told him as we swayed back and forth.

"You're beautiful."

I reached up on my tiptoes as he bent down and pressed his lips against mine. My hand moved along the ridges of his abdomen. I wanted more, but Lincoln pulled away.

He softly sang the chorus to me, rocking us to the slow beat. One thing I learned in that music store, in what felt like forever ago, was that Lincoln could sing and dance.

He did it often, and I loved that he wasn't afraid to do it. Before him, I never felt confident in my own skin, at least not the way he did, but Lincoln had changed that. He changed so much.

The song ended, and Matchbox Twenty started to play.

"Would you like to sit?"

"Okay." Lincoln led me to the small table and pulled out a chair for me.

"God," he breathed, "I was so relieved your Dad said yes."

I was too. After my dad recently found out I had a boyfriend, I thought he'd never let me leave the house. He sure made it tough for me, doing things like unplugging the phone in the evening. It took a lot of persuading by my Mom to get him to come around. Since I finally turned sixteen last week, dad didn't argue; that was until he found out Lincoln graduated.

"I guess he figures since you're leaving soon that it would be better for me to have a boyfriend I can't really see."

Lincoln's face fell, and I instantly regretted saying that. We talked so often about him leaving, and it was almost time. It just felt so real, and I was trying to be supportive. I really was, but I felt like he was leaving me, and he had a choice not to. I knew that wasn't really true. He signed a contract already, but my irrationally young heart felt like he was making this choice.

"Lols," his nickname for me, and the soft way he said it melted my heart.

"I'm sorry. You did all this, and it's so beautiful. I shouldn't have brought it up."

"It's hard for me too, you know."

"I do. Can we just forget I said anything?"

He reached his hand across the table, linking our fingers together. "I'm going to write to you all the time. It's going to be okay. This will just be a small blip. We have our whole lives ahead of us. Plus, I'll get leave after boot camp for a visit."

"I know." And I did. We hashed this out already maybe a dozen times, but no matter how often we talked about it, I still had fears. Every time I turned on the news, I was met with another story of another young man having his life cut short because of this stupid war. I had to try to not think about the fact that Lincoln would be fighting for his life while I'd be in an eleventh-grade trig class.

Ty cleared his throat, he might be only sixteen, but he was huge. He was taller than Lincoln, and Lincoln was tall. It wasn't just his height. His shoulders were broad and built like a linebacker. He carried a couple of glasses of water and sat them down in front of us.

"Thanks, Ty," I said

He gave Lincoln a nod of his head, "I'll bring your dinners out in a sec."

"Thanks," Lincoln gave him a chin lift.

"Oh, my God. What did you have to do to get him to do this?" I laughed.

"Ah, nothing really Ty's a big softy at heart. He might be a giant, but he's got a heart of gold."

Ty brought out two large plates of pasta. "Thanks again," I told him.

"I got your back while he's gone. I've never seen my boy this happy—anything you need. Anyone messes with you, they'll answer to me. Got it?" Ty's voice came out kind of scary, and if I was honest, he intimidated me.

"I got it," I answered as Lincoln squeezed my hand.

"Oh, I almost forgot." Ty reached into his pocket and pulled out a white envelope, handing it to me. I opened it and saw two Lollapalooza tickets. I couldn't help my excitement. I jumped out of my chair and threw myself against Ty, hugging him. I squealed. "Lincoln, I'm so excited. Oh my freaking God, Jane's Addiction will be there. I can't believe it! Thank you, Ty. Thank you so much."

He laughed. "Don't see what's so great about that music, but whatever. Glad you're happy."

"Thank you!"

"Damn, bro. She better be this excited about my birthday present."

I sat back down and stuck my tongue out at Linc as Ty left us. It was stupid of me, and I regretted it almost immediately, so I tried to move the conversation right over it. "This is so cool, Lincoln." I looked at the date. It was just two days before he would leave. He noticed my face fall a bit and grabbed the tickets from my hands.

"I'll be there. Don't worry."

"All right." I changed the subject because I hated thinking about his impending leave. "Did you cook?"

Lincoln laughed, and the corner of his mouth tipped up. "Would you believe me if I said yes?"

I thought about his failed attempt to make boxed mac n' cheese. "Not really."

"Alex has been perfecting it. His sauce has been on all day."

"You mean gravy." I corrected, taking a bite of his pasta.

"Um, Lols, in case you haven't noticed, gravy is an Italian term, and Alex is far from that."

"Shh," I shushed as I closed my eyes, savoring the gravy with garlic and hints of oregano. "Mmm," I all but moan, "this is so good," I opened my eyes.

I looked at Lincoln to see if he was tasting this deliciousness, but when my eyes connected with his, they somehow looked darker. He licked his lips the way he usually would just before he kisses me.

"Did you try it?" I asked.

"Um, sorry." He cleared his throat, startled.

"Linc, take a bite," I giggled.

"Jesus, hearing you moan. You have no idea what you do to me."

I watched as he closed his eyes like he was in physical pain, then reopened them. "You take my breath away," he said in an almost whisper.

I blushed then, unable to make eye contact any longer, I stared at my pasta and said what I'd been thinking about lately but had been too afraid to say. "I want to, Lincoln. Before you leave. I don't want you to go and us never..."

My eyes met his as he cut me off, "You know how much I want to. I want you so bad. I think about you... what it'd be like..."

"Why do I feel a 'but' coming on?"

"Because we're in Illinois. If anyone found out, I could go to jail. The age of legal consent is seventeen. You know this. I can't take that risk."

"Can't or won't."

"Lola, don't be like that. I want our first time to be pure, not some threat hanging over our head."

I felt the burn of embarrassment and guilt in the back of my throat as tears welled in my eyes, threatening to fall.

He was by my side before I could pull in another breath. "Don't. Tonight was supposed to be romantic and sweet. Don't get upset. Please. We have time until things hurt. Can we just enjoy what we have? If you push it, Lols, my resolve will break, and you don't want that. You want it when we're both ready. I love you. What we have, I know it in my gut that we're going to have it forever. I don't care about distance or how long we have to wait because I'm never letting you go."

"You're that sure?" I had to ask because he said it with so much conviction, like the idea of him and I forever was truly going to happen.

"I've never been more sure about anything."

"I love you, Lincoln," I said, even though fear still clung to me.

"We're going to be okay." He cupped my cheek and brushed his lips against mine. I couldn't help it. A tear slipped free, and his thumb wiped it away.

"I have something for you, and I guess now's as good as time as any." He reached into his pocket and opened a deep blue, ring sized jewelry box. Inside was a small ruby ring surrounded by silver petals, making it look like it's the center of a rose.

"I want this to be a promise ring. I know we're young. I know I'm leaving. I know it's not fair to ask you to wait for me. But I'm asking it. Wait for me, and I promise I'll always come back to you."

My eyes filled with tears again. "I'll be here. I promise."

"You wear it on your right ring finger. That way, the left will be open when I can give you the real thing."

I took it from the box and slipped it on my right finger. "It fits. I love it so much." He brushed his lips against mine, then sat back and began eating.

"Holy shit! This is really good." He said, breaking the intensity of our promise to each other.

"Don't tell Alex, but I think it's better than my Ma's."

I sat back in my seat, and I stared at my beautiful ring. It was going to be all right. Everything between Linc and I would work out. I just knew it.

Chapter Seven

Dear Lols,

How are you? I'm okay. Tired. We had a long day of training. It's all right, though. I don't mind it. I'm fast at pretty everything. If they give me a gun to assemble and disassemble, I'm the first one done. If we are running an obstacle course, I'm always first. If we are doing something with endurance, I'm usually the last man standing. I'm good at it. It feels good to be good at something. I feel like I do everything they say, and I do it with ease. Some of the other guys get jealous. But fuck 'em, I'm gonna do me. Ya know what I mean? I'll never let someone else's inadequacies affect my reality. Check me out, I sound like Buddha or someone. Ha!

God, I miss you.

I wish I knew what you are doing right now.

I think a lot about when we first met.

Penso che to sia anche bello, that's what you said to me. I looked it up as soon as I left the football game. I know I've told you, but I swear the moment I saw you, it was like my entire world changed. The way you moved, the way your hair fell, and that ass. ;) God, I love your ass. Seriously, babe, it's a thing of art. I miss you. Did I write that already? I think you're really beautiful too. I miss laughing with you and arguing over music. I miss dancing with you. I miss holding you.

The barracks are crowded. I never feel like I have a minute to myself. There's at least twenty of us showering at the same time, so I never have any privacy.

Ty told me he's been by to see you and that you're doing all right. I hated seeing you cry when I left. I almost didn't leave, but I know it will be the best thing for our future. I think about our future all the time. I wish I just gave in and that we were together the way a man should be with his woman, but then I think we have time.

You still wear the ring I got you, right?

Has anyone been messing with you? What about that Camille chick? Does she still think she's queen bee? How's everything else been?

All right, they just told us lights out, so I have to get going. I will write more soon.

I love you more than words.

I love you more than touches.

I love you more than anything.

Yours, Linc.

Dear Lincoln,

Hi, how are you? I'm doing good. School started. I can't stand my Biology Two teacher. She makes these noises with her mouth—it's totally disgusting. Anyhow, I'm in AP calc right now. I finished the assignment that Mr. Collins had us work on, so I thought I'd write you back. I got your letter this morning. I am so happy to have an address to write to you. I'm not going to lie, I've been checking the mailbox a few times a day. Homecoming is coming up. I wish I could go with you. Ellie says I should just go stag, but I don't think I really want to. I think that if I go, I'll just be missing you. Not sure what to do. :(

Tell me about boot camp? What's it like? What do you have to do? I can't believe you have to shower with a bunch of dudes. I know, you're a dude, but still, not having privacy, yuck! What do you eat? I want <u>all</u> the details, so I know what it's like for you. I try to imagine you there, but it's hard.

Hang on, teacher's coming.

Okay, I'm back. Sorry, I'm in study hall now. I've decided to throw my social standing—as if I really had any—away and join the math club. I know I'm a total math nerd, but it's so easy for me.

Of course, I'm still wearing your ring. I love it. I love you. Whenever the light catches on it, I think of you.

I've been listening to Evanescence. They have this song that just came out called Bring Me To Life. One of the lyrics is, 'Wake me up inside' I guess I connect with that part of the song because somehow it feels like that's what you do to me. When I'm with you, I feel so alive. It's like my heart faded since you've been gone. I'm trying not to be a downer. Ellie has been on me, but it's hard. You know? It's like no one understands how much I love you and how it feels like there's this enormous part of me missing right now.

Gosh, I'm sorry. I don't want you to feel bad or anything. I just know that you're the only person who can understand what I'm going through.

Okay, I've rambled on a ton.

I love you soooooooooooooo sooooooooooooo much.

P.S. I forgot to tell you something huge. Dad got me a car. Crazy right! I'm excited about it. It's an '89 Corolla, so nothing impressive, but at least it runs. I'm going to stop by your house and bring Marlene something. I haven't decided what yet, but being with her helps me miss you less.

P.P.S

I really wish we would have made love. No one would've had to know. I love you, and when I'm missing you most, I imagine your hands on me.

Okay, goodbye for real, but not for long.

Yours, Lola

Dear Lola,

I got your letter, and I can't tell you how great it was to hear from you. I hate that it seems like you're sad and that I have to give you worse news. Better to just tear the Band-Aid off, right? I can't come home after boot camp like I initially thought. I guess with everything that's going on in Iraq right now, they're sending everyone directly to their specialty school. Don't cry or be upset, please? I hate to think of you upset when there is nothing I can do to comfort you. I want to hold you in my arms and tell you that this won't be forever. I want to tell you that time apart will make it easier. I don't know if that's true, though, because honestly, it feels horrible the longer I'm away from you, the more it feels like a piece of me is missing. I heard the song you mentioned. It was okay. I can think of way better songs. Ha, but I'm sure you wouldn't agree. :)

I'm sorry that you have to go stag to homecoming. I wish I could take you.

You wanted to hear about what it's like here. It's pretty much day after day of training. I've never made my bed so much in my life. Every corner has to be perfectly precise. They pretty much tell me when I'm allowed to eat, sleep, and breathe. It's not as bad as I thought it would be, though. Maybe years of foster homes and living in crappy places with shitty people makes this seem easy?

I've made a couple of friends, so it's not horrible here. The worst part is not being able to use the phone. I'll be able to call you after boot camp, though.

One day, this time apart is going to make a difference. I'll be able to provide for us. We're going to have an amazing future, you'll see.

Even though we can't talk, just know that my love for you is as strong as it's ever been. I dream of you. I hope you dream of me too. All right, beautiful. I better get going.

Oh, yeah. Thanks for bringing Marlene mums for her porch. She wrote and said, what a good girl you were. Fuck, writing that just now made me wish I could make you dirty.

Fuck, now I'm getting hard in a room full of dudes.

Night, babe.

I love you more than words.

I love you more than touches.

I love you more than anything.

Yours, Linc

DEAR LINCOLN,

Damn you and your last letter. I'm not going to lie. Thinking about you getting turned on makes me turned on. I wish you were here to take care of me. Who am I kidding? You probably would tell me how we need to wait. I hate that you're older than me and that you've been with other women.

Meanwhile, I'm over here in Virgin-Land taking care of myself. Okay, all right, I don't need to go there. I'm trying to pretend that I'm not super disappointed that I won't see you soon. I had been holding onto that. I know it's not your fault, so don't feel bad if I'm sad. It just means I love you.

Since you said it takes time to get these letters, I wonder if I won't get one in return until you transfer to your specialty school? I hope not.

I love getting your letters and look forward to them. I think about seeing you again. Sometimes I'm afraid that time will change us. Don't let it, promise? Now that you are there, do you think you'll end up going overseas? I'm so afraid of that.

Gah, I'm sorry. I think I sound down in this letter, and I don't want to sound down. I want to sound happy. Don't think that I'm all down, and there is nothing you can do about it. As promised, I'm living my life. I'm hanging out with friends. Don't worry, every single guy knows I'm taken. I know you. I know that even though you want me to hang out, you are afraid that some guy will swoop in. Don't be. I never want you to have that fear. I'm beyond in love with you.

Oh, I almost forgot. I think I might start looking for a job. I'd like to have some extra cash, and now that I have a car and am mobile, I think that's exactly what I need.

All right, I'm heading to bed, where I'll be under my covers thinking of you.

I love you so much.

Love you, Lola

Dear Lols,

I was thinking about our second kiss. Do you remember that? It had been a while since I'd seen you after our first kiss at the mall. At least our late-night phone calls kept me company. I remember missing your lips. They were so sweet. Even now, I can close my eyes and remember perfectly how they feel. Your parents thought you were staying in at Ellie's watching movies, and her parents were out at some show till well past midnight. When I got your call, I was in the car with my brothers. Man, they would make fun of me so badly for how I'd make them all be quiet anytime you'd call. We were all in the car just driving around, and I let Alex take my car, which you know, I never do, so that I could see you, but I didn't want the whole gang barging into Ellie's house. Ellie invited, God, I can't even remember that dude's name anymore, and he showed up first. I remember how excited you were when I showed up. You snatched me at the front door and kissed me—right there—that quick. You made the first move. God, you were bold. I loved it. Then I walked in the rest of the way and saw that you were being subjected to a hardcore make-out session on the couch while waiting for me. I loved that kiss. It was so you. The way you were always unapologetically you. That was one of the first traits I noticed about you, and it was one of the most refreshing things about meeting you.

The ringing phone stopped me from reading any further. I closed the book of our letters that Lincoln gave me. I treasured them, and it was no surprise to me to see that Lincoln saved his and cherished them just as I had. The book was a present on our first wedding anniversary. He was always sweet like that. A photo of the two of us from when we were teenagers was on the cover. The majority of the book was black felt, but our picture was sepia with curled edges, making it look older than it was. Underneath the happy, smiling couple was the title: *Our Beginning.* I shouldn't have tortured myself by going through the book. I should've gotten rid of it.

I let the phone stop ringing, too exhausted from the emotions that reading Our Beginning brought out in me. A minute later, I heard a ding, signaling a voicemail. I got up from my bed and stored the book in a large box on my closet's top shelf.

I checked my phone and saw that it was Ellie. I listened to her voicemail, which was full of concern, and decided I'd call her back later. I shouldn't let Lincoln get to me. It had been long enough that I should let him go. I was moving on. I was doing good, right?

Lincoln was my addiction. He was the only man I'd ever been with. Loving him had been like a drug, filled with all the nasty side effects. When I had him, it felt like the greatest high. When I didn't, it was like my world fell apart. Over the years, I realized so much of my time had been a craving—praying for the next hit. Was there a support group for this—In Love Anonymous? If so, I suppose I was working through my steps. I admitted I had a problem, and I wasn't using anymore, but maybe looking at the book was a slip in my recovery. Perhaps I was delusional that there was a cure for this kind of sickness? All I really knew was that if I took another chance and let him in, it might be that final dose that made me broken beyond repair.

I went to the bathroom to splash some water on my face and noticed the look of anguish coating my features. This is not who I wanted to be. I needed to be stronger. I needed to move on. After a quick scrub of my face, I decided that staying in was only feeding the fire. Perhaps the best way to stem my addiction was to reach out to my support group. I quickly dialed Ellie.

She answered on the first ring. "It's about time! Seriously, I've been calling you for days."

I sighed, "Shit, I'm sorry. I'm a crappy friend."

"No, you're a friend who is going through something, and instead of leaning on your people, you're becoming a recluse."

"I know I was thinking the same thing, and it's not good for me. Do you want to meet me at The Hidden Tap for a few drinks?" I asked.

"Is that the new bar not far from you?"

"Yes. I haven't been there yet and was hoping that going out and finding some normalcy might do me some good. Plus, I hear that there's usually live music, and what can I say? I'm a sucker for a band."

"You sold me at drinks. Can you give me an hour?"

"Yep. See you soon." I disconnected, feeling like I was doing something for me. I was making progress. Tonight was like any night. Just because he was released, it was no different than a week ago or a month ago. I needed to put on my big girl panties and do this.

I spent a little longer on myself in the mirror, taking more time on my eyes than I have in a while. It might be to cover the worn out look in my eyes, or maybe I'm hoping that looking good on the outside will make the inside match. Either way, by the time I was finished, I was decked out. I had on black strappy sandals with a three-inch heel, black fitted capris, a cute nude colored top that somehow complemented my dark skin tone and not wash me out, and a small clutch. I left my hair down and ran a straightener through it for a second time today, just to give it an extra boost. It looked sleek and shiny. I felt good about myself. Stealing one more glance in the mirror, I let my confidence shine and locked my worries away.

Chapter Eight

I waited at the bar for Ellie. She texted me from the cab a few minutes ago that she'd be here any second. The bar had a homey feeling to it. It was trendier than a sports bar, but casual enough that I would've felt comfortable wearing jeans. The lighting was dim, but not so dark that you couldn't see the person next to you. It was slightly crowded, but I could still see the door from my seat at the bar. I flashed Ellie a smile, then waved as she walked in.

Ellie looked incredibly put together with her wide-leg off-white pants and black blouse tucked into her high waist. Her light brown hair was pulled into a small bun, and her black frame glasses accentuated her nerdy-chic-look that she had perfected.

"Hi," I greeted Ellie standing from my seat at the bar. "I saved you a seat. Looks like it's filling up in here pretty fast."

"Thanks, sorry it took me so long to get here. Traffic was a bitch. You look amazing, by the way." She took her seat, and I did the same, motioning for the bartender to make his way to us. He was cute in his own hipster way. Ellie ordered a dry martini and handed the man her credit card, telling him to keep the tab open.

"Have you heard the band that's playing tonight?" I asked the bartender as he handed Ellie back her card.

"I have. They've played here before. They're pretty good," the bartender explained.

"Thanks." I smiled at the bartender one last time before he turned and continued to work the bar.

"He's cute." Ellie sipped her drink as if she didn't just try to plant a seed.

"Meh, he's a hipster."

"Listen, there is nothing wrong with a hipster. It means they have style, and they care about the way they look."

"I hear you. I actually met one the other day on the train. He was kind of cute. I thought about giving him my number."

"Really? That's an awesome start. I know you're sometimes conflicted about Lincoln, but..." Just hearing Ellie say his name made guilt wash over me. Ellie, being the perceptive best friend, noticed the look on my face. "It's a good thing, Honey, and don't look at me like that. You have nothing to be guilty for. He's the one who's in jail."

"Was in jail. He's out, and I feel like I'm the one in the wrong. I mean, I told him if he did it, that I'd be done. I knew he'd get in trouble, but did that stop him? No. It didn't. We should have a family started by now. We should have an entire life laid out. But we don't, and why? Because Lincoln thinks he needs to defend everyone. He thinks he needs to be the fucking savior, but where the hell does that leave me?"

"He's out! Why didn't you say anything sooner?"

I looked at her sheepishly. *Yeah, I should've led with that.* "I'm sorry. It all just feels like a lot. I'm just trying to figure out how I feel about everything. I mean, I know I already have made up my mind, but it still feels emotional, and it still feels like I'm all over the place emotionally."

"It's okay to feel however you want. Don't try to hold your feelings up to any standard." She took a sip of her drink and continued, "He's out, but it doesn't change anything. He is who he is. You know... I don't really believe that you get just one love. I think as you change, so can who you were meant to be in love with. It's all right to move on."

I placed my hand on top of Ellie's because she was right, and everything she just said is exactly what I needed to hear. "You're right," I sighed.

"When are you going to serve him?"

I'd met with a divorce attorney a while back. I already felt guilty for not seeing Lincoln while he was incarcerated. That would cut him deep. I couldn't be so heartless as to serve him while he was there too. I wanted him to make it out of there. I didn't want him to get pissed and do something stupid and be in there even longer. Gah, as I thought about it, I knew that sounded like codependency.

"I'm not sure. Serving him will mean we have to have contact, and I'm afraid of that."

"Why? Lincoln would never hurt you."

"Gosh, no. I know that, but I'm afraid that if I see him, I won't be able to keep my distance. I need to do it soon. My attorney will have someone serve him. I just need to make sure that he's settled and okay. I don't know if that makes sense. I know I'm going to hurt him, and I want to do it as gently as I can. Do you understand?"

"Honey," she said with a gentle tone, then continued, "He's already been hurt. It's been years since you've talked to him. I don't think it would surprise him to receive papers confirming what he already knows."

I took a sip of my drink, not loving the truths that Ellie spoke.

The band must've set up while Ellie and I were talking. I heard the singer say into the mic, "Check, check."

I looked to the stage that was about twenty feet from our seats at the bar.

"Holy shit." I grabbed Ellie's arm.

"What?" Ellie asked, unsure what the fuss was about.

"That's the guy from the train."

"The hipster?"

"Yes!"

"Oh, he's cute."

The stage, which was probably only six inches off the ground, had just three men on it. Jet was standing near a mic with an acoustic guitar, wearing jeans and a light blue t-shirt. The other two men were dressed similarly, and both were attractive in their own way. One man, holding a bass guitar, took a swig of beer while his slightly baggy jeans still made him look relaxed and at ease. The other was sitting on a stool without any visible instruments. I watched intently as he took a harmonica from his back pocket. His jeans were almost black with intentionally faded grey spots. Who knew I paid so much attention to jeans? It's like all three of these men were saying something about themselves with just the way their jeans looked and fit.

The man with the harmonica began to play. The guitar soon followed along with the bass. It wasn't anything I heard before—kind of an Indie Rock vibe mixed with Blues. It wasn't so loud that I couldn't continue to carry on a conversation with Ellie. However, I found that I didn't want to. I watched and listened, getting lost in the quiet lyrics.

Eventually, the band took a break. I looked over and noticed Ellie was watching me. "They're good. You should talk to him."

"No." I shook my head. "I just like the music. They're pretty good."

"Well, you might not have much of a choice about talking to him." She tilted her head, and I looked up to see Jet approaching. "Crap," I muttered.

"Lola?" Jet asked like he couldn't believe it was me.

"Hey," I looked between Ellie and Jet and saw her grinning.

"Jet, my man!" The bartender greeted Jet. "Your set was dope. You need something? On the house."

"I'll take a water."

"That's it?" The bartender confirmed.

"You can let me buy these pretty ladies their next round."

The bartender set a coin down in front of us to trade for a drink when we were ready for another. Jet grabbed his water and said, "Thanks, man," to the bartender.

"Lola, I can't believe you're here. How's your head?"

"My head?" I asked, confusion marring my features.

"You hit your head so hard you don't even remember doing it?" he asked with a smile and turned to Ellie. "See, I was minding my own business sitting next to this beautiful woman on a train when our heads accidentally collided."

"That's not exactly how it went." I laughed nervously, unsure where that came from. Something about him made me feel out of sorts.

"So, Lola, how's your complications? Uncomplicated yet?"

"You sure don't beat around the bush, do you?"

"Well, fate must've brought us together again for a reason." He touched the side of my face affectionately. It was too personal for a stranger, yet those butterflies felt like they were taking flight, followed by that familiar guilty feeling.

"Stick around for the next set. I'd like to talk a little longer. Get to know you a little."

Ellie nudged me with her knee, and I knew that she thought I should talk to him.

"She'll be here," she answered for me.

"Great. I have to get back up there." He looked at his watch. "But I'm counting down the minutes." He winked, then walked away through the small crowd of people and picked up his guitar.

"That was awesome," Ellie said, sipping her drink. "I think this is precisely what you need. I'm going to finish my drinks and see about the guy to your right." I paused mid-sip, looking over her shoulder to where a man who was completely her type was sitting three stools down. I was surprised I didn't notice him sooner with his high thread-count suit tailored to perfection. He was a little bit older than us. I could see grey speckled throughout his temples. Still, he was attractive, and he reeked of money. He was the type of man that Ellie would be interested in.

Jet's band began playing again, and the music was a soothing backdrop for us. We finished our drinks and quickly got another round using our tokens from earlier.

"I'm not sure if I can do it," I admitted. I had been mentally debating if I could sit and talk to Jet. I kept eyeing the door, hoping for an escape route.

"Of course, you can do it. Jet seems sweet. Just talk to him. What harm can it do? And besides, I see something that I wouldn't mind doing myself. "

I sighed. I knew she was right. What harm could a conversation have? Besides, there was something charming about Jet. I just had to work through my guilt. I should've been able to move on.

"All right, I'll do it." I convinced myself that if I was ever going to get over Lincoln, then I had to at least give it a shot. I guess you don't know what you don't know, right?

We sipped our drinks and listened to the music. I watched as Ellie flirted with the man a few stools down without even speaking to him. It was all in her body language and in her eye contact. I've never done that. It's always been Lincoln and me, so picking up anyone was beyond something that I was comfortable with.

The band stopped playing their music, and before long, Jet walked over to me.

"Hey," Jet greeted, and I saw a fine sheen of sweat coating his forehead from his performance on stage.

"That was awesome. You have a good voice."

"Thank you." Jet motioned to the bartender, who quickly brought a glass of water.

"I think that's my cue," Ellie said as she got up from her seat. "Here, Jet, take my spot."

Ellie walked the few seats down to the man, who quickly took her hand and placed a soft kiss on it. It's way too forward, in my opinion, but to each their own. How Ellie did all that without even talking to the man, I had no clue. I didn't think I could ever be in a place in my headspace that I ever would feel comfortable being that forward.

Jet took a seat, and I saw the crowd thinning out in the bar a little now that the band was finished playing. "Lola, God, you're beautiful. Sorry to just blurt that out, but man, you take my breath away. It almost hurts to look at you."

I couldn't tell if it was a line or not, but it made me blush, nonetheless. "Wow, thank you."

"I don't mean that as some cheesy pick up line. I swear it. It's just bad. I watched you during my set, and you can't even imagine how many people's eyes just turn to look at you. You're that gorgeous." Okay, now my face was a deep shade of red.

"And now I've embarrassed you."

"It's okay, really," I giggled. I actually giggled. Who was I?

"So, Lola, how long have you been at Black Label?"

"I interned there during college, and they offered me a job, so I've been there ever since." I studied him for a moment, taking in the carefree way he carried himself. He seemed so confident, so sure of himself in his own skin, and it was always something that had attracted me to Lincoln.

"How about you? How long have you been at Sound Machine?"

"I've been at Sound Machine for a little over three years. I've worked with a few different companies. I'm sure you've heard of them."

"That's cool. Where else have you worked?"

"I was at E Inc, Apostle, Sound Systems, and now finally Sound Machine."

"Wow, you really have been everywhere. I really like working with Apostle and Sound Systems. E Inc, now they have a lot of work to do to be anywhere near the same level as the others."

"Is that your way of saying that they suck?"

"I didn't say that exactly."

"You didn't have to," he laughed, " I worked there, remember? I know how they are."

I nodded, agreeing with him. We continue to make small talk. Ellie came over and gave me a quick kiss on the cheek, saying goodbye as she walked out the door with a man following closely behind her.

Well, that didn't take long.

We stayed chit-chatting for another drink. There was something charismatic about Jet. Maybe it was the way he flirted or the way he carried himself, but I enjoyed his carefree nature. When my drink was finished, I told Jet I had to go. Even though I was enjoying sitting and talking with him, I still didn't feel completely comfortable.

"It's still early. Are you sure?"

"I'm sorry. It's already later than I intended to stay."

"I've enjoyed talking with you, Lola. I hope our paths cross again soon."

"It was nice." And I wasn't even lying. I really thought it was nice. I left the bar smiling, and for the first time in lord knew how long, I thought that maybe I could get over Lincoln. Maybe it was possible.

Chapter Nine

My ringing phone woke me. I reached my hand over to my nightstand and fumbled around, almost knocking over my glass of water.

Ty's name flashed across the screen. Swiping the little green circle on my phone, I sleepily answered, "You better be calling to tell me you're downstairs and bringing up coffee." I mumbled.

There was silence on the other end.

"Hello. Ty? Did you butt dial me? You better not be waking me up this early with a butt dial."

More silence.

My stomach filled with dread. Lincoln.

I immediately hit end on the call.

My heart beat rapidly in my chest, and now I was wide awake.

Sooner or later, I was going to have to face him.

My alarm clock went off, making me jump. I was no longer half asleep as I moved to the kitchen and pressed brew on the coffee pot that I forgot to set last night. Iz rubbed against my ankles and took a swat with her claws. I moved my foot just in time, or I would've had an evil kitty gash.

"Hold on, Iz!" I got her cat food, then did my regular routine. I showered, blew out my hair, slipped on my pencil skirt, a different color blouse than yesterday, but the same fit, and before I knew it, I was boarding the train and headed to work. My desk already had a stack of mail on it when I got in. I sat down, powered on my PC, and began my day's work.

Busy work, that's exactly what I needed to keep my mind off Lincoln. Hours passed, and I was interrupted by a knock on the door.

"Come in," I called out, not paying attention to whoever was there. I was too lost in a spreadsheet.

"Hey," Katie, one of the receptionists for the label greeted. I was immersed in work and just waved my hand for her to say whatever she needed.

It was a little rude of me, but people around here knew when I was so involved in what I was doing that I didn't make time for pleasantries.

Katie was on the funky side. She always wore bright hues of eyeshadow. Her hair was bleached and spiky, but she was utterly stunning in her own self-confident way. I liked her.

"These came for you."

I was startled and finally lifted my eyes as she presented me with a vase filled with long stem roses. If she was observant, which she wasn't, she would've noticed the small disappointed look that passed over my face. Lincoln would never send me roses; he knew they weren't my favorite. If it were from Linc, it would be lilies or an orchid. I thanked her and found a spot for the flowers near the window. I took the card out and read it.

Dear Lola, I enjoyed getting to know you a little last night, but I'd love to get to know more about you. Have dinner with me? Jet

His phone number was listed. I placed the card in my bag, unsure of what I wanted to do. Should I go out with him? Maybe? I definitely enjoyed his company, but the fact that my belly dipped knowing those flowers weren't from Linc should've told me something.

I took out his business card he gave me on the train and purposefully typed out an email to him instead of calling. I knew it might be the cowardly way to go, but so what. I thanked him for the flowers and explained that even though we had a lovely time, I wasn't quite ready for that date, but I'd hope that maybe one day I would be. He responded right away with: **I really hope so too. I knew it might still be too soon, but I thought I'd throw it out there. Jet**

All right, I kind of felt like a jerk. I didn't reply, though.

I worked through lunch and continued working later into the evening. It was nearly seven by the time I left the office. There were a few cubicle lights on. It looked like all the other offices were vacant. I took the elevator down and winced when I saw how dark it was outside. I hated taking the train in the dark. Whatever, Chicago is what it is. At least it wasn't raining. Richard must've left hours ago as well. I pulled my bag close to me. I didn't like walking alone in downtown Chicago after dark.

A weird feeling passed over me, like I was being followed. I looked behind me and saw nothing. I walked a few more steps, and the feeling never passed. An alley was a few feet ahead, and I increased my pace, wanting to make it to the train as quickly as possible. Goosebumps covered my skin. Someone was there; I just knew it. I stopped and leaned my back against a brick building as soon as I passed the alley, then dug out my mace from my bag.

I zipped my bag closed and was about to walk again when I was suddenly pulled into the alley. It happened so fast. I didn't have a chance to lift my hand to spray the mace. I couldn't even get a scream out because a hand covered my mouth. I began to struggle, gearing up to fight. Lincoln taught me how to fight, but fear still gripped me.

"Lols, stop. It's me."

My world tilted, and my heart beat for an entirely different reason.

Lincoln.

His body was pressed against mine. He was bigger than the last time I saw him.

I didn't say anything as he removed his hand from my mouth. My breathing was heavy, and my fear was quickly replaced by every emotion.

Lust, love, hurt, want, pain.

Pain.

So much pain. It hurt to look at him. His dark eyes stared back at me. His chest rose and fell with deep breaths. He was as affected by my nearness as I was by his.

"Linc," I breathed out his name. It was a whisper—nearly a prayer. My lip trembled, and I wanted to cry.

He cupped each side of my cheek and bent low. I was afraid he was going to kiss me. I was scared I wouldn't stop him. Instead of kissing me, he tilted his head towards my ear.

"We need to talk, Lols."

I shouldn't have avoided him this long. I knew I fucked up and caused this. If I'd answered a call or reached out to him, he wouldn't be here. I couldn't put it off any longer.

"Okay." I agreed. I knew I needed to talk with him. It was past time.

Lincoln grabbed my hand and led me down the alley. I didn't question him. I didn't ask where we were going. We came to a black SUV, and I watched as Lincoln reached in his jean's pocket and took out a set of keys, beeping the locks. The alley was small, and the passenger side was too close to the next building for me to get in.

Lincoln opened the driver's side door, letting my hand go as he did. "You'll have to climb across. Sorry."

I moved to get into the SUV, but Lincoln turned me towards him at the last second. My body stiffened in reaction to it.

"I just need to hug you. It's been too long, Lols. I need to hug you," He repeated. There was so much pain behind his words that I couldn't prevent myself from moving into him, allowing his arms to wrap around me. I held him to me, and he squeezed me so hard it was nearly painful. I didn't even try to stop it as a tear broke free. After a few moments, I attempted to loosen the hold to ease the pain, but Linc said, "Not yet, Lols. I need a little longer."

"It hurts," I told him, not talking about how hard he was holding me.

"It's been hurting for years. Give me a couple of seconds to let it hurt a little less." His voice broke, slicing me wide open. I couldn't deny him; I never could. It was part of the reason I avoided him. I let him hold me. I wasn't sure how long we were like this. His face was pressed into my hair. I could tell he was breathing me in, and God help me, but I was doing the same. I turned my head and pressed it against his chest. I could feel every beat of his heart, and it became too much. It was like he sensed that I'd given all I could give. He let me go, and I climbed into the SUV.

After a few minutes in the SUV, I asked, "Where are we going?" I was nervous, and I found myself fiddling with my left ring finger sans wedding ring.

His eyes gazed down at my hand, "No ring," he said as an accusation instead of answering my question. I didn't meet his eyes. I tucked my hands under my thighs, so I didn't fidget, then looked out the window. It wasn't long before I could tell we were headed to my place. *He knew where I lived.* Of course he did. He's Linc.

The ride was quiet. There was no small talk. Nothing at all to fill the void. He parked the SUV and got out. I waited while he rounded the hood and opened my door. I learned a long time ago that Lincoln liked to open the door.

I got out, then reached into my bag to take out my keys. I liked to have them ready before I got to the door. Linc grabbed them from me, and I didn't argue. It was like he knew exactly where he was going and which key to use.

We entered my apartment, and I didn't miss the click as he locked the door behind us. Maybe he needed to ensure our privacy? He flicked on the light, and I could see him clearly now. It looked like he bulked up even more in prison. His hair was short, and it almost reminded me of how he wore it when he was enlisted. His eyes were the same, with those thick lashes that drew me in. I had to look away. It was too much. I knew I could get lost in those eyes.

"Meow," Iz practically ran to Lincoln.

"Hey, Kitty." She purred as he scooped her into his arms and pet her.

"Traitor," I mumbled under my breath.

"What's that?"

"I'm going to change. Wash my face. Make yourself..." I was about to say 'at home' and stopped myself, then amended, "There are drinks in the fridge."

I didn't turn to see his expression. I knew I'd see disapproval written all over it.

In my room, I threw on black yoga pants, a tank, and a large baggy grey sweater that was netted and hung loose on a shoulder. They were my comfy clothes. For what I was about to go through, I needed to be comfy. I had a feeling it was going to be a long emotional night. I washed my face free from eye make-up that might end up running all over the place.

I spent far too much time trying to prepare myself. I knew it was going to be emotional. I texted my boss, Griffin.

I need a personal day tomorrow, but I stayed super late today and worked through lunch, so I won't be behind.

He texted back almost immediately: **Don't worry about a thing. Is everything all right?**

I answered: **I'm just going through something personal.**

Griffin: **You know I have always thought of us as friends. If there is anything you need to talk about, I'm here.** He was always stopping in to make small chat, and it hit me for the briefest of seconds that I hadn't really been that open to that friendship.

I texted back: **Thanks, I'll be okay.**

A few more seconds passed, and I received one final message. Griffin: **Okay, doll. I'll see you Monday.**

I was salary, and my boss was pretty good about being flexible with my schedule as long as my work was done. Still, his concern for me had me taken aback. I wanted to think about this more, but I knew at this point I was stalling.

With nothing left for me to do to avoid Lincoln, I left the safety of my room. Lincoln was sitting on the couch with his head hung low. He had a stack of papers in his hand. Shit, I didn't even realize that I had left them out on the credenza. Dread filled my stomach because I knew exactly what he was looking at. His head lifted, sensing me in the room. "So, it's true. You're divorcing me."

Chapter Ten

I sat on the opposite end of the couch. I couldn't be too close to Linc. I felt his eyes on me, knowing he was searching for an answer. I didn't know where to begin. He didn't wait for me to start.

"You won't see me or speak to me for nearly three fucking years. Three years where every single day felt like you were ripping my fucking heart out. And now I see this." He threw the papers across the room. "You're fucking killing me, Lols." I watched a tear trail down his cheek, and I lost it.

Anger and pain sliced through me.

"Don't," I bit out. "Don't you act like you're the victim here. You left me for the Army, and I waited for you. I stood by your side when you went overseas. I stood by your side when you re-upped. I was young and living in some fairytale land. I married you on leave. On fucking leave. Then you're home, and we finally get to start a life together, and Alex fucks up. Do you let it go? Do you let him make his own mistakes? No, not you. Always the hero for everyone else. You get so caught up in his bullshit world and trying to pull him out of it that you'd leave in the middle of the night to have his back whenever he got into shit."

"He's my brother. He needed me."

"I'm your wife!" I yelled. "I was alone. Again. I'd lay in bed all hours of the night fearing the worst until you'd return, and I'd worry. I questioned if I was strong enough, but did I do anything about it? Nope, not me. I stood by your side. After all, you're Lincoln Fuckin' Paige, the man I held on a damn pedestal. Alex gets caught dealing. Dealing! And he goes to jail for a little bit, life finally seems like it's getting normal. You're working. So am I. We seem like everything is going to be all right, but what happens, huh? Trey happens."

"Don't throw Trey in my face."

"Why not Linc? Guess what happened when you went to Florida to help him get sorted? For four fucking months, I was alone a-fucking-gain. Marlene would've gone. Hell, Ty would've gone too."

Lincoln grimaced at my tone, but I was too far gone from all of my pain.

"I spent so long hoping we'd get our time. Finally, I had you. We were happy. Then Alex is out, and he calls again. I begged you not to go. I knew that it wouldn't end well. I fucking knew."

Tears ran down my face, and I knew I had to finish even though this part would hurt him as much as it hurt me. I was too far gone.

"I was pregnant. I was going to tell you that night you left to go with him. Then you were arrested, and the day you were being sentenced, I miscarried our child. I laid in the hospital room, too ashamed to call anyone because I was going through this while you were leaving me again. I can't do this anymore, Linc. We've been together since we were kids, and do you know how many of those years we've spent together that I actually had you? What we have isn't a marriage. I'm just a sad excuse for a lonely housewife. I deserved more. I deserve to be first." My voice cracked while tears ran down my face. I started to feel like I couldn't breathe and hiccupped between sobs.

Lincoln moved to me, and I was in his arms. "I'm sorry, Baby. I didn't know. I love you. I'm so fucking sorry." He was trembling too. Tears streamed down his cheeks, which made me sob harder. He was desperately kissing me all over my tear-streaked face. "I didn't know," he said again, and he found my lips, kissing me with everything he had. Willing us to be okay. But I think we both knew that there was no going back.

He broke our kiss. "Tell me you love me," he pleaded like he needed to hear it.

With a cracked voice, I admitted, "You're the love of my life. I'll always love you."

"Don't say it like that. Don't say it like we're over. We'll never be over."

I couldn't respond to that. I was crying too hard. Years of telling myself I was over him were so I'd be *okay*. I wasn't okay, and I never would be. I just got by, and as the years without him passed, I got by a little easier, but I was far from healed. He picked me up and carried me to my bed. I didn't fight him. I didn't have it in me.

"I need to feel you." Lincoln took my sweater off and then his shirt. I laid in his arms with him kissing me and telling me how much he loved me. He stroked my hair, then my body, and I somehow stopped crying and found the comfort his arms provided me. My eyelids grew heavy and fluttered as I tried to stay awake, but it was useless.

"MMM, LINC," I FELT kisses along my collarbone, trailing up my neck.

"Wake up, Baby."

Just a little bit longer. I liked my sleep. I liked waking up to my husband.

Oh, shit. Everything rushed back to me as I opened my eyes and began to dart up and out of bed.

Linc put a firm hand against my shoulders, pushing me backward. I could move if I really wanted to. The truth was, I was half asleep and having my husband wake me up for the first time in years confused me. My head wasn't alert enough to say no. My libido, now that was roaring back to life.

"Let me love you, just for tonight."

I couldn't deny him. I never really could. So when he lifted my tank over my head and took my nipple into his mouth, I didn't stop him. I moaned into it, too emotionally exhausted and physically frustrated to do anything but moan.

"God, you have the best breasts. They're so responsive." I ran my hands over his chest, loving the feel of it. Loving the feeling of him. I didn't want foreplay. I didn't want to wait. I just wanted Linc inside of me.

I pushed my sweats down with one hand, then rubbed my other hand over his hard length. He was still wearing jeans. That wouldn't do. "I need to feel you inside me." I opened my legs, making my intentions clear.

He searched my eyes, looking for the sincerity of my decision. He must've liked what he saw because he stopped kissing my breasts and sat up to take his jeans off. While he was doing this, I got naked the rest of the way.

"Come here, Linc." He didn't move. He was staring, and it unnerved me.

"I'll never let you go. You know that, right? You'll always be a part of me."

It felt like he was committing me to memory, and maybe he was. Perhaps this is what we both needed? He moved up the bed, hovering above me, yet holding his weight, so he didn't crush me. I wrapped my legs around him and delighted in the feel of him as his hard shaft pushed against my entrance. He searched my eyes one last time, making sure I was okay with this. He must've liked what he saw because he pushed inside.

"Yes," I moaned out, loving the feel of him. It had been too long. He was so big, it felt like I was a virgin all over again. I guess three years and no sex could do that to you.

"You're so tight. You feel so good."

He barely moved and just stayed completely seated inside of me. I could feel his dick throbbing. I wanted to move, but I let him lead. He kissed me. It was all tongue, deep and unrelenting. We kept our eyes open, staring at each other, making love as he slowly moved. Our hands gripped each other's bodies with more fervor. We both got to a place where slow and tender just wouldn't do. My heels dug into the back of Linc's thighs. My hands grabbed onto his firm ass, pushing him into me.

"You're killing me, Lols. You're everything."

I didn't respond. I couldn't. A moan was all I could muster. It felt too good. I thought I'd never feel this again. It was so beautiful. So amazing. So much fucking bliss. I could hardly stand it. He met my thrusts, lifting my leg so he could get in just a little deeper.

My nails dug into his shoulder as I held on.

"Linc!"

"God, yes, Baby."

"Take me there."

"I don't want it to be over," he whispered with so much sincerity.

"There's been no one else but you, pretty sure I'll come again."

He pulled out of me, and I saw his beautiful dick glisten with my wetness as he moved, so he was sitting on his heels.

I felt bereft without him.

"I'm going to taste you."

Placing his large hands below my ass, he lifted me to his mouth and began feasting on me. Holy shit. I forgot about the heaven that was his tongue.

He licked, and he sucked, and it was literally only seconds later that I came.

"Fuck!" I called out, so lost and taken out of reality.

He moved me onto his achingly hard dick so quickly I might still have been shuttering from my orgasm when he impaled me. He thrust in and out of me, kissing me as he moved. I could taste myself on his lips. I didn't care. I didn't care about anything but the two of us and how we were together. I was ignoring all of my pain, purposefully pushing it aside, living in the moment with him, and taking all I could from one second until the next.

He released my mouth and moved his head to my nipples. God, the way he made me feel. My nails raked his back, and he released my nipple with a pop, "I love you," he said, and I could tell he was getting close.

"I want to ride you."

"By all means, Lols," He said, laying back to let me do the work. I began to move, and I put everything into it. I moved my hips and gave him my all. Every feeling, every ounce of love I had, went into the way I moved on him. He could see it in my eyes. I knew he could. He gave me this look, the one where his head tilted to the side, and his eyes went all soft.

He reached up and grabbed my breasts with both hands. My head fell back, and I realized that somehow, he regained control. His hips were pushing forward, and he was meeting me thrust for thrust. My head snapped forward, and my eyes connected with his. He let go of a breast and moved his hand to my clit and began circling it with his thumb.

"That's right, Baby, I'm right there with you."

Suddenly, his thrusts were manic, and I was so lost in my second orgasm that I nearly missed the beauty that passed over Linc's face as he came.

He held my hips in place. I could feel the throb of him as he emptied himself inside of me. He began to lift me off of him, and I became desperate for him to leave me where I was.

"No, Linc. Stay right here for just a little while longer."

He tilted his head, then brought me down on top of him so that our chests were still together. His arms wrapped around me, holding me to him. My head was to the side, lying against his chest, and I listened to his heartbeat as it slowed from exertion.

"I wish I did so many things differently. You're the best thing that's ever happened to me. Don't ever forget that. I love you."

I wanted to cry all over again because it felt like goodbye. And perhaps that's what this was. The best damn goodbye that we'd ever have. I laid awake in his arms for some time. The room began to get lighter, filtering in through the curtains, and I knew I'd managed to stay awake all night. My eyes were very heavy when Linc kissed my lids and told me to sleep. I curled into him and did just that.

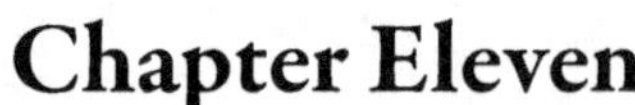

Chapter Eleven

I opened my eyes to the fresh smell of coffee and immediately noticed I was alone. Lincoln was gone, and I wasn't even a little surprised. I think we both knew what last night was. I got out of bed and saw a sticky note by Iz's bowl that said, 'She's been fed.' I poured a cup of coffee, noticing it was almost noon. Linc probably set a timer on the pot. I moved to the living room with my coffee and was reminded of how Linc looked with his head down. He was so dejected. I did that. Then, I noticed the divorce papers were in a pile on the table along with a letter. I guess it was poetic that he'd write me a letter after all the letters we'd sent to each other. Perhaps our last goodbye would be by a letter as well.

Dear Lols,

My beautiful angel. Words can not express to you how sorry I am for all the decisions I made that took me from you. I'll think about our baby every day for the rest of my life and what we could've had. I didn't ask you all the things I should've last night. Like how far along you were or if they knew what the sex was? Did they know what caused it? I fear it was the stress I caused you. I'd love to know the answers to these questions, but I know I'm not deserving of them.

In prison, all you have is time. Time to think about all the what-ifs. What if I'd told Alex no? What if I listened to you? Or better yet, what if I didn't save him from himself and he was in jail for a long drug-sentence and not in jail for the rest of his life for murder? Maybe, if I'd done that, I wouldn't have been charged with involuntary manslaughter? I also know what it was like that night. There is a part of me that knows that if it was just Alex, he'd be dead, and as much as I wish things were different, I'm glad my brother's alive.

You'll never know what hearing the pain I caused you all the years we were together does to me. The only thing I know to do to lessen it some for you is to let you go. I won't fight you. I love you too much to put you through that.

You were right. For all the years we've been together, I was gone for far too many of them. I'd change it if I could. I'd cherish every single second of it and not waste any of it. When Trey was hurt, I could've let Ma take care of him, but I went. I should've stayed. I should've seen what all the time apart was doing to us. Maybe I took us for granted? We were Lincoln and Lola. I thought we were stronger, but I didn't see what my absence was doing. I didn't see what it was doing to you. I should've seen it. I should've done a lot of things differently.

Thank you for last night. It was the most precious gift you could've given me. I know I didn't deserve it, but the beauty that is you will forever be with me. Always.

I'll never forgive myself that you felt like you couldn't turn to anyone while you were in the hospital. I won't ask for forgiveness. Just know that I get how big what I did is.

I signed the papers. And, though, it breaks my heart to do so, I'm letting you go. All I can do is pray that you'll do better than me.

I love you more than words.

I love you more than touches.

I love you enough to say goodbye.

Yours, Linc

My stomach roiled, and I ran to the toilet just in time as I emptied the contents of my stomach. This was it. We were done. Officially over. The finality of everything felt like it was ripping me apart all over again. I laid in bed and cried until I fell asleep.

A day passed, then another. I hadn't eaten and wasn't taking care of myself. It was like I lost him all over again. The heartache I felt was immeasurable.

I was watching Lifetime. I couldn't even tell you what the movie was about, just that Jackie, who was played by some actress from my youth and I couldn't remember if it was 90210 or Saved by the Bell, was ticked off and going for revenge. I was hoping to get lost in TV, but just when I thought I had no more tears to cry, I was wrong. I realized up until this point with Lincoln, I'd been ticked just like Jackie, and now, I was just sad. I was grieving in a way I'd never done before, not even when Linc went to prison. The stages of loss were real, and I'd officially entered a new stage. After years apart, I was finally grieving.

There was a pounding on my door that I desperately wanted to ignore.

"Lola Paige! You open this door right now!" Shit, it was Ellie. "Now, dammit!" And Ty.

I'd ignored their phone calls and eventually let my voicemail fill up, not listening to a single one of them. I knew what they'd say. "Call me. We're worried about you. Yada, yada, yada."

Clambering to my feet, with my hair a mess from not washing it for days, I turned the deadbolt on the door, not even bothering to open it.

Ty pushed in with Ellie right behind him.

"What the fuck?" Ty hissed, seeing the sorry state I was in.

I laid back down on the couch, and Ellie moved *Our Beginning* to the coffee table. I read it way too many times over the last few days.

"I'm going to fucking kill him," Ellie said under her breath.

"Not if I don't get there first," Ty said, and any other time that would worry me. If the two of them fought, it would be horrible. I wasn't sure who would win, but I didn't want to come between brothers. I couldn't say anything, though. I felt numb and broken.

Ellie sat beside me, moving the hair away from my face. "What happened?" she asked.

I still couldn't say anything. I was too afraid that if I opened my mouth, the tears would begin again.

Ty stomped around my apartment in his ticked off brooding way. I faintly heard him walk into my bedroom to use his phone. "What the fuck did you do to her?"

Shit, he was calling to yell at Lincoln. I couldn't let that happen. I didn't want him to know how hurt I was. I moved off the couch and quickly to my room where Ty was yelling, "Motherfucker, you..." I placed my hand on his arm and shook my head. "Stop, please," I whispered. Ty seemed shocked, and his eyes flickered.

"You know what. We're going to talk about this later." He hung the phone up, and my heart ached knowing Linc was on the other end.

"I'm going to shower. I'll be out soon," I told Ty. I needed to escape my friends and collect myself.

In the bathroom, I stared at myself in the mirror. I was a wreck. My hair was a disheveled mess. My eyes were swollen, and my face was puffy. I'd yet to shower since Lincoln was inside of me. It was time I washed him away.

In the shower, I gave myself a pep talk. I'd done three years without him. I could do forever. I just had to keep moving on and taking each day as it came, right? It hurt so freaking bad, though. I wouldn't allow any more tears to fall. I'd cried enough to last a lifetime. I had to be all right. I could see concern covering Ty and Ellie's faces, and that wasn't fair. I couldn't check out.

I finished my shower and dressed. It was the first time I was in clean clothes in days, and I had to admit that it made me feel the smallest amount better. When I came back out to the living room, I noticed Ty and Ellie had picked up some around the space. It was no longer completely disheveled. The soft hum of the dishwasher ran in the background.

"She looks a little better," Ellie said to Ty.

The outside buzzer buzzed, making me freeze. They wouldn't have called him here, would they have?

Ellie must've noticed the look on my face and said, "Ty, tell the pizza guy to come up. Lola, you need to eat."

I nodded my head and sat on my couch, watching as Ty answered the door and paid a man for several large pizzas and a couple of two liters. I didn't question why he bought so much. Ty was huge, and I knew he could eat.

Ty threw one of the Pizza boxes open on the coffee table then sat beside me, taking a large bite.

"I'll get glasses with ice," Ellie said from the kitchen.

She returned and poured me a glass of ginger ale. "You need to eat, and you need to drink."

I took a sip and picked up a slice of pizza. I could do this. I could act normal and get through this, right? I nibbled on the pizza and did my best to appease Ellie and Ty. Ellie sat on the other side of me, and it wasn't lost on me that they were closing ranks around me.

Finally, after several long, tense minutes, Ty asked, "You want to talk about it?"

"Can I just tell you guys that Linc and I spoke, and he signed the papers, and leave it at that?"

Ellie looked at me sympathetically, and Ty cursed under his breath. "You want to watch the Bears game?" Ty asked, trying to lighten the mood. I was sure he could tell I needed a distraction.

I nodded, and Ellie grabbed my hand, whispering, "It's going to be okay."

I was tight-lipped, nodding my head once. I could see the worried glances that passed between Ty and Ellie throughout the game. The tension was palpable. I couldn't take it.

"Guys, if we're going to watch football all night, beer would be great."

"I'll run out," Ellie said, standing almost immediately.

"You know there's an app for that. We can just order it," Ty explained.

"There is?" I asked.

"There's an app for everything. I could take out my phone and in ten minutes have strippers, clowns, booze, and exotic animals all at our disposal."

"What kind of parties do you have?" Ellie laughed, and I giggled, then added, "Seriously, who are you, Mike Tyson?"

Ty laughed, "You know I'm like half a foot taller than him, right? Seriously, Ellie, you don't have to go out."

"There's a store nearly next door to her apartment. I'll be back in ten minutes. I could use a drink myself."

Ty reached for his wallet, and Ellie shooed him away. "I'm not taking your money. It's just a little bit of beer, but if you want me to go buy a couple of bottles of Cristal, then, by all means, hand over your card."

He shook his head at her. Ty always complained that because he's a large black man, whenever we went out to fancy clubs, they thought he wanted Cristal.

Ellie grabbed her coat, saying, "I'll be right back."

There were a few minutes of silence between Ty and me when he finally went for it. "Are you really going to be okay, Lols? I'm worried about you. Wondering if we need to get you some help. Maybe someone to talk to." I could tell this made him uncomfortable.

"I'm just mourning. I'm going to be all right. I just feel a loss, like someone died. It just hurts, but I've gone the last three years like this. I can keep going on."

He linked his fingers with mine. "Some*one* didn't die, but you're allowed to feel loss because some*thing* did. You hear what I'm saying? It's all right to hurt, but what's not all right is to shut everyone out and not take care of yourself."

I nodded, "I'm sorry, I worried you both."

"We care about you, Lols."

I nodded my head because I knew that they did.

The Bears scored a touchdown, and Ty and I both jumped up to cheer for our team. I couldn't help it, even though I was crushed, our football team was killing it.

Ellie came in a few minutes later and dropped a twelve-pack of beer next to the pizzas. I leaned forward and grabbed a beer from the case. "What is this?"

"Some local craft beer. The hipster guy said it was selling like crazy." She shrugged, then grabbed a beer and tried to twist off the top to no avail.

"Here," Ty reached for our beers, then took his keys from his pocket, which had an opener on his key ring, and opened them.

He handed me back the beer, and I took a swig, "Not bad." We both agreed, and we continued watching the game. By the time they left, I had a slight buzz, and I wasn't as distraught as I was before. I had to stay busy and keep on moving on. That was what was going to get me through this.

Chapter Twelve

I returned to work the following day. I was the first one to get there and the last one to leave. My mind stayed on work as much as it could. I needed to be invested in something, and what better to consume my mind than work? I heard a knock on my door and looked up to see my boss in the doorway.

"Hey, Lola. Do you have a minute?" Griffin stood there waiting on me to give him the okay to enter. He was my boss; he could enter whenever he wanted to, but he tried to treat everyone's time with respect. I always found it to be an admirable quality.

"Of course." I closed the window on the spreadsheet I was working on.

Griffin sat across from me and sighed. "I can't believe I have to say this to you."

I suddenly panicked. Surely, I couldn't be getting fired?

Sensing my discomfort, Griffin waved his hands in front of his face. It was a thing he did, speaking with his hands. Some people thought it was funny, but I enjoyed the extra amount of flare it added to the conversation. "It's nothing like that. Here's the thing. You've been paying bills too quickly. Invoices change. You know this. You're paying them so fast it's like they don't have time to adjust for simple things like tips."

"I always go back in and adjust later."

"I know you do, and you do an impeccable job at it, but I need you to do it a little slower. It makes no sense for you to do double the amount of work. HR alerted me to how many hours you've been putting in, and they said that it has to slow down."

I sighed. "So, you're mad at me for working too much?"

"Not mad. Not at all. It's just that those hours go into our numbers for coolest place to work, and they said you're throwing our numbers way off."

I couldn't believe what I was hearing. The ridiculousness of not wanting me to work more was staggering, but what else could I say.

"Um, okay, I'll just finish this, and then I'll leave."

Griffin sighed again. "It's Friday night. You're a beautiful woman. Go home, hell, go out. I'm going to this fab club called Hydration. You can join me if you like. But you need to put down the mouse, Lola."

I knew he wasn't hitting on me. He wasn't like that, but I hadn't really made friends with him. In truth, since Lincoln had gone away, I stayed mostly to myself, but the idea of just hanging out and trying to have fun seemed refreshing.

Unable to stop myself, I cracked a smile. Griffin was amusing. I reluctantly closed down my computer while Griffin sat there. He was not going to leave unless I left. "So, what do you say, Lola? Do you want to come with me to one of the coolest bars in all of Chicago?"

I thought about it for a minute. What would I do if I was home? I knew what I would do. I would obsess about everything that once was, and I needed to keep busy. "Okay," I agreed, because what did I really have to worry about?

He clapped, "Great, a cab will be here in fifteen."

"Fifteen minutes? I'm not changed."

"You always look amazing. Come on, it will be fun."

I'd never been out with Griffin before, at least not when it was only the two of us. I'd met up with large groups of the office staff, and he was there, but this was new territory for us.

"I'll fix my make-up, and I'll be right there."

"Perfect," he said gleefully.

THE CAB STOPPED OUTSIDE of a quaint looking restaurant called The Dirty Martini. "I thought we were going to someplace called Hydration?"

"We are. It's next door, but I thought you might feel a little more comfortable here first." I shrugged. Inside it looked like a regular Chicago bar. Businessmen and women sat at various tables and along the bar. It was quiet, and the atmosphere was calm.

I followed Griffin to a seat at the bar. Griffin was maybe ten to fifteen years older than me. He had salt and pepper hair that was always styled. His suit was a fine material that I was positive cost a mint, and his shoes were most likely from this year's men's runway line. He was also well-built. The way he spoke with flair contradicted his attire. I watched as he leaned forward and kissed the bartender's cheek. "Malik, this is Lola."

"Hey, sweets!" Malik said, "What'll it be for you?"

"How about a drink menu?" Griffin asked.

"Absolutely." He walked away then returned a second later, placing it in front of us.

"The bourbon lemon drop and the bourbon martini sounds good."

"It does," Griffin agreed, "Malik, can you get us two bourbon lemon drops?"

I sat with Griffin making small talk, and sipped on my drink, "This is quite good."

"It is," he agreed.

I looked around the bar and noticed many of the couples that were together were the same sex, and it finally dawned on me that we were in a gay bar.

"Is this place? Are you? I mean, I thought, but I wasn't sure." My questions all came out muddled together. I had no idea we were going to a gay bar. Not that I cared, I was just surprised.

Griffin laughed at my nervousness. "Yes, Lola. This is a gay bar, but straight people come here too. I can go either way if that answers your question."

"Oh," I replied.

"Don't worry. I don't date employees. Strictly platonic, I swear," he said, making me smile.

I drank another cocktail and found myself laughing with my boss. He was funnier than I'd ever noticed.

"All right, girl. There is going to be some seriously entertaining stuff happening next door. You ready to head over?"

I was having a good time, and I shrugged, "Why not!"

We walked the short distance to Hydration, the Dirty Martini's much more risqué sister club. The doorman seemed to know Griffin and ushered us right in. Inside was a large bar in the center of the room with a giant circular chandelier reflecting all the lights in the room. It was crowded in here, and so many men walked around with no shirt on. Lordy, there were a lot of pecs and six-packs, and I was staring. I don't know that I'd ever seen so many beautifully toned men at once.

"Let's get drinks," Griffin said over the music.

I followed him to the bar where he ordered for us. He handed me a martini then nudged my shoulder, directing my gaze to a stage where two men were completely greased up wearing nothing but speedos and wrestling.

"They're covered in lube," Griffin said into my ear.

I gave him big eyes and watched as the two men slid all over each other. It was interesting and entertaining. I noticed some men in the room found it a little more than entertaining because they got much closer to each other as the wrestling went on. Someone was pinned, and they were getting ready for another wrestler.

"Are you going on tonight?" Someone asked Griffin. *Holy crap! Griffin lube wrestled!*

"Not tonight," he responded, leading us back to the bar.

"This place is wild," I said, grabbing another drink. My eyes widened, and my mouth was slack as I took in the scene. I'd never seen anything like this before. I wasn't judging, but it was a sight to take in. He chuckled at my obvious astonishment.

"Drink up, Lola, let's dance." He chugged his drink and escorted me to the dance floor.

I felt carefree and lighter than I had in lord knew how long. At the end of the night, I was more than a little drunk, and Griffin shared the Uber with me, even though we lived on opposite sides of town.

Once home and in my room, I laid in my bed and thought that I could do this. I could move on. I had fun tonight. I was going to get by.

Chapter Thirteen

Monday morning rolled around. I took Griffin's advice, and I didn't go to work early. Instead, I caught the train like I normally would. I took a window seat and was surprised when I heard, "Is this seat taken?" I looked up and saw Jet standing in the aisle. There were plenty of other seats around, but I really didn't mind his company.

"Hey, Jet, by all means." I motioned to the seat beside me.

He sat and stared at me for a second. It was a bit unnerving, and I wondered out loud, "Do I have toothpaste on my face or something."

He laughed. "No, it's just I'm still so taken aback at the sight of you."

I found myself blushing, and I knew that if I hadn't had the carefree weekend with my boss that I probably wouldn't even be open to having Jet sit with me.

"I was hoping you would've called."

He was persistent.

"Are you ready for another beautiful Monday morning?" I looked outside at the overcast, rainy day, then quirked an eyebrow at Jet.

"It will be a good day, you'll see. Do you have a busy day ahead of you?"

"Not too bad. My boss yelled at me for working too hard, so I need to pace myself better."

"Since when does a boss not want his employees to work hard?"

"That's exactly what I thought. But apparently, they are trying to make some top ten best places to work list, and all my overtime is killing their chances."

"Is it a good place to work?"

"I like it there. My boss is a riot. I never really thought so before, but he brought me out over the weekend to this gay bar that, I kid you not, had lube wrestling."

"No, shit. How was that?"

"Slippery..." I shrugged.

"I bet."

"How about you? Do you have a busy day planned?"

"It depends."

"Do you have a difficult musician coming in?"

"Well, it depends on whether I need to bust my ass, so I can take the pretty girl I'm talking to out for lunch, or if I'm going to be working through it."

Man, he made me smile, and smiles were good for me.

The train slowed, and without answering his lunch question, I asked, "Isn't this your stop?"

"So, it is. What do you say, lunch?"

I bit my lip thinking about it. Was I ready for lunch with Jet? I knew the answer. I was not. "I'm sorry, not today."

"Working through lunch it is. Hope to see you again, Lola."

I waved as he exited the train, and my phone beeped, signaling a text.

Ty: Hey, Lols. Lunch?

Apparently, people wanted to feed me. I texted back immediately. **Sure 12?**

Ty: I'll be downtown. Pick you up at the office.

I replied with a big thumbs up then stood to exit the train. I made the short walk to work, grateful that the rain stopped, and greeted Richard at the front of the building.

"Morning, Mrs. Paige."

"How's the baby?"

"I have pictures. Do you want to see?"

"Of course, I do." He pulled out his phone, showing me photo after photo. I smiled at him and hid the crushing weight I felt. I should've had a baby. She would've been a toddler.

I wished him a good day and took the elevator up to Black Label. I paused when I made it to my desk. There was another large spray of roses. This time they were white. There had to be at least two dozen. I grabbed the card and read, knowing that it was from Jet.

Another time? Regards, Jet

I had no idea how he got the flowers here so quickly, but I wondered if he'd already had them arranged.

I worked hard all morning, deliberately trying to go slower than I normally did, but it was no use. Griffin stopped in for a quick hello which broke up my morning nicely.

I was getting ready to power my computer down when I heard a quick tap on my open door. I looked up, and Ty was there. "I was just coming down."

"I was a few minutes early. Thought I'd come up."

He walked over to my desk and looked at the flowers, plucking the card out and reading it. "Who's Jet?"

"Just some guy who has been trying to get me to go out with him."

I watched Ty's smile turn into a frown, but he refrained from commenting.

"Are you about ready to go?" I grabbed my purse and walked to Ty, giving him a squeeze around his waist.

We were heading past a series of cubicles when we saw Griffin. Griffin's body language straightened, and he turned towards me, stopping us. "Lola, is everything all right?"

Ty was a huge man, and I often forgot how intimidating he looked. "Oh, I'm sorry. Ty, this is my boss, Griffin. Griffin, this is my," I paused about to say brother-in-law but finished with, "brother," instead.

"Hey, man," Ty said, extending his hand. Griffin shook it, then asked, "You headed to lunch?"

"We are. Do you want to come?" I asked selfishly. I didn't want Ty to question me about the roses because the more I thought about it, the more I felt guilty having them on my desk, but screw that! Lincoln made his choices.

"Can't today. Raincheck?"

"Sure."

"Nice to meet you," Ty said, putting his arm protectively around my shoulder and walking me to the elevator.

We went to lunch at an upscale sushi restaurant that wasn't far from the office. It was already crowded, but I had no doubt that Ty had reservations. The hostess greeted Ty right away and showed us to our table. She poured us both water, took our drink order, and said our waitress would be right over.

"Your boss a good guy?"

"Yeah. He is. We went out over the weekend, and it was a ton of fun."

Ty raised an eye questioning me.

"Just as friends. It was fun."

"You seem a lot better this week. Did you take me up on my suggestion to talk with someone?"

"Not yet. I will," I lied. That was the last thing I wanted to do. I didn't want to talk with anyone about my feelings. If I did, my dam would break, I knew it, and Lincoln didn't deserve any more of my tears.

Ty read me well. We'd known each other for ages, so I knew he knew I was bullshitting him, but he let it go.

The waitress came over, and Ty ordered us an enormous platter of sushi that would probably put me in a food coma.

While we waited for our food to come, I asked Ty about his dating life, and he was as vague as ever. No matter how many times I tried to inquire, he shut me down. I was not getting in there. Eventually, our food came, and I had to stop my inquisition.

Changing the subject quickly, he brought up what I was dreading. "Jet?"

"A man I met on the train. I've run into him a few times since, and he's pretty relentless."

"I need to have a word with him?" Ty sat up straighter and puffed out his chest.

"Relentless but harmless."

"What do you know about him?"

"He works for Sound Machine and is also a musician."

Ty nodded his head.

"Do not go all private investigator on him." Ty owned one of the largest security firms in Chicago. He hated it when I referred to him as a PI.

"I'll be discreet. Looked out for you most of your life. I'm not going to stop now just because you and my brother are getting divorced."

Divorced.

Hearing that word felt like a blow. Tears welled in my eyes, and I frantically blinked them back.

"Shit, Lols. I'm sorry."

I squared my shoulders and stood from the table. "I'm going to use the restroom. I'll be right back."

I took the time to collect my thoughts and repeatedly told myself that it was all right that it was what I needed.

I returned to the table, and Ty was paying our bill and boxing up our lunch. "I'm going to take the leftovers to the guys unless you want them."

"No, it will be nasty by the time I ride home."

"You're right. Old sushi is the worst."

Ty dropped me off at work, and I stared at my roses, wondering if I should accept Jet's invitation and have lunch with him. I needed to move on. I'd been grieving my marriage for too long.

Chapter Fourteen

It had been two weeks since my lunch with Ty. During that time, I ran into Jet several times on the train, and he'd sent me roses of all different colors another four times. I hadn't heard a peep from Lincoln, and I didn't suspect I would. Ty had also been tight-lipped now that he knew I wasn't falling apart. I went right back into survival mode like I had been in the last three years.

I saw Richard as I approached the Hancock building. "Hi," I waved. "I have something for you and Sam."

"Awe, Mrs. Paige. Thank you. You didn't need to get us anything else."

I shrugged. "I know. I just see something cute, and I have to buy it."

"When you have kids, no doubt in my mind, they'll be more than a little spoiled."

I felt my insides fall while putting on a happy smile. "Have a nice day, Richard."

"You too."

I left Richard and wondered why I kept bringing up his baby when I knew it would hurt me. I had to stop doing that. Maybe Ty was right, and I could benefit from talking with someone. I thought about that while I waited for the elevator. A delivery man carrying a large arrangement of roses stood next to me, waiting as well. I eyed him for a second, then asked, "Where are you bringing those?"

"Black Label."

"Let me guess, they're for Lola Paige?"

He looked at the card then asked, "How'd you know?"

"I'm Lola." I reached into my purse and grabbed some cash for a tip. "Here, I'll take them from you."

"You sure? I can carry them. It's really not a bother."

I waved him away and grabbed the vase from him. I got on the elevator and could see the card. "Drinks?" was all it said. I couldn't help the small giddy feeling in my stomach. It was nice to have someone pay so much attention to me and to do it so relentlessly.

I rode the elevator up and smiled at the receptionist, then passed Griffin in the hallway. "More flowers? Whoever this man is, he has class, that's for sure."

"Morning, Griffin. Want to help me swap out a few of the vases and put them at reception? I have so many."

"Not sure I ever heard a woman complain about too many beautiful things." I shook my head at Griffin, and he followed me to my office. He set the roses down and grabbed a few vases. "I think you should go out with him."

"You do?"

"Only if you want to. But I'm guessing you would've turned him down flat if you weren't considering it."

I nodded my head at him as he left to bring the flowers up front, then moved to my desk and opened my email. I decided what the hell. I emailed Jet and typed. **Drinks–Six–Auggies.**

I hit send, unsure if I just made a colossal mistake or not.

The response was almost immediate. **I'll be there, Beautiful.**

My workday was going quickly. I called Ellie to let her know that I finally said yes to going out with Jet. "What are you going to wear?"

"I hadn't really thought about it. We're just meeting for drinks."

"I'll come to your office at four. Let's do some shopping first!"

I couldn't talk Ellie out of shopping if I tried. "Fine," I agreed and let her go, telling her to text me when she was close, and I'd go downstairs.

I finished my day and met Ellie, who was waiting in a Town Car. She was dressed in a bold red dress that hit just below the knee. I never dressed that bold to work, or ever for that matter. "Driver, take us to Saks," she ordered as soon as I slid in beside her.

"Busy today?" I asked as the car drove forward.

"No more than usual."

"You?"

"It was fine."

"Are you nervous at all?" she asked, not letting our small talk continue.

"A little. He's... nice. This will be good." I wasn't sure if it was her I was trying to convince or myself.

She sighed, "I'm all for you getting back out there, but I just want to make sure you're ready."

I sat quietly for a few long seconds. "I'm not one hundred percent sure if I'm ready. He's easy to talk to. It's just drinks, so if it feels like too much, I can always leave. I suppose it's time for me to at least try to move on, right?"

"It is. You ready to make a dent in my wallet?"

"Oh, no. You are not buying."

"Let me do this for you. I want to help you feel all special and pretty for your first time," she said cheekily.

I giggled. "It sounds like you're trying to get me into bed."

She laughed, "You couldn't handle me in bed, Miss Vanilla."

"I am not vanilla," I huffed as the car came to a stop.

She raised an eyebrow at me before getting out of the car.

"What? I'm not."

"Sure, when is the last time you even dusted off those cobwebs? Have you even had an orgasm in three years?"

It occurred to me that I never told her that Lincoln and I had sex. I gave her a guilty look as we stepped onto an escalator.

"Is this not your first time going out with Jet? Was it that night at the bar when I left with that guy?"

I shook my head, feeling even guiltier, then kept my eyes averted, watching the escalator move upwards.

"Lola. You didn't!" she scolded, knowing that I slept with Lincoln. "That's why you were as torn up as you were. Isn't it?"

I stepped off the escalator and admitted softly, "Yes, and no. It really felt more like a goodbye than anything else, and that's why it hurt so badly."

She patted my arm in sympathy then led me to a clothes rack where we began sifting through various items. I attempted to buy black, but Ellie wasn't having it. She convinced me to buy a baby blue blouse with cap sleeves and a tight-fitting skirt with a flower print. I never wore prints. I always wore black, but I had to admit it looked good.

Ellie all but squealed at a white and gold pair of Louis Vuitton heels with thin ankle straps and peep toes. They were beautiful shoes, but I was hesitant to try them on. They were a tad bit pricey but not that bad for Louis Vuitton.

"Try them on," she prompted, handing me a pair in my size. "They're gorgeous."

I bit my lip, "I don't know."

"Do it! You never let me do anything nice for you, and lord knows, I'm loaded. Try them on."

I grabbed the shoes and slipped them on. They were fantastic. Ellie took one look at the shoes on my feet, and she waved the saleswoman over and handed over her credit card. "She's going to change into this fabulous outfit. Can you ring it in while she gets ready?"

"Of course," the well-dressed saleswoman, whose hair was coiffed at the nape and too much sweet perfume wafted from her, said grabbing the box the heels would go in.

"You didn't need to do all this," I said as I exited the dressing room wearing my new outfit and feeling good. There was something to be said about clothes and how they made you feel. Don't get me started on the magic of heels. You could be having a shit day, but put on a good pair of heels, and it will make you feel like a queen.

I WALKED INTO AUGGIES and spotted Jet immediately. His face lit up when he saw me, and he stood from the bar and walked directly to me. "Hey there, Beautiful." He bent in and gave me a quick hug. I wasn't sure how it made me feel.

"There's a table in the back." He placed his hand on the small of my back and directed me towards it.

He waited for me to take a seat before sitting himself, and it made me think he had good manners. He already had a beer in his hand.

"What are you drinking?" I asked, eyeing his glass.

"It's Noon Whistle's Smack That. You want to taste it?"

"Is it hoppy?"

"It's not too hoppy, but it's a little sour."

I reached for his glass, and he intentionally touched my fingers as I did. I took a small sip and scrunched my nose at him.

"Not a fan?"

"I'll stick to a Martini."

Jet waved at a passing waitress who told him she'd be right there. I took off my coat and placed it over the empty chair next to me.

"My God, you're stunning." I blushed under his scrutiny then briefly thought that he said that a lot.

I smiled. "Jet, the flowers are nice, but it's a little over the top. Thank you, though."

"Well, it got you here, didn't it?" He smiled, took a sip of his beer, then added, "I'll slow it down, but I'm the kind of guy who sends flowers."

"I saw that," I muttered under my breath. The waitress came over, and I ordered a dirty martini. We talked about work, and I knew a few people Jet worked with.

He was funny and charming in his own way. He laid off on the 'beautiful' comments, which helped me feel more at ease. I was enjoying myself and sipping on my second Martini when I got a prickle on the back of my neck. I looked around the bar to see if there was a reason, and that's when I spotted him.

Lincoln.

He had a hooded sweatshirt on over a baseball cap. My attention left Jet as I watched him take a sip of his amber drink that I knew was whiskey. His eyes were on me, and he tilted his drink towards me. Fire blazed in those eyes. He was half a room away, yet I could tell he was pissed.

I suddenly felt guilty for being with Jet, which I shouldn't. At all.

My hand was squeezed, making me break eye contact with Lincoln. I looked at Jet and saw a worried expression on his face.

"Are you okay? You suddenly got quiet, and your face looks white."

I gulped, not sure what to say. "Yes, sorry. What were we talking about again?" I tried to pretend that Lincoln being across the room from me didn't affect me, but every few seconds, I glanced away from Jet and met Lincoln's fiery gaze.

I winced as I watched him do a shot. He sucked at drinking. He could sip on whiskey, but he was a lightweight when it came to shots. Always had been. It didn't matter how tall he was or how much muscle he put on; shots got him hammered and quickly. The bartender immediately poured him another shot. I looked away, not wanting to see him take it down. Jet was talking about something. I really should've been paying more attention.

"Okay, Lola. I lost you." He looked around the room to see if there was a reason, and he immediately noticed Lincoln staring at us.

"Is that guy creeping you out? Do you want to go?"

"What? No, it's fine. I know him. It's just... Can you excuse me for a second?"

"Are you going to go over there? He looks like bad news. You should stay."

His comment about Linc looking like bad news irked me, and I felt protective. "He was my husband," I said quietly.

On second thought, I decided to call Ty and see if he could come and get Lincoln. I didn't want Lincoln to get trashed. He was on parole. Was it even legal to drink on parole?

"I'm just going to make a call first."

Jet nodded. His brows furrowed as he skeptically watched me.

I found Ty's name in my contacts and hit send. It rang several times before he finally picked up.

"Lola, everything all right? It's not really a great time."

"Shit, I'm sorry. Listen, I'm at Auggies, and Linc is here." I paused for a second, then said quietly. "He's getting drunk."

"Shit. I'm in a meeting. I can't get out of it. Lols, I hate to ask you this. God, I really do. But I don't want to see him go back in because he's a light-weight. I know this is asking a lot of you..."

I sighed, "Fine."

"I'll make it up to you. I promise."

"I'm on a date, Ty."

"I'm sorry, Lols. Listen, I have to go. There are twelve men staring at me right now, wondering why I stopped the meeting."

"Shit. Okay, Honey. Bye."

I disconnected and met Jet's eyes.

"I hate to do this. I was really enjoying our night. But I have to see that he gets home all right."

"He looks like a grown man that should be able to handle himself."

"I know. It's complicated, though."

"Is he the complicated part you told me about when we first met?"

I nodded. "We've been uncomplicating things for a while, but he was a part of my life for a long time, and I need to help him."

"Is he a drunk? Is that what's happening? Because if he is, maybe it's not the best idea for you to go with him."

My defenses were raised again, and I spoke a little louder than I should've. "No. He'd never hurt me. It's not that, more like the opposite. He's the biggest lightweight I've ever met, and he'll be falling all over the place before we know it. He's got to get out of here."

Jet looked back at Linc then to me again. He stood and waited for me to stand. Once I did, he reached in for a hug. "Will you text me to let me know you're okay?" he asked hesitantly.

"I'll be fine," I said, not wanting to commit to calling him.

"I'm going to grab another drink at the bar, so if anything gets out of hand, I'm here, okay?"

"Okay."

I said goodbye to Jet and approached Lincoln, feeling all the butterflies on the short walk over, and I prayed that I didn't fall back into the same old same old with him.

Chapter Fifteen

Lincoln stared at me as I approached and continued to sip his whiskey. Another shot was already lined up, ready for him to shoot back.

"What are you doing, Linc?" My voice was firm, and I was proud of myself that I didn't let it waver.

"I didn't know you were going to be here."

God, just the sound of his voice made my chest ache.

"Why are you drinking like this? If you get hammered, and anyone finds out, they'll send you back Linc. You know it."

"Lols, if I want to get drunk because my wife and I are getting a divorce and I see her out with another man, then I'm pretty sure I have the right to get drunk." He lifted the shot glass and slugged it back. "I had to sit here and watch as another man put his hands on you. And there's not a damn thing I can do about it."

He lifted the glass of whiskey next and was about to sip that, but I shot my hand out and began to try and grab it from him. A small amount splashed out onto my fingers, but my hand touched his, and all of those sparks and feelings seemed to burn right through me.

"Stop, Linc. Please."

He set the glass down. "I could never deny you."

"Thank you. Did you drive here?"

I waved the bartender over. "He needs to close out his tab," I said while waiting on Lincoln to answer my question about driving.

"Is your boyfriend going to watch us all night?" He tilted his head towards Jet, and guilt coursed through me.

I knew Linc loved me, and I knew this had to hurt him. No matter how much time we were no longer together, it would always hurt me to see him with another woman, so I understood where his pain and bitterness seemed to stem from.

"Jet's not my boyfriend."

"What kind of name is Jet?"

Annoyed, I asked again, "Did you drive?"

Instead of answering, he touched the sleeve of my blouse. "Is this a new top? It looks nice on you. Of course, it's new. It's probably all new. I miss you in Chucks."

I sighed, and when the bartender dropped his tab for his signature, I reached down, added a tip, and signed it like it was second nature.

"Come on, Linc. Let's get you home."

"I don't have a home anymore."

"Let's get you to Ty's."

He began to stand and wobbled a little. "Fuck," he hissed. I wanted to shake my head but refrained. Instead, I slipped my arm around his waist to help keep him steady. Touching him was hard, and it took all of my willpower not to bury my head into his chest and feel him against me.

"I'm guessing you drove. Give me your keys, Linc."

He clumsily reached into his pocket and pulled out a set of keys, and handed them to me. My heart sank when I saw the keychain I had engraved with our names and our wedding date.

We walked out of the bar, and it didn't hit me until much later that I didn't look back at Jet.

I found his SUV with no help from Linc. I had to hit the button on his key fob until we got close enough to where I could hear it in a neighboring lot.

I helped Lincoln into the SUV, which wasn't easy since the longer he stood, the more he became unsteady on his feet.

His nearness hurt. I wanted to touch and hold him so badly, but I knew where it would end. I knew our time had passed, but it didn't make it easier. I got in the driver's side, adjusted the seat and mirrors for my much smaller frame, and buckled in. I started the car and began to head towards Ty's place. Linc was quiet for a minute, and when he talked, it shocked the hell out of me.

"I had a brother."

"I know Lincoln. You had three."

"No, a biological one. His name was Andrew."

I gasped. How had he never told me about him? I felt myself gripping the steering wheel as he spoke.

"He was a year younger than me. Before CPS took me, he would get sick all the time, and between the physical abuse we took and not having food, he hurt all the time. I tried to get out of there. I tried to find something to eat, but he was too little. He was just so small."

"Lincoln."

I watched him grab his head like the memory hurt him. "I couldn't save him, Lola."

He looked away from me, and his pain became my pain. We weren't together, but I loved him and would always love him. All of these years together, and he never told me about Andrew.

I pulled into a spot in front of Ty's place. I wanted to comfort him. I wanted to be there for him, but it wasn't who we were any longer.

I turned off the SUV and began to get out. "I'm fine, Lola. You don't have to come up."

"This is your car Linc. What am I going to do with it? I'll make sure you get up there okay, and I'll call an Uber."

"Fine," irritation laced his words, and his eyes looked dim, like the spark inside of him wasn't there. I didn't feel like he was truly with me after his confession about his brother.

We walked into Ty's, and I asked, "Were you with him when he died?"

"Do you really want to know Lols?"

"I do." I sat on the leather sectional in the big open living room, and Lincoln sat, keeping his distance from me.

"I never wanted you to know how bad it was. I never wanted you to see my pain. I've been seeing a counselor. He thought you should know about him. He thinks it's why I'm always doing everything I can to protect my foster brothers."

He watched me for a few brief moments, and I let it all sink in. Something tragic had happened to Linc, and he wanted to save everyone all the time because of it.

"You know it was just the old man and us. My mom OD'd when Andrew was two. I was only three, so I didn't really get it. One day she was there, and the next, she was gone. The old man was a drunk. He hit us, but that wasn't the worst of it. He'd leave, sometimes for days at a time, and there was no food. Andrew was sick a lot. I don't know why he got sick all the time and I didn't, but he was just so much more fragile than I was. He kept getting sicker and the old man wasn't there.

"There were no houses by us. We lived in a trailer that was secluded from everyone. Andrew was sleeping all the time, and we had nothing to feed him. I tried to find something—anything to feed him. I went outside and searched for food. There was nothing. I was six years old. Six fucking years old." His voice broke, as it filled with anger and desperation. He closed his eyes for a second, then reopened them and continued, "I was starving, and I knew my brother was passed that. He wouldn't wake up. I didn't want to leave him because what if he did and wanted something to eat, but I couldn't help him.

"I didn't know what to do. I felt so helpless. I remember when he stopped breathing. One second there was breath, and then there wasn't. His chest no longer rose and fell. I sat by his side, praying he would get up, but he never did. He never woke up. I was with him another day before CPS came to the house. Apparently, the old man was in the hospital dying of liver failure. It took him some time before he let anyone know there were kids at the house."

My heart ached for him, and I couldn't stand the distance between us. I moved to him, and I hugged him. His arms squeezed me, and I felt him shake. I realized he must be crying, but his hair was buried in my neck, and he gripped me so tightly.

"You were just a boy, Linc. There was nothing you could've done. They were selfish and cruel, and none of it was on you."

He didn't speak about it. He just let me hold him. All the hurt between us was irrelevant at the moment. He was showing me his pain, and for the first time in our life together, he bared it all. He needed me. I didn't let him go. I held him to me, and eventually, his head was against my chest, and I stroked the side of his head. It was always something he found comfort in, and after, I felt him fall asleep. Once he was sleeping soundly, I covered him with a blanket and reluctantly decided it was time to leave.

I was about to call an Uber when I saw Ty pulling into the drive.

"Hey. Did everything go all right? I'm so sorry I couldn't be there to help."

"It was heavy. Listen, I was about to call an Uber. Can you give me a ride home?"

"Of course. Get in."

"Thanks."

"Do you want to talk about it?" Ty asked once I was buckled into the car.

"So much happened tonight. He told me some things he's never told me. It was heavy. I'm not sure what to do with it, but it explains why he always felt the need to protect Alex."

Ty was quiet for a second, then it was as if he decided he shouldn't push—that what Lincoln told me was for me alone. "I'm sorry about your date."

Rubbing my temple, I realized I'd forgotten about Jet. I was supposed to call him. I fished my phone from my purse and saw a missed text from Jet, asking if everything was all right. I quickly texted that it was fine and put my phone away.

"Don't worry about the date. You were in a meeting." I shrugged then yawned because I was seriously tired. I wanted to ask Ty how Lincoln had been recently because tonight had been such a break-through. I wondered if he knew Lincoln was seeing a therapist. I was worried, but in the end, I decided to let it go. It wasn't my place to ask.

Part of me wondered if knowing about his past changed anything. Did knowing the reason someone made the decisions they made have any effect on forgiveness? Does it negate the fact that I wasn't first? The only thing I knew for certain right then was that I had a lot to think about.

Chapter Sixteen

"Let's hear it," Griffin said as soon as we sat down at the restaurant.

"I want to wait for Ellie to get here. I don't want to repeat this twice."

Griffin looked at his watch, "Is she always late?"

"It's only a few minutes past the time we were set to meet. She's usually a few minutes late, though, but she'll be here."

It was the first time Griffin and Ellie were meeting. Both had wanted to know about my date, and I felt like it would be easier to tell them both in person. I still felt so conflicted. Ellie walked into the crowded restaurant and spotted us immediately. "Sorry, I'm late. Chicago traffic." She shrugged, this was a common problem for her, then she bent low and kissed my cheek. Griffin stood while Ellie took her seat. "Ellie, this is Griffin."

"Nice to meet you." She held out her hand to shake his, and I could immediately see interest on both of their faces. Strange, I would never have guessed it.

"I'm so glad you've made it. I was waiting for our Lola to tell me what happened."

Ellie smiled when he said 'our Lola.'

"I already ordered your drink," I told Ellie. "The waitress should be back any minute with it." I knew Ellie had no aversion to having a cocktail in the middle of the day, but I was sitting with my boss, and I didn't feel comfortable doing that. Plus, I thought it would just make me tired.

"Thank God. The client I just left was truly atrocious. Her taste was as gaudy as it comes."

"What do you do?" Griffin asked.

"Interior design," she shrugged.

"It's not just interior design. Ellie is the most sought after interior designer there is." I was proud of Ellie and hated when she down-played her importance in the industry.

"Give me your card. Sometimes I have clients who are looking for someone," Griffin said.

She pulled out her business card and handed it to him. I knew that they were scented, and I'd joked with her that it was typical Elle Woods behavior.

Our drinks came, and we ordered lunch. Once the waitress walked away, the looks from both Ellie and Griffin we're impatient. I turned to Ellie, "Griffin doesn't know the backstory."

"What backstory? She met Jet on the train. There, he's up to speed."

I shook my head and shot her a look, and I saw her eyes go wide as she figured out that there was more to last night than drinks with Jet.

"Jet and I were having drinks. It was nice. Conversation flowed well. Then I looked up and saw my ex at the bar getting drunk."

"No!" Ellie exclaimed.

"What's the big deal here?"

"First, Lincoln Paige can't hold his liquor at all. And secondly, that wound is kind of fresh," Ellie said.

"You mean your ex-husband? I thought he's been out of the picture for years?"

"He was in jail. I didn't want to say anything to anyone about what happened between us. I guess I was embarrassed. I mean, who really wants to lead with the fact that they're getting divorced because their husband is in jail?"

"Did he hurt you?" Griffin asked immediately in defensive mode.

"No." I waved my hand defensively. "It was nothing like that. He would never hurt me. He was helping his brother Alex out of a situation and got mixed up in it. He was gone for almost three years."

Griffin nodded, his eyes pleading with me to continue at the same time conveying sympathy for everything I'd been through.

"So, I was out for drinks, and as much as I would've liked to just go somewhere else with Jet, I didn't want Lincoln to do something stupid and get picked up. I called Ty."

"Ty's the one who shows up at work sometimes, right?"

"Yes, he's my brother-in-law."

"They're foster brothers," Ellie chimed in.

Griffin nodded.

"So what did Ty say?" Ellie asked.

"He was in a meeting and couldn't get out of it. So, I did what I thought was best and cut my date short, confronted Lincoln, and drove him to Ty's."

"Ouch. Poor Jet," Griffin said, on an exhale.

Ellie, knowing more about Lincoln and my history, asked, "How was it? Are you okay?"

I gave her a wide-eyed look, wordlessly saying how much I wasn't sure how I felt. "Lincoln was pretty drunk, and he opened up about something that, in all of our years together, he never told me about, and it sort of explained why he's the way he is?"

"What do you mean?" Griffin asked.

"Linc's always trying to save everyone. I don't know how else to explain it. But even before he went to jail, he was gone a lot, and I guess I just started to feel like people were first because of it. Anyway, Linc was pretty emotional, and the entire night felt pretty heavy. Eventually, Ty got home and gave me a ride." I shrugged like that was the whole story, but I could tell they were both watching me carefully to try and read what I wasn't saying. I began to feel a little uncomfortable by their scrutiny, so I looked away.

Ellie grabbed my hand, pulling my attention back. "Seriously, are you okay?"

"I really don't know. Part of me wants to forgive him and go back to him. He was so sincere, plus he said he's been going to counseling. I just don't want to be the second fiddle anymore."

"Well, last night should've taught you something obvious," Griffin chimed in, relieving me from Ellie's searching gaze.

"What's that?" Ellie asked at the same time I raised a questioning brow.

"You're not that into Jet. I think you want to be, but you're not. If you were 'there,' there would've been no reason that you didn't put Lincoln into a cab and continued on with your date."

I deflated a little with that knowledge. He was right. I think I wanted to be into Jet. I liked the attention Jet gave me, but he didn't really do it for me.

I let out a puff of air and nodded my head.

"It's okay. There is no reason you have to be into him. From the flowers he seemed like a decent enough guy, but I'd let him know that you're not there. No sense in stringing the guy along," Griffin added.

I nodded, knowing he was right. "You're probably right about all of that," I agreed, feeling a small weight lifted off of my shoulders by letting my friends in on where my head was at.

The rest of the lunch went well. Ellie and Griffin hit it off, and I wished I'd gotten them together much sooner.

"Call me later. We can talk through things more if you need," Ellie said as we were saying our goodbyes. I knew she wondered what it was that Lincoln told me, but that was only for me. I wouldn't share.

Griffin and I made the quick walk back to the office.

"You know, no one would blame you if you went back to your husband," Griffin said before we walked into the building.

I sighed. "It's more complicated than that."

"Does it have to be?"

"We've been together since we were teenagers. He has a pattern of leaving and putting other people first. He's Lincoln Paige. He'll never change."

I felt a small amount of guilt saying those words. He opened up to me last night in a way he never has before.

We took the elevator, and Griffin kept side-eying me. "What?" I finally asked.

"It's... nevermind."

"Go on, say it."

"I don't think you're ready for it." He motioned his head toward a large vase filled with roses. "I'm betting those are for you."

I took the card off the roses and realized he was right, another gift from Jet.

MY FINGER HOVERED OVER the cursor. I took a deep breath and hit send, then immediately reread my small note to Jet.

Jet,

Thank you for the roses, but I think that you should stop sending them. I have a lot of feelings mixed up with my ex, and I'm not ready to date anyone or be pursued at this time. You're a really great guy, and I think that there is someone wonderful out there for you.

Best of luck,

Lola

Best of luck? Why the heck did I type that? Like, hey, good luck out there in the dating pool. You're going to need it.

I powered off my PC and decided to let it go. It was sent. There was nothing I could do about it, and besides, I really did think he was a good guy and that he deserved to find love. I just knew it wasn't going to be me.

I didn't stay late at work. I was trying to take Griffin's words to heart about working too much. I took the train, then grabbed takeout, and headed home. My evening was quiet, no calls or texts and nothing from Lincoln. After the previous night, I half expected that he would be here waiting when I got home from work, and when he wasn't, I wasn't prepared for the slight drop in my stomach.

Chapter Seventeen

All this noise. I wanted to stick my head under my pillow, but a quick glance at my phone read **Ty Calling**. He knew I hated mornings and wouldn't phone early unless it was important.

"Hello?" my voice was scratchy as I spoke.

"What did you do to my boy? I've barely had him back, and now he's gone. I knew it. I knew you'd be his downfall, and now he's gone. Gone!" Marlene shouted at me over the phone. After losing Alex and Lincoln, Marlene's patience had waned.

My stomach dropped, and I shrieked, "What do you mean gone? He can't be gone. What happened? Was it Alex again? Oh, my God, I can't believe this is happening." Tears streamed down my face, hearing that Lincoln was gone.

"Mom, what happened?" I cried out.

She sighed, "He's not dead, child. He's gone, as in he left. I'm at Ty's now, and he said he left yesterday, said he needed to clear his head. That boy seemed dead inside for weeks, and I know it was you. What kind of wife leaves her husband when the going gets tough? Then he gets released, and you serve him? There's only so much a man can take. What did you think this was all going to do to him?"

Marlene was downright scolding me. I felt my anger rise. We'd been close, but then I had to cut her off when I cut Lincoln off. She didn't understand. She blamed me for not sticking by him, and it all hurt too much, so I decided that I wouldn't do it anymore. I couldn't do it, and I stopped answering her calls. She was my family, but I couldn't deal with how she blamed me, so I just stopped, and it hurt, but right then, when she was yelling at me, I was pissed.

"Marlene, you don't get to do that..."

"I'm Marlene to you now, huh? I'm not even Mom anymore. I see how it is. You throw me away just like you threw your husband away."

"Stop, I didn't mean..."

"What, you didn't mean to break a good man's heart? You didn't mean to break mine?"

"Mom, you know that's not fair. You know it was Lincoln." I couldn't take it. My anger was at an all-time high, and maybe it was because it was just the pain of it all coming through, but I snapped. "Mom, do you know how many times he left me? It was always someone else's needs first. Always. I begged him not to go with Alex. Begged. It hurt so much, and if he would've stayed home, I wouldn't have lost the baby. We'd be a family. You'd be a grandma. So what Mom? What should I have done? Continued to stay with a man who always left me? Who broke my heart so bad I miscarried?"

I was breathing heavily, and I waited for a response. She wanted to spar with me; I was all in, but there was no response, just silence.

"Mom?" I questioned.

I heard Ty in the background. "Mom, you okay? Mom?"

Ty spoke in my ear, "Lols, it's Mom. Something's wrong. I'm calling 9-1-1." Then he disconnected. I sat staring at my phone, scared out of my mind, then without thinking, grabbed my phone, and headed to the hospital.

I BURIED MY FACE IN Ty's chest as soon as I spotted him in the waiting room. "What happened? Is she okay?"

"She was talking with you, and then she clutched the phone, and it was like she was frozen. I didn't know what the hell was happening. I grabbed the phone to call 9-1-1, and she collapsed. She just collapsed," he repeated. I squeezed him around his middle.

"Have you called anyone?" I asked and looked up to see Ty shake his head.

Ty let me go, and I pulled out my phone and searched for Trey's name. We hadn't spoken in some time, but I could call him. I could do this for Ty.

"Surprised to see your name flash across my screen," he answered, not letting me get a word in. "You got some nerve, Lols."

"Stop," I cut him off. "I'm with Ty at the hospital. It's Marlene. Ty said she just froze then collapsed. We don't know what's going on yet. We're in the waiting room waiting for the doctors to tell us something. Can you catch a flight and get here as soon as possible?"

"What hospital?"

"Chicago."

"I'll be there. Can you keep me posted with any news?"

"Yeah, Honey," I paused. "Have you heard from Lincoln? Marlene and I were on the phone when this happened, and she said he left town. She didn't know where he went."

"Shit," he hissed. I talked to him a few days ago. He said he needed to get away. A buddy of mine has a cabin southeast of you. Service is crap out there."

I released a deep breath. If anything happened to Marlene and Lincoln wasn't here, he'd never forgive himself.

"We'll figure it out," I encouraged even though I had no idea how we'd get a hold of him.

"Going to make arrangements now. Call me if anything changes."

"I will. Bye, Trey. I love you."

He was silent for a second, then murmured, "Love you too, Sis," and disconnected.

"Trey's catching the next flight out. I told him we'd keep him posted on Mom. He said Lincoln's at his friend's cabin and that there's shitty service."

"I'll try him again," Ty responded, pulling out his phone.

A few seconds later, Ty put his phone back into his pocket and shook his head. I called my parents next. They no longer lived close by, but I knew they would want to know. They were both getting older and didn't move around the way they used to. I loved my parents, but we weren't that close. I hated that for us, but it was what it was. They never really seemed to support my relationship with Lincoln, and so we grew distant. My mom asked if she should come, and I told her it wasn't necessary. I felt like she asked just because it was what she thought she should do, not what she wanted to do. I didn't want to deal with the dynamics of our relationship on top of everything else, but I thought they should know, and truthfully, I longed for their support.

It was just anotherrelationship that I needed to work on, and I didn't have that in me right then.

After I made the call to my parents, I called Ellie, who told me she would be right here.

Then we waited.

And waited.

And waited.

When the doctor finally updated us, there were a few words that stuck out to me.

Hemorrhage.

Stroke.

Wait and see.

It was all too much, and I felt like I was in a state of shock. I held Ty's hand as the doctor explained that they would have to operate and were putting together a team. Trey's fight would land soon. Ty tried calling Trey's contact to see if anyone could reach Lincoln, but we were having no luck. As strained as things were between Lincoln and I, the pain we would all feel losing Marlene overrode all of that.

After the doctor left us, I held Ty's hand and softly cried. Ellie sat on my other side and held my hand in a show of solidarity.

"We were arguing," I confessed. "This all happened because we were arguing on the phone. I called her Marlene and not Mom, and then I told her about..." I trailed off, not having told them.

"You told her you were pregnant," Ty finished my sentence.

My mouth fell open, shocked that he knew. "Linc told me. Bottom line, you should've said something. You shouldn't have carried that alone. We're your family."

"When were you pregnant?" Ellie asked. I couldn't meet her eyes.

Ty answered for me. "She lost the baby when Linc got locked up."

"Lola!" Ellie scolded then gentled her voice, "You should have said something."

"You're right, but I was messed up with losing Linc. Do you know how many times I had to say goodbye to him and then knowing that the last goodbye cost me our baby? I was a wreck. I am a wreck. I can hardly look at a baby without thinking of everything I could've had if Lincoln would've, for once in his damn life, chose me. But none of that matters. In my anger at Linc, I shut out Mom. Then I yelled at her, laid it all on her about the baby, and she collapsed. I caused this. It's all my fault," I cried, dropping their hands and cradling my head in my hands.

"She already knew." I heard from the doorway. I looked up from my hands to see Trey in the doorway. He looked good. Better than when I had seen him last. It looked like he put a lot more muscle on too. He used to play football professionally, and his spinal cord had been severely damaged. He'd been in a wheelchair ever since.

Confusion marred my features as I heard, "What do you mean she already knew?"

"Linc told her. We don't keep big shit like that in Lols. You hide stuff like that from your family, it'll just eat you."

"It's not your fault," Trey said, wheeling close to us. Ty stood then bent low to embrace his brother. He moved away, then noted, "You look good. That new trainer has been working you hard."

"Yeah, in more ways than one," Trey smirked then got serious. "Lols, you've got two seconds to drag your ass out of that chair and give me a hug before I haul my ass out of this chair and sit next to you."

I didn't hesitate to get up and move to Trey. He grabbed my arm and pulled me down on his lap. I buried my face in his neck as he held me while I silently shook. I turned my back on Trey just like I turned my back on Marlene, and I hated the way I felt because of it. He's been my brother, just like Ty.

"I'm sorry," I murmured.

While I sat there curled in his lap, Ty filled Trey in on what was happening with Marlene. "When will they do the surgery?" he asked.

"It'll be a few hours. They're putting together a team. If she makes it through that, it'll be a long hard recovery."

"Fuck," Trey hissed.

"Tell me about it, Brother."

I stayed in Trey's arms for a while. Somehow it comforted me in more ways than I could explain. I felt forgiven for turning my back on him. There was comfort in his arms as if feeling his strength shouldered some of my burden. Finally, I pulled away, "Do you think she'll be okay?"

"I think we need to pray," Trey said, and I knew he was right.

It had been years since I'd gone to church, but my Catholic upbringing never really left me. I ordered everyone to grab each other's hands, then I began, "Hail Mary full of grace..."

Chapter Eighteen

"She's stable but in a medically induced coma. Call me when you get this, Linc. We need you." Trey put the phone down on the table next to him.

"Still no luck, huh?" Ty asked.

Trey shook his head. "He should be here. I hate that we can't get a hold of him."

"What did his parole officer say? He's got to check in with him, right?"

"He said he just talked to him yesterday, and he isn't due to check in for another two weeks."

"Shit," Ty grumbled.

It had been two long days since Marlene collapsed. The boys talked me into going home and getting some sleep last night and a fresh change of clothes. Ty had someone from his office bring fresh clothes for him and Trey, and they got a hotel room across the street so they could freshen up and try to get a little shut-eye. They wanted to be close by in case anything changed.

Marlene's surgery went well, except now we were in a waiting game for the doctors to decide when it was time to wake her up, then we would have to hope and pray that she did, in fact, wake up. The doctors were preparing us for a long recovery, which I took as a good sign. They must believe she was going to recover. I knew they said that there was a chance things could change, but for now, she was stable. We sat by her bedside and held her hand. I prayed with her more than I'd prayed in a long time. Ty and Trey would talk to her as well, but I knew we were missing Lincoln. I knew he should be here. For him. For her. For all of us. He had been the one everyone turned to. He went to Trey when he was injured and spent months helping him rehabilitate. He was Ty's best friend. He wouldn't let a Sunday go by when he was around without checking on Marlene.

"I'll find him," I blurted. It wasn't until that moment that I knew it was what I needed to do.

"Lols?" Ty questioned, taken aback by my declaration.

"You both need to be with Marlene. I love her too, but if anything happened and either of you weren't here, and I was, I'd never forgive myself. I'll find him and bring him back. He needs to be here."

"Are you sure, Honey?" Trey asked, wheeling closer to where I was sitting and grabbing my hand.

"Yes. I've been thinking about it, and it needs to be me."

Trey studied my eyes and must've been confident that my mind was made up. He nodded. "I'll get you the address."

Ty sighed, "Take the Range Rover at least. I want you to have something dependable."

"It's only three and a half hours from here. I'll drive straight there, get him, and come right back."

Ty reached into his pocket and pulled out his keys. "I'll grab the car from the garage across the street."

"Thanks."

Ty bent low and kissed me on the top of my head.

"Sweetheart, while he's getting the car, I'll give you a few minutes alone with Ma." Trey didn't say what we were both thinking. He was giving me a few minutes in case she didn't make it. In case I was too late.

He left the room, and I switched seats, so I was closer to Marlene. I grabbed her hand, noticing how frail it felt. Had she been getting smaller, and I hadn't seen her to notice? Had her health been declining before this, and I was so caught up in my resentment toward Linc that I didn't give her any mind?

I had to dispel the what ifs. I needed to hurry. I knew there wasn't a whole lot of time to waste. Things could change at any moment.

"Mom. I'm sorry I shut you out. I didn't do it because of anything you did. I did it because it hurt to be around you. You always brought him up and could never understand why I had to leave him. I know it's difficult to understand, but it always felt like he was leaving me. When he was enlisted, we were together, but we were so far apart. That never worked for me, that lifestyle, it felt lonely. He knew it and urged me to be here close to you guys, but then my parents moved, and he was gone. When we were together, it was off the charts, but it was also difficult.

"I know he knew it was hard on me. When he finally left the Army, I thought, this is it, we'll finally have a life together. But then Alex would call, and Linc would disappear, and I'd feel so alone. And then he left again after Trey's accident. I know it wasn't Trey's fault, but Ty would've been there, and he was gone for so long. I mean, couldn't he have helped get him situated then sent one of you in to help? Finally, for once, he was back, and I had him. It was so good. I felt like we were living the fairytale he promised me.

"Then Alex was out, and he kept going to Linc for things. Lincoln came to me and told me Alex needed him at his back. I begged him not to go. I knew that if he did, things would never be the same. He kissed me and told me it would be okay and that he'd be back in a little bit. He promised everything would be fine, but it wasn't. The pain of him going away for that long and how alone I felt again, I know it deep in my gut that's what caused me to lose the baby. I was so distraught. And no one understood why. I should've let you in. I shouldn't have turned my back on you.

"I love you, Mom, and I pray that you wake up so that I can explain all of this to you in person. I need you to get better. I know Lincoln is your boy, and I know you need him here. I know your sons need him here. I'm going to bring him back to you. I promise, Ma. I just need you to hang on. Promise you'll hang on. Fight, Mom. We're not ready to let you go."

I kissed the top of her head and squeezed her hand one last time and then left the room. Trey was in the hallway, and I could tell by the sympathetic look on his face that he overheard everything I had to say. He didn't say anything to make me feel awkward. "I wrote down the directions for you. Since we know cell service can suck out there, I didn't want you to have to rely on the GPS."

"Thanks." I grabbed the paper from his hand, and he pulled me down for a hug.

"When this settles, you and I are going to have a talk about where I was when Linc came down. Not saying you're totally wrong in that he could've had other people come help, but I want you to know how messed up my head was. He saved my life, Lols. I wouldn't be here if it wasn't for him."

I swallowed back tears, nodded, then pulled away from him. "We'll talk," I agreed, then left him to meet Ty in front of the hospital.

Ty was idling in a no parking zone in front of the hospital.

He hopped out, and I heard a person yell at him, "Hey, you can't park there."

"Two seconds," he shouted back and ignored the approaching man in the red valet coat.

"There's a full tank of gas. Check in with us if you can. I love you."

He gave me a quick hug and shot the valet a look that could kill. "Be safe and bring him home."

"I will. Love you too."

DRIVING FOR HOURS WITH a heavy heart gave me a lot of time to think. It started off with me thinking about all the holidays I spent with Ma when Linc was in the Army. In my senior year of high school, I remember her inviting me. Linc was gone, and my family always did a huge Christmas Eve dinner and a bigger Christmas Day brunch, so when she asked me to come over for dinner, I was excited and nervous. We never did much of anything at night, and my parents were fine with me going. I remember opening the door, and the boys were laughing. Alex had cooked a huge meal. The Christmas tree was fake, but it was still pretty. There were a ton of ornaments on it. When I looked closely, I remember noticing how many were from different foster children that Marlene had helped. How it ended up that she adopted the four she did, I wasn't sure. Then again, they were all special.

Everyone hugged me one after another. I thought the day would be hard. I thought that being with everyone, without Lincoln would devastate me. But the guys brought me into their fold, and I quickly felt like I was just spending Christmas dinner with family. After the best holiday meal I'd ever had (don't tell my mom), we all sat around eating dessert and making each other laugh. Alex got up and mimicked 'white people' dancing that had us all laughing until I reminded him that Lincoln could out dance him any day. Everyone agreed, and the room got a little quieter.

"Oh, Lola. I almost forgot. Lincoln left something for you under the tree." Marlene motioned to an unopened box that I'd previously noted but didn't pay much attention to.

Trey moved his big body under the tree, grabbed the package that weighed more than I'd expected it to, and set it on my lap. All eyes were on me as I tore into the paper. I opened the red and green striped wrapping paper excitedly. There were a few CDs I really wanted, and at the end, there was a thin package that reminded me of something my cousin Tommy used to do when he was little. Tommy would wrap up handmade cards. It was sweet. You had to be extremely careful not to rip what was in the wrapping paper, but it was always some type of heartfelt message.

I eyed the wrapping paper, trying to decide the best way to go about opening the green and white striped paper. I found a corner and slowly peeled it away. Inside was a piece of cardboard that read, '**Open the front door.**'

A knock startled me. I looked around and saw everyone smiling at me. I cautiously moved to the front door. I had no idea what kind of surprise Lincoln would have sent me, but knowing him, it could be anything. I opened the door and squealed.

Lincoln stood there in his military uniform. It didn't even take me half a second to throw myself in his arms, and then he was kissing me. *God,* that kiss. I remember feeling starved for it. It was like the first drink of water after nearly dying in a desert.

Marlene snapped a few pictures of us while we kissed, and eventually, she broke up the kiss saying, "Are you going to come give your Mom a kiss, or what?"

He broke our kiss and pressed his forehead against mine. "Merry Christmas, Lols. God, you're even more beautiful than I remember."

"You're here! This is real? I'm not dreaming?"

He chuckled, "I'm here. Are you surprised?" I shook my head excitedly. "God, I love you," he replied.

"I love you too. So much! Merry Christmas."

He gave me another soft kiss then gave Marlene the biggest bear hug. His brothers were next with hugs, and everyone talked about how I had no clue whatsoever that Lincoln was going to surprise me.

"Best Christmas ever, having my whole family here," Marlene declared, squeezing my hand. I knew right then that she considered me part of the family. Thinking back on it and looking at the photos Ma snapped, she must've sensed how much we loved each other and knew that it was the forever kind of love.

That Christmas break was the best. Lincoln only had a few days home, and we'd spent every minute of it together. My dad reluctantly let me stay the night on Christmas once he spoke to Marlene and she promised Lincoln would be on the couch and I would have his room. And it was in the late hours that night, when everyone was asleep, that Lincoln woke me, and we finally made love for the first time.

There were a lot of holidays after that where Lincoln couldn't be there, but somehow it became tradition to sleep at Marlene's on Christmas night whether he was there or not, and Lincoln always found a way to have something special for me under the tree.

I hadn't gone to Ma's since Lincoln had been incarcerated. That thought struck me. I took that tradition from her. I missed those Christmas dinners. Even after Alex was gone and Marlene cooked, it was still special, and I stopped going.

I thought about that for a while. I thought about all the things I stopped doing since Lincoln left. I vowed to myself that if Ma made it through this, I wouldn't let a Christmas go by again where I wasn't with her.

I passed a road sign that told me I needed to exit the highway soon. I knew I still had about an hour to go, but I also knew I needed to pay more attention now. Once I exited, it was all country roads. I rolled down my window to let the fresh air in and could immediately smell dampness in the air. It would rain soon, I was sure of it. I checked my phone and saw that I still had a signal, and I called to check in on Ma. They assured me she was the same and thanked me again for going to get Lincoln. I hung up with them, nearly missing a turn.

The rain began to fall, slowly at first, then it picked up so rapidly I had to pull off the road. I was a good driver, but still, I'd never driven Ty's Range Rover, and I was in a place I'd never been, driving on a road that was quickly changing from crushed stone to dirt road. The rain let up, and I drove on following the meticulous directions. This place really was in the middle of nowhere. I made a few turns and drove for another fifteen minutes or so when it began to pour again. I parked then waited, and the slow dance with the rain began again. If it wasn't coming down as heavily, I would drive on, but I cautiously waited as it poured.

I was driving again when lightning cracked through the sky overhead, making me jump. The handwritten directions fell to the passenger floor. Instinctually, I reached for them, jerking the wheel slightly. It was that tiny jerk that caused me to hit a mud puddle. That was my first mistake. My next mistake was immediately hitting the brakes and losing my momentum. My wheels spun as I tried to get out of the puddle, which suddenly seemed more like a giant mud pit than anything.

I was from Chicago; I was used to driving in shit weather. Maybe I could rock my way out of this? I switched between going in reverse and moving forward, hoping to rock myself free from the mud, but it seemed the more I did, the more mud kicked up and hit the back windshield.

Shit.

Another streak of lightning flashed across the sky, and although the sun should still be shining brightly overhead, it almost appeared that night had fallen. I stopped rocking the car, realizing that it was getting me nowhere. I looked at my phone. No service.

How long had I been driving?

Grabbing the directions off the floorboard I noticed there were only a few more directions to follow. It wouldn't take me that long on foot, would it?

I second-guessed myself over and over again. I wanted to get to Lincoln. Time wasn't on our side, but I also knew I needed to be safe. *What to do? What to do?*

The rain seemed to lighten up some again, and I decided that was my window. I grabbed the few things I had, including my directions, and did a quick search of the Range Rover to see if there was anything else that could help me. Luckily, when I opened the glove box, I found a flashlight. I hit the power button to test it, and nothing happened. I banged on it a few times, and it lit up. *Thank God.*

I put the keys in my jean pocket and grabbed my purse, securing it over my shoulder before placing the directions inside. I already read them and knew that I had a turn in the next half a mile or so. As I opened the door, I felt the drop in temperatures immediately. I cursed myself for only wearing a long sleeve shirt. I should've worn a jacket. It was a warm day when I left, and my choice of wardrobe wasn't really on my mind. I was glad that I'd remembered to call Ellie and ask her to check on Iz, at least, but beyond that, I didn't prepare to come get Lincoln. I just went.

My feet sloshed in the mud, and every step was taxing. The more I walked, the more the slight incline of the road became steeper. I slipped a few times. It felt like I was walking forever, and I second-guessed the directions and my ability to follow them, more than once.

Finally, I saw a small road that looked more washed out than the road I was on. It almost looked like a small river flowed down the road instead of dirt. I cursed again then walked with the trees on the side of the road, using them to prevent myself from falling. The rain began to come down again, and luckily, the trees helped provide some cover. The trees whooshing with the rain and the heavy patter of droplets sounded violent. I didn't see any wildlife. They must've all been smart enough to seek shelter.

I trudged on and stopped against a wide tree to check the time. I'd already been at this for a little over an hour. I carefully put the phone back and double-checked my directions. The drive to the cabin should be just ahead.

I walked several more yards and eventually saw the drive on the other side of the street. I cursed that I wasn't already on that side. Crossing the road didn't look like it would be easy. I moved to it, and my first step on the road seemed like it wouldn't be that bad. One foot after another, right? My feet were covered in mud and flowing water, so every time I moved my foot, there was a sloppy suction of sorts, but I took another step. Below the surface, there was a rock or a stick that I couldn't see, and I completely lost my balance, falling forward into the mud. I braced myself with my hands, but my palm hit something sharp, and I could tell that it was scraped. I had also submerged the flashlight into the mud, and it went out. My jeans were completely soaked, and I started to doubt myself that this was a smart idea. Maybe I should've waited it out longer in the Rover?

There was no turning back now. I picked myself up, and when I took my next step, I noticed that I must've twisted my ankle a little because bearing weight on my foot sent a sharp pain throughout my ankle. I was frustrated, exhausted, and emotionally drained. I wanted to cry at the difficulty.

Another streak of lightning took me out of my self-pity.

I'd just have to deal with the pain. I was almost completely across the road when a large stick washed past me. I reached out and grabbed it. I could use it to help bear my weight. It helped, and the rain slowed again, making it so I could at least see in front of me more easily.

With the rain lessening, the sky changed from almost black to a dark grey. I could finally see the cabin up ahead. Each step was painful, and I knew I looked a ragged mess. I had mud everywhere. God, I hoped there was running water in the cabin.

The cabin wasn't huge, but from the outside, it looked like it was cozy. There was a small glow coming from the window that I could see as I approached, and it made me feel better. A few more steps and I'd make it to Lincoln.

"Lincoln," I yelled out his name, hoping he would hear me, but I could tell my voice just carried away in the wind. Finally, I made it to the door, and I banged as loud as I could. "Linc," I shouted his name again.

Finally, the door was thrown open, and there he stood.

"Linc," I whispered his name, relieved to be safe.

Chapter Nineteen

"Lols?" Lincoln looked baffled as he stood in the doorway. Even in my state, covered in mud and in a lot of physical pain, the sight of him was like a punch to the gut. He was beautiful. Still the most beautiful man I'd ever seen. He had stubble on his face, which wasn't like him. He wore jeans and a light grey long-sleeved Henley.

"It's really you. Are you okay? What are you doing here? Come in."

I tried to take a step into the cabin and winced as I did.

"You're hurt." Lincoln didn't hesitate. He picked me up and slammed the door behind us. I made it. I was safe in his arms. Now that I was here, I didn't know what to say or where to begin. How did I tell him about Marlene? I hadn't even given it much thought, and now I was hurt, and the roads were washed out. He set me on a counter next to a sink.

That answered that question; there was running water.

"Lola, where are you hurt? Why are you here? Talk to me. You're scaring me."

I shook myself out of my jumbled thoughts. "I... I think I sprained my ankle," I stuttered out.

He was standing in front of me but reached over and turned on the faucet. I could smell that he'd washed his hair recently. The fresh scent of soap mixed with earthy undertones was all Linc. I began to shiver, not even realizing I was cold.

Lincoln grabbed a grey hand towel by the sink and wiped my face first. "We need to get you out of these clothes. You're soaked to the bone." He moved to my hands with the towel, rinsing it out every few seconds. I watched as the dark brown water went down the drain.

"All right, let's get this shirt off of you. I'll get you one of mine. And a blanket. Then we'll get these jeans off, and we can see what you did to that ankle, okay?"

"Okay, thank you." I nodded my head, thinking that all sounded like a good plan. Lincoln left to get me a shirt, and I had the overwhelming need to go after him. I wanted to scream at him not to leave me, that I needed him. I shook those thoughts away; I didn't need him. Not anymore. I felt confused and conflicted as he reappeared, holding a red and black flannel.

In a flash, my shirt was up and over my head. Lincoln moved quickly, dropping the flannel that he was holding over my head. It was enormous. I loved wearing his flannels, and I briefly wondered if that's why he chose this one. Of course it was. It was Linc; he didn't do things without thinking about them.

With my hands inside the shirt, I unclasped my soaking wet bra and put my arms through the sleeves. "Help me get these jeans off. I don't want to get your shirt wet from the muck."

Linc nodded, "Put your arms around me." I did as Lincoln said. He lifted me up, and he helped me take down my wet pants and underwear. The shirt fell, covering me. Lincoln set me back down and removed my muddy shoes, then took my pants off the rest of the way. "Baby girl. It's already swelling. What did you do?"

He grabbed the towel and wiped at my legs and ankles. I winced as he brushed over the ankle. "I want to get that elevated and get ice on it. I'm going to move you by the fire and get you a blanket. You're still shivering."

He picked me up again as if I weighed nothing and brought me to a small couch by the fire. I watched silently as he moved about. He grabbed a pillow, propped my foot up, and then got some ice out of the small freezer. He came back with a blanket and the ice. And set the ice on my ankle and tucked the blanket around me.

Then I watched in fascination as he moved back to the kitchen, heated up a cup of tea, and brought it over to me. It was so like Lincoln to just take care of me. He handed me the cup saying, "This should help warm you up."

I took a sip, and he was right. I could immediately feel myself warming. I realized I hadn't answered any of his questions. He had to have so many, and Linc being Linc, was patient as ever.

I took another sip and watched Lincoln as he stood leaning against the wall, watching me.

"Lincoln, I have to tell you why I'm here. Sit down. Okay?"

He watched me for a beat then asked, "Who is it? Is it Alex? Ty? Trey?"

"Sit down, Honey," I gentled my voice.

"Fuck," he hissed. "It's Ma."

"Sit down," I pleaded again.

Lincoln carefully lifted my feet, sat, then placed them back on top of his lap, and held the ice to the ankle. He was so careful with me, and it struck me how, since the moment he saw me, I felt completely safe with him, and I knew he'd take care of me. Then again, isn't that one of the things that kept me going outside? *Just a few more steps and Lincoln would be there. He'd make it better.*

I stared at Lincoln. The soft glow of the fire illuminating his face. He'd aged in the few years we were apart. I already knew that he bulked up, but this was more than that. There were a few subtle creases around his eyes that somehow made him all the more attractive.

He rubbed my uninjured foot. "Lols," he called my name, taking me out of my reverie.

"It's Mom," I confirmed and watched as he briefly shut his eyes. He was hiding his pain from me, and I didn't want him to do that. I wanted to be there for him. We'd been through too much to not to.

"She had a stroke two days ago, and they needed to operate on her brain to stop the bleed. She's alive, but it's not good. I'm so worried. When I spoke to your brothers a few hours ago, she was still in a medically induced coma. Trey flew in, and him and Ty were with her. The more time that passes, the better. The doctors are hopeful that she will wake up, but she'll have a long road ahead of her.

"We couldn't get a hold of you, so I decided that I would come and find you. It's only supposed to be a three-and-a-half-hour trip. I thought I could come, tell you, and be back in a few hours. But then I got stuck in the mud, and I wasn't that far away, so I braced the storm. The road leading to your drive is practically a river, and I fell when I crossed it."

I looked down at my palms to assess the scrapes now that I thought about everything I had just been through.

"You came here for me, to tell me about Mom?" I met his eyes and couldn't quite read the emotions playing behind them. How did he do that? Why did he look so guarded suddenly?

"I couldn't bear it if something happened to her, and you didn't know." I swallowed down the lump in my throat that formed as I spoke those words.

"But something did happen to her."

"You know what I mean."

He nodded his head because he did.

"Thank you."

"Well, a lot of good it did. All I managed to do was get stuck in the mud and twist my ankle."

"No, you did a lot more than that, and you know it." I knew what he wasn't saying. We weren't together any longer. I didn't need to come.

"Even if the rain stops. The road is washed out, and I won't be able to get very far. They'll have no idea if I made it, and I'm afraid in the end, I'll have just caused Ty and Trey to worry even more. I think I messed up."

"You didn't mess up. There's pop up storms all the time. Do I think you should've waited out the storm in the Rover? Yes. But also, no. You would've been safer there. Dryer for sure. But if the road out front is washed out, all of that water had to go somewhere. We won't know until it dries out if it would've headed toward you in the Rover. It would've been a hard decision for anyone. There's an emergency satellite phone in the closet. I'll call my brothers and check-in."

"You have a satellite phone?"

"Relax, it's only for emergencies, so it's not set up all the time."

"You're being awfully calm about this."

"Calm is the last thing I feel right now. You showing up the way you did, scared me out of my goddamn mind. Knowing my Ma is lying in a hospital bed has me freaked the fuck out. But that's out of my control. We can't do anything about Ma. But what I can do is make sure you're taken care of. I'll call my brothers, then I'll run you a bath. There's no shower, but your hair is caked in mud. Sound like a plan?"

I nodded, and I wasn't sure why, but the back of my throat began to burn, and I felt overwhelmed with emotion. Maybe it was everything I'd just been through, or maybe it was Lincoln. He always had a way of undoing me.

He noticed me fighting back emotions and moved quickly, scooping me under the knees and cradling me on his lap.

"Lols," he cooed gently.

A sob tore free from me, and he wrapped his arms around me as I clung to him.

"I was on the phone with her when it happened, and I called her Marlene. Not Mom. What is wrong with me? She was so ticked at me, Linc. And then she just wasn't there anymore. Ty got on, and he called 9-1-1. It all happened so fast. I'm sorry," I cried out. "It's my fault. Then I was outside, and it didn't feel like I would ever make it to you. All I kept thinking was that you'd never know about Ma, and that would be my fault too. I'm so sorry, Linc."

He rubbed my back. "Shh, Sweetheart. None of this is your fault. You didn't cause Mom to have a stroke. I've been on her about her blood pressure for a long time. She hates going to the doctor. It's been a constant fight. You didn't do that. And you made it here. You found me, Lols. Don't take that on. You braced that storm out there for me, for Ma."

He rubbed my back and soothed me. It felt so natural for me to move my head into his shoulder and fold into his embrace. He moved the hair away from my face, tucking it behind my ear. "It's okay. You're here. You're safe."

I sniffled one more time. Like a confirmation that it was a total shit show outside, thunder rumbled through the sky, and the room flashed from another bolt of lightning. I took a deep breath, realizing I was in Lincoln's arms, and this wasn't fair to him. I ended things with him. Sitting in his lap and leaning on him would only send him mixed signals. I pulled away. "Thanks. I don't know what came over me."

He dropped the strand of my hair he held as if he too felt there was a line he was crossing. "We should run you that bath."

I nodded and braced as Linc effortlessly picked me up and redeposited me, then moved to the bathroom and turned on the water. I heard it running and watched Lincoln move from the bathroom to a small closet where he grabbed a black case down from the top shelf. He set it down on a small table in the kitchen area and came back to me.

"Let's get you in there right away. I can't believe I didn't lose power yet, and I want to make sure you have hot water."

"Okay," I whispered, unsure of why I was whispering, and started to stand. Linc shot me a glare that said he was picking me up and that I better not even try it. He scooped me up and carried me to the bathroom, setting me on the closed toilet lid. "There's some shampoo and soap in the corner."

He motioned, and my eyes followed his hand to see a small shelf next to the clawfoot tub.

He stared at me. "Lols, take off my shirt."

I bit my lip, thinking I was crossing a line getting naked in front of Linc.

"You need help getting in the tub. And trust me, it's nothing I haven't seen. Every inch of your flesh is burned into my brain. It's all I see when I close my eyes. It's all I dream about. It was the only thing I had of you for nearly three years. Being modest won't make a difference now. It will only make it harder for me to put you in the tub."

I closed my eyes for the briefest moment, wanting to cry all over again. Being this close to Lincoln was its own kind of torture. My body wanted to react to him. The proximity of us made me instinctively want to touch him. But that wasn't who we were anymore.

I unbuttoned the flannel, and Linc watched me as I did. His eyes trailed each button as it came undone. There was another flash of lightning, and it cloaked me in darkness as I let the shirt fall away. Linc reached over to me and my breath hitched. The door to the bathroom was open, and his silhouette was visible from the glow of the fireplace. He was so close, and I was completely naked. I heard a slight crackle, and the room came to life as Lincoln lit a small candle.

"It's not much light, but it will have to do. You ready?"

"Yeah."

He again grabbed me behind the knees and cradled me. I was naked in his arms for the tiniest of seconds, and I couldn't help the way my nipples tightened automatically being this close to him. I just hoped he didn't notice. If he did, he didn't show any signs of it. He set me in the tub, and the warm water felt nice.

"I'll see if I can find you a washcloth and a towel. I'd turn the water off too. It's going to turn cold any second."

"Okay," I nodded, sinking into the hot water. I bent my knees to my chest to hide my nudity and moved forward to turn off the faucet.

He left the room and came back with a cup which I wasn't sure what that was for, a folded towel that he set down next to the flannel, and a washcloth that he handed me. "Let me help you with your hair."

"I got it, Linc."

"It's dark in here, and we can hardly see. Let me help you, Lola."

"Fine," I acquiesced. The longer he was close to me while I was naked, the more I felt like my body was betraying me. My heart thundered in my chest as I watched as Linc grabbed a stool and sat behind the tub. He reached into the tub with his cup and poured it on my hair. I grabbed the bar of soap and tried to focus on creating a lather on the cloth, even though my entire body felt alive with him behind me. Over and over again, he poured water on my hair, then he reached over me and grabbed the shampoo from the corner. I heard the lid as he opened it and snapped it shut again. His fingers worked through my hair, and at some point, he started to massage my scalp. I felt myself relaxing into the tub and into his gentle scalp massage.

"Hmm," I hummed, "That feels nice."

He didn't respond. He just kept at it. I sank into the water, letting my knees unbend as much as they could, and I laid as much as I could in the tub. It was bliss. I closed my eyes and enjoyed how relaxed he was making me. He continued to wash my hair. Then he rinsed it out. He had me so mellow that I didn't notice the way he was pausing or how his breathing had changed.

"You're killing me, Lols," the deep huskiness in his voice made me snap my eyes open. I knew that lust-filled tone. "I want to fuck you so bad. The way those perfect nipples of yours are poking out of the water, taunting me. You're like the perfect dream and nightmare all in one. You're my fantasy come to life. The forbidden fruit that's no longer mine. There's only so much a man can take with his ex-wife who no longer wants him." He stood and left the bathroom, closing me in.

His abrupt departure left me feeling guilty. I hurriedly finished and grabbed the towel from the side, then carefully lifted myself up without putting any weight on my ankle. The toilet was next to the tub, so I could slide myself on that without bearing any weight. I dressed quickly and wrapped the towel around my hair.

Once dressed, I wasn't sure what to do. I didn't want to annoy Lincoln, not that he annoyed easily, but I thought I pushed him. It wasn't intentional. I didn't mean to turn him on. I didn't mean to tease him. Maybe that's not what he was thinking about, but I knew him. I knew it would be difficult to keep boundaries. Especially after the last time we were together. Hell, every time we've been together.

With Lincoln and I, there had never been a time when we were in the same room and hadn't felt that pull. There was always an invisible thread that connected us. This time it was like a jumbled mess of knots, but it was still there. It was just more complicated.

I decided I could use the furniture as a crutch, and I would be able to make it to the couch. He wouldn't have to carry me. I braced my hand on the side of the tub and stood on one foot. I hopped to the door handle and opened the door.

"Hold on. She's trying to walk on it again," Lincoln said into a large black box that resembled a walkie talkie, agitation laced his voice.

He set the phone down, met me by the door, picked me up in a quick swoop, and then was setting me back down to grab the phone.

"I'm back. From what Lola described, the road isn't drivable. Once this rain stops, I'll scope it out and see if there is a way for us to safely get back to the main road." There was a long pause, then I heard, "Tell her I love her. Tell her to fight." Then another long pause, "Yeah, brother. You too. I'll call you in a few hours." A crack of thunder tore through the sky, making Lincoln pause, then he said, "I'll tell her," another pause, then, "Yeah," and he was pressing a button on the satellite phone and hanging it up.

"The doctors are bringing her out of the coma. So right now, it's a waiting game." I yawned, suddenly feeling very exhausted from everything.

I nodded, and in the firelight, I wasn't even sure if he could see me. "You're exhausted," Linc said, leaning against the wall. Somehow, only illuminated by the fire, he looked larger than life.

"You bulked up in there," I stated the obvious.

"All there is in there is time. I'd have hours to think about where I went wrong. I had hours to think about how I would win you back, but that was before." He didn't say it, but I knew he meant before he knew what happened with our child. "I spent hours trying to clear my head by lifting weights."

"Did it help?" I hated feeling like he was tortured in there.

"Not really."

There was a long pause, and my chest tightened, thinking about him in prison being tortured with his thoughts.

"What was it like?"

"I'm bigger than a lot of dudes and trained a fuck of a lot better too, but even the biggest motherfuckers get tested from time to time. Skinheads thought they could get me on their side since I'm white. That was probably who I fought with the most. After that, and a few long nights in solitary, they mostly got the point."

He moved to the kitchen area, and my eyes tried to follow his movements, but it was too dark.

"Do you want something to eat?"

I was feeling pretty anxious, so food felt like the last thing on my mind. I shrugged. He didn't see me.

"Lols, food?"

"I have some lunch meat. I can make you a sandwich."

"That's fine, thank you."

I was quiet again, thinking about him in solitary. I wanted to know about his time there. I had my share of sleepless nights wondering if he was okay. I guess I always thought he would be fine in there because of who he is. There are not a lot of people who would try to mess with Lincoln. "Did other groups mess with you too?"

"Alex had some friends in there. He had some enemies too. I just did my best to navigate it all, but if something came up, I had to defend myself and not get caught."

Processing what life was like in there was hard. Even though I wondered if he was okay, I often tried to pretend he wasn't there. If I pretended he was deployed or somewhere else, it was easy to ignore what he was going through. I hadn't really thought of it as another type of war, but what he described seemed exactly like that. His enemies were different than what he was used to, but he had to be ready for battle all the time. It made me think about how when he was deployed, at least he had my letters to get him through. I began to feel guilt, but then I quickly shut it down, telling myself he made his choices.

"So, you were all alone?" I don't know why I was pushing this. I guess I needed to know what he endured.

"I met some dudes. I watched out for a couple, and they kept their ears open so that if anything was brewing and I needed to know, they told me. It wasn't all bad. I joked around sometimes, found moments where I pretended I wasn't locked in a cage."

Linc handed me a plate with a sandwich on it and a bottle of water.

"How about you? How's work been?"

"It's been good. Mostly I found myself immersed in it. Griffin, my boss, has been trying to get me to slow down, though."

"Is he the one that had taken on that role not long before I left?"

"He is. He took me out to a club a little while ago. He's nice. It was fun."

Linc exhaled loudly, and I knew I needed to clarify. "We went to a gay bar. Not that he's gay, he said he's into both, but not the point. He's not trying to get in there."

"Man got eyes?"

I looked incredulously at Linc. "Yes."

"Then he's into you. There's no way a man can see all that is you without being into you."

I rolled my eyes, "Whatever. I think I can tell when someone is into me, and I'm telling you he is not. He's just cool. I think you would've liked him."

Linc seemed to relax, and he lifted my feet again and took a seat on the couch, placing my swollen ankle in his lap with fresh ice.

"That's good that he isn't letting you work yourself to the bone."

"He met Ellie the other day, and that went good. In fact, I think there could've been some mutual interest there."

He shook his head at the mention of Ellie. "How is she? Has she settled down yet?"

"As if. I don't think she could find someone who could keep up with her."

"I don't believe that. I think she's just searching, and she doesn't give them long. She tries them on for size, and if they don't work, then she moves on. She's been that way as long as I've known her."

"Do you think she's searching, or do you think she's lost?" I asked between bites, then added, "This is really good."

"I think she knows what she wants. She just hasn't found it yet."

I nodded because that's what I thought too. I think deep down, she was getting tired of the endless search.

I took a bite, then another and felt Lincoln's eyes on me. It didn't unnerve me, though. It felt natural, like old times when we would sit and talk for hours. Besides Ellie, Linc was my best friend. It struck me then that turning your back on your best friend was like shutting off a part of yourself. I'd somehow managed to shut out a lot of people I cared about when Linc left.

"What's going through that pretty little head of yours?"

I shook my head, not wanting to say.

He reached forward and placed his hand on mine. It was a simple gesture, but it made me feel at ease. "It's nothing. Just... this is nice. Us talking. I was thinking about how you were my best friend, and I could talk to you about anything and how I stopped talking to Trey and Ma when I stopped talking to you and that it was hard and kind of lonely."

"Why did you shut them out and not Ty?"

"You've got to know why," I countered.

"I think I do, but I want to know why you think you did." *What the heck did he mean by that?*

"I talked to her when you were first arrested then through the trial. I talked to Trey too. They couldn't understand why I was mad. They thought I was betraying my vow as your wife. I loved them dearly, but I felt like they had your back, and no one had mine. They were my family too, you know? Even when Mom yelled at me on the phone the other day, it was like everything was at the beginning all over again. Honestly, I felt like they were abandoning me. Marlene never took the time to find out why I was so destroyed—never seemed like she wanted to understand. It was like she blamed me for leaving you."

"And Ty?"

"He didn't do that. He just let me be me and was there for me when I was in so much pain. He didn't judge me. He didn't push."

"I'm glad he was there for you."

"He always has been. Every time you deployed or shipped out."

"Yeah," was Linc's only reply.

We fell into another kind of silence, and I felt my eyes drifting, but this time with Linc was rare and right or wrong, I needed it. I sat up a little straighter, not wanting to fall asleep.

"Can I ask you something?" I twisted in my seat, hoping to get a better look at Lincoln's eyes.

"Always."

"Would you change anything if you could?"

Chapter Twenty

"Would I change anything?" He repeated. "Yeah."

He was quiet for a long moment. "Joining the Army made me into the man I am today. It changed my life and my mentality. It made me want to work hard, and it gave me skills I wouldn't otherwise have. It kept me out of the life I was probably headed for. You know how Chicago is. I wouldn't have been able to provide for you. So I wouldn't change that.

"Maybe I should've talked with you more about when I was gone. I think you were falling apart when I left, and I thought you were good. I had this unmistakable feeling that we would always be good."

I blew out a deep breath, feeling a tightness in my chest. This was a good conversation for us to have. I knew it. We were here, and it would give me closure, but the pain was real, and my feelings were still so tangled up in his, even after all of this time.

"I would've talked Trey into letting me confide in you about what was happening with him. I didn't realize the resentments that you held onto from me being there with him. I promised him some things, and in hindsight, I should've told him I needed to confide in you. I should've had you to lean on and let you help shoulder my burden so you wouldn't have felt like I chose to leave you."

My curiosity about what really happened with Trey was again at the forefront of my mind. Trey had said something at the hospital, and I should've paid more attention to what he said. I was so lost in my overwhelming feelings that I didn't question him, but maybe it was time I did that.

"I feel like somehow I failed to let you know how much I love you. That maybe if I'd been more open with you, things wouldn't be the way they are."

I swallowed, then swiped a small tear that leaked from the corner of my eye. "I knew," I admitted.

"Not enough. Not if for a moment I was away from you had you believing I wasn't thinking of you. Or didn't wish to be anywhere else than beside you."

He didn't elaborate any more on if he would change anything with Alex. Maybe everything he told me in the car was all I was going to get. Would Alex have been dead? Truly? I wasn't sure I could live with that, either.

"Why couldn't you have gone to the cops or taken Alex out of town? You had other options."

"You know Alex. You think he would've done anything else but go after Dante? He was pimping kids. He pimped Alex's sister."

I gasped, never having heard that before. "Alex has a sister?"

"Had. We were too fucking late."

"Was it drugs?"

"He was a fucking pimp, of course drugs were there. These guys, they don't mess around with pimping kids *and* stay clear of drugs. They're scum. It was all of it. But Alex was clean. He wasn't there for that. We were trying to take him down. It's just it all went to shit once we were there. Somehow, Akeila, Alex's sister, told Dante what we were doing, and he was waiting for us. We got set up. Akeila was found a few weeks after I was sentenced, and she died anyway. It all turned out to be a clusterfuck."

"Why didn't I know about Akeila?"

"You wouldn't talk to me."

"I was there for the hearing."

"The lawyers said it would've made us look like we were vigilantes. Said it would give us a motive going in and that if it came out in court, Alex would be looking at death row."

"Do you think if you would've just hauled Alex to Florida to live with Trey for a while that none of this would've happened?"

"I don't know. But what I do know is there'd still be a pimp out there, peddling kids to sick fucks. It crosses my mind, ya know? Alex was using, kept getting in trouble. Maybe I should've tried to take him to Florida. It's not that easy to kidnap a grown man against his will, though, still if I could've convinced him... I don't know. I gotta think that if I saved just one kid from that kind of torment, then I did the right thing. It's the only thing that can let me sleep at night, and trust me, the hours I do get are far and few between."

"You're not sleeping."

"I lost the love of my life, and she's seeing someone else. What do you think?"

I noticed the bags under his eyes and saw how truly exhausted he looked. The need to take care of him superseded the need to protect my heart.

"I'm not seeing anyone. I tried to go on a date, but I was forcing it. Thinking I was ready when I wasn't."

I watched Linc's chest decompress as he let out a huge breath. Another crack of lightning lit up the cabin, followed by thunder so loud, the boom shook the room, making me jump. The ice slid off my ankle, and Linc's fingertips brushed my skin as he readjusted it, sending chills down my spine. How was it that after so many years, he still affected me?

"I know I should want you to be happy. I should want that above all else. But maybe I'm a selfish bastard, and I can't say I'm not pleased as fuck that you haven't moved on."

I didn't know what to say to that. I suppose there wasn't much I should say. After all, if the roles were reversed, how happy would I really be watching Lincoln with someone else? Just the thought made jealousy burn through me.

We were quiet then. Several minutes passed as the storm rumbled around us. I yawned again, and Linc moved my foot and stood.

"I'm going to grab some more wood for the fire."

I watched his departing back, then stared at the dancing flames. My eyes grew heavier and I drifted to sleep.

"Mmm," I mumbled, pulling myself into Linc's warm chest.

"Shh, I'm just moving you to the bed. You fell asleep and were hanging halfway off the couch."

I didn't argue. My eyes were heavy. I was in a dazed, sleepy mode. I don't know why my mouth said what it did. I was barely even conscious of it when I murmured, "Stay with me."

THERE WAS A SOFT PILLOW beneath my head and heat at my back when Linc shifted beside me.

I blinked my eyes awake. I was hot, like inferno-hot, and it was a heat my body craved. Not thinking about it, I snuggled into the warmth. I heard the soft inhale and exhale from the sleeping Lincoln, and my eyes shot open. What was I doing in bed next to him, my arm around his chest, and his leg slung over me, pinning me? How had I gotten here? Then I remembered sleepily asking him to stay. I couldn't fault him for being here. Then, I remembered how tired he looked and how he said he hadn't been sleeping.

I stared up at him, and I wished it wasn't so dark in here. He'd left the door open to the rest of the cabin, and when I moved my gaze that way, I could still see a small glow from the fireplace.

I thought about everything Linc had told me. How he had a brother that he watched die. He didn't say it outright, but I knew that was why he helped Alex. He couldn't let Alex go after his sister alone and maybe die. He couldn't let another brother die. Would I have loved him differently if he was the type of man who could sit back while Alex put himself into a dangerous situation? I thought about Trey, had there been more going on that I didn't know? Did any of that really matter? We were still where we were. I loved him and always would, just as he loved me, but I carried around so much pain.

Being an Army wife wasn't easy. I mostly felt alone. He was gone, and I had to live my life. I had to get my degree and start my career. I didn't move to wherever he was stationed. He wanted to make sure I didn't put my dreams on hold. I thought about when he was in Iraq for the first time and how the government mandated a fifteen-month stay. It was hard finishing school and starting college while my boyfriend was gone.

I remembered how different college was. My friends were all boy crazy, and I stayed in my dorm room instead of going to parties. I went sometimes, but it never felt right. Some random guy would always hit on me, and it made me miss Linc. He was in hell, and I was drinking cheap keg beer and having drunk dudes fawn all over me. Still, every single time I would see him, it was like he erased all the time he was gone with just one look, just one smile. Maybe I didn't open up to him enough about how that constant back and forth between loneliness and high of being around him affected me?

Did any of that really matter anymore?

I was afraid it didn't. We were past that. The divorce papers were signed, and sometimes, no matter how much you loved someone, there was no coming back from all the hurt and pain.

Still, he was beautiful. I sighed, staring at him and thinking that I'd never fall in love again.

It was what it was.

Linc moved, and the arm under me pulled me closer, and the leg thrown over me locked me in more. I could tell he was still sleeping, but I was trapped in his embrace.

God, the nearness of his body.

My treacherous reaction to him.

I could feel my breasts swell. The hardness from his muscled physique caused wetness to pull between my legs. I squirmed, trying to ignore it. He tensed for a moment, and I felt every solid inch of his hardness press against my leg. I closed my eyes, unsure if I wanted this moment to stop, but knowing that it probably should. I knew what being with him again would feel like. It would be amazing. It would feel like everything until it was all taken away from me.

I began to pull away.

"Don't go yet," Linc's sleepy gruff voice said into my ear, "Just give me another minute to pretend that this is real."

I swallowed, and as tears filled my eyes, I was grateful to be cloaked in darkness. Feeling incredibly torn, I laid there unmoving, surrounded by his heat and *all* of his hardness.

He ran his fingers through my hair and stroked the side of my head.

"Do you remember when we used to do this at Marlene's house? Or how about that tiny apartment you rented with those three girls? What were their names? Anne? Roberta? No, that wasn't it."

"Rhonda, Anne, and Eloise," I corrected.

"That's right. Rhonda would play that terrible death metal. We just hid out in your room, tangled up in each other. Kind of like this."

I wanted to stop him from reminiscing. I wanted to remind him that we were in the past, but my body was still so attuned to him, and every inch of my body felt at war with my heart. This was dangerous for me, and I knew it, but like the junkie I was, I stayed still and let him stroke my hair.

"I'd leave Bragg and drive straight through the night as soon as my shift ended on Friday. We'd stay in bed all day Saturday, barely coming up to eat, and that stupid music would finally end around six when her girlfriend got off work. Then I'd leave exhausted Sunday afternoon, so I could make it back again for duty Monday morning."

"I think you only did that a few times, Linc. You got deployed again, not that long into my sophomore year. I swear you were only home for a few months before they were shipping you out again."

"It was seven times," He said matter-of-factly. "But you're right. I was gone way too soon."

Feeling this intimate moment between us begin to shatter, I started to pull away. Linc moved his leg from on top of me, then unexpectedly wrapped his other arm around me and hugged me. "I'm sorry you didn't feel like I was there for you." He kissed the top of my head and released me. I watched as he stood and checked his watch.

"We slept for about four hours. I'm going to call and check on Ma and throw some more wood on the fire."

I watched his back as he left the room, and as I did, I thought about how much this hurt. Would there always be this pull to him? Was it a mistake for me to come?

No. I had to get that thought out of my head. It couldn't be a mistake. He needed to know about Marlene.

Marlene.

That's what this entire trip is about.

I needed to get my butt up and see how she is. I attempted to move my ankle and was met with a ton of resistance. *Ouch! That hurt.*

I sat up and swung my feet over the side of the bed. "Lola Paige, if you move another inch from that bed, so help me God," Lincoln called from the other room.

How the hell did he know I was going to get up?

"I was just sitting up," I lied.

Linc walked in with the large satellite phone. "Thank God," he said into the phone. "Can you hold the phone up to her ear?" There was a pause, then I heard, "Hey, Ma. I'm sorry I'm not there with you. Don't try to talk. It's okay. I love you. I'm here with Lols, she loves you too. She hurt her ankle trying to find me, but she's okay. It might take us a little longer than expected to get back to you. You 're the strongest woman I know, so you stay strong, and you heal up, okay? I wouldn't be the man I am today if it wasn't for you. You've done so much for so many people, and the world still needs people like you in it." There was a long pause, and I could tell either Ty or Trey was on the other end.

"It's still raining outside, but it doesn't seem like it's as bad. Still, the road out front is washed out from what Lola said. Once I get her situated, I'll check it out and see if there's anything to be done. It's dark in here, and I can see it's swollen." Another pause, then, "You know how stubborn she is." He was quiet as he listened, then I heard him say, "There's no power. I'm going to check the shed for a generator. If the roads are as impassable as she described, we might be here for a day or so." I waited for Linc's next response to whatever his brother was saying. He walked around while he talked, and every few seconds, I could see him as he crossed my peripheral from the bedroom.

"I know. I'm so glad she woke up and has you both. We'll be there as soon as we can." Then, "Right. You too," and I could tell from the change in Linc's shuffling around that he disconnected.

Lincoln appeared in the doorway a few seconds later. "Are you still tired? Do you want to stay here or go back out to the couch?"

"I want you to tell me what is going on."

Linc looked at me for a moment, "Right, couch it is," he declared, then before I even had a second to say anything, he was picking me up again and setting me down on the couch. It happened that fast.

"Linc, how's Ma?" I asked, not having much patience for being manhandled.

"She's awake. The doctors are very hopeful. She was conscious, and it is too early to tell how the stroke affected her motor skills. They're going to continue to monitor her and do more tests. Most likely she will eventually be moved to a rehab facility. It's good news."

I placed my hand on my chest and looked up to the heavens, "Thank you," I whispered. Even though I didn't go to church like I did when I was younger, I still believed, and at that moment, I felt like God had been looking out for Ma.

Linc sat down on the couch and gently lifted my foot to inspect my ankle. "This is one of the worst sprains I've seen. I'm worried that there's a break in there. It's bruising pretty nice."

I looked down at my ankle, and in the firelight, I could see that he was right. It looked pretty gnarly.

"I'm sorry I got hurt. I'm sure you want to be on your way to Ma," I said, feeling guilty.

"You didn't cause it to rain. Do I wish you stayed in his car until the storm wasn't as bad? I don't know. Who knows how bad it could've been in there? I'm just glad that it's only your ankle. That will heal. I don't know what I would've done if something had happened to you."

His eyes were locked on mine as he said that, and I felt everything. All the love and the pain that those words entailed. Right then, I felt caught, like a small animal ensnared by his trap. He was definitely the predator. Always had been and always would be, and the way he watched me and stared into my eyes felt like it was everything. His words said he was glad I was okay, but his eyes said so much more. They told me that if something had happened to me, he wouldn't recover. There was longing and frustration.

And pain.

So much pain.

I hated feeling like I inflicted that. I had my reasons, and he knew that. Still, I was here, where he came to escape, and I knew it wouldn't be easy. I also knew that I could never have lived with myself if I had the power to let him know about his mom and didn't do anything about it.

I was the first to break eye contact. "Do you think there's any Tylenol or Ibuprofen here?"

"Shit. That should've been my first thought. Let me check for you."

He set my foot down and rummaged through the bathroom. He walked out empty-handed, so I assumed that was a bust. He shuffled through the cabinets in the kitchen and also came up empty-handed.

"It doesn't look like there's anything. I want to wrap it up, though. Hopefully, that will reduce the swelling." He opened and shut more cupboards, and a few minutes later, he sat down with a towel and a pair of scissors. He began to cut the towel into large thin strips, then carefully lifted my foot as he wrapped it around and around. "Not going to lie, that freaking hurts."

"Shit, I'm sorry. I'm almost done."

"It's not your fault. Thank you for taking care of me."

Linc propped my leg up on the back of the couch and stood. "Always, Lols," he said. It was quiet, making me feel like there was an intimacy behind those words. Then he was gone. He moved into the bedroom, and I saw that he returned with a jacket and his shoes.

"Going somewhere?"

"Yes. I'm going to check out the road and see if there is a generator in the shed. I might be gone for a little while. Is there anything you need before I go?"

"Can you get me some water?" I asked.

He nodded, then moved to the kitchen, setting his things down on the small kitchen table as he got me a bottle of water.

"Thanks."

He responded with a grunt, and I watched him put his shoes on.

"Don't get up, Lola."

I waved him off with my hand.

"I mean it. I know you. Wait for me to come back. I don't want you to hurt yourself more."

"I'll be fine."

He shot me a skeptical glance.

"Be careful." That was met with a lift of his chin as he opened the door to brace the elements.

I WAS OFFICIALLY WORRIED. I had no idea how much time went by, but had I noticed that it was dark outside, I would've begged him to wait until the morning. How much time had passed? An hour? Two? Or was it more like thirty-minutes? With nothing to do but stare at the fire, time was ticking by incredibly slowly.

I stared at those dancing flames, and my mind drifted back in time to the day that changed everything.

I finished tying the black ribbon on the small box and placed it back in my underwear drawer. Inside was my first sonogram. Tonight was the night that

Lincoln found out he was going to be a father. I had dinner from Parvi's, our fa-vorite Indian restaurant, delivered. It was in the oven to stay warm.

I double-checked myself in the mirror and added a dab of Linc's favorite per-fume on my wrists and neck. My hair was down and wild. I didn't straighten it. It was always a pain for me to work with because I had so much of it, but Linc loved it. I had on his favorite pair of jeans. I could've gone for a dress or some-thing fancy, but I knew how much he liked my ass in these. I also had on a vin-tage Stones t-shirt that was worn out like crazy. The neckline had been cut, and the sleeves were also cut off. I only had my bra on underneath, and you could see hints of the black lace as I moved my arms.

This outfit wouldn't have been sexy to most men, but Linc loved when I let loose and let my inner-rock-goddess, as he would call it, shine through.

After making sure I looked exactly how I wanted to look, I double-checked the apartment. It was cleaner than normal. Not that we were messy people, but with Linc always on a job with Ty and me busy at work, finally getting my foot-ing with a new boss, things could get hectic, including our home. I got home early this afternoon to meet the cleaner I splurged on. Note to self, do that more often.

A few candles burning smelled of lemon and sage, adding to the clean, fresh smell in our little space. I felt anxious. I'd been sitting on this for a few weeks, and I finally had it confirmed by the doctor. I knew that this would irrevocably change our lives. I knew that Lincoln would be over-the-moon ecstatic.

I stared at the clock. Any minute he'd be home.

Iz purred against my legs, and I could tell that she was excited for Linc to get here too. Maybe she sensed my feelings. I wasn't sure, but I seemed to think ani-mals had a way about them where they could definitely pick up on their human's energy.

A few more minutes passed, then a few more.

An hour passed from the time Linc was supposed to be home.

He was late and didn't call. I was worried, so I phoned him, but he didn't answer. The night was turning out to be a bust, and disappointment settled in my gut. I'd told him earlier to make sure he was home by six, that I had a special surprise for him. And he wasn't here.

Another hour passed, and I was hungry and sick of waiting for dinner. I grabbed the takeout from the oven. It was slightly dried out now, but it would have to do. I served myself up some Tandoori chicken and sat at the table. This sucked.

When I finished, I blew out the candles, put the food in the fridge, and then changed my jeans for some comfy pants. I took off my bra and grabbed a tank from my underwear drawer. I touched the lid of the box, thinking, 'not tonight', then I tried Linc one more time before I turned on the TV and put on my favorite rockumentary.

I must've dozed off. Linc was in our room in the closet. "What are you doing? Where've you been?" I sleepily asked. He set something down on the side of the bed, and I immediately sat up because I knew what was in that bag. Guns.

"What's going on?" I shrieked.

"Shh, Lols. Go back to sleep. I didn't mean to wake you. Everything is going to be all right."

Fuck that!

I sat up and turned on the bedside lamp. "You didn't answer my calls tonight. You were supposed to be here hours ago, and now you show up in the middle of the night, and it looks like you're gearing up for World War Three. No, I will not go back to sleep. What the fuck is happening?" I shrieked.

Linc sighed and sat down next to me on the bed. "Alex got himself into some trouble. He needs my help. I have to go to him."

I saw the clock on the nightstand and noticed it was just after midnight. "You mean, you're going after him in the middle of the Goddamned night with guns? What kind of trouble is he in? Please don't go, Linc."

My emotions were everywhere. I was somewhere between pissed, let down, and scared out of my ever-loving mind.

"It's going to be all right, okay?" Linc bent low to kiss me on the top of my head. I smacked his hand away. I didn't normally react this way, but I was pregnant. My hormones were raging, and tonight was supposed to be special, and now this.

"It is not okay, Linc. Whatever you are helping him with is not going to be okay. It never is when it comes to Alex. I know you love him. I know he's your brother, but please don't go. I'm begging you, Linc. Don't." Linc stared at me, and I could see an internal battle waging behind his eyes.

Finally, he sighed, "I have to, Lols. He's my brother."

I knew my husband. When he made his mind up on something, there was no changing it.

"I swear to you, Linc. If you go and something happens, this won't be like last time," I threatened. He didn't know that we had a baby on the way, but I felt like he was letting me down in every way possible.

"It's going to be fine, you'll see. I love you."

I closed my eyes, hating how I felt. My entire world felt like it was shifting and that it was out of my control.

"Please, don't go," I begged one final plea.

His eyes gentled on me. "I'll be back in bed before you wake up. You'll see."

Tears filled my eyes. This wasn't how our night was supposed to go. I was supposed to be telling him about our baby, not watching him double-check his bullets in his gun.

"Baby," his voice gentled even more. "I'll come home to you."

I looked away from him, not wanting to let him see the tears that fell. "I can't believe you're doing this. I can't believe you're letting Alex come in between us again."

"I gotta go, babe." I wouldn't turn and look at him. If I did, he would know how crushed I was.

"Please," I whispered one last time.

Linc ignored it.

He turned off the bedside lamp and said, "Go back to bed. I'll be back," but he didn't come back. I laid in bed and cried. It was supposed to be one of the most special nights of our lives, but he couldn't put us first. He might not have known that I was having his child, but I felt beyond let down. For the first time in our life, I doubted what we had. Was this the life I was going to give our child? A life where my baby's dad made choices that had him getting guns in the middle of the night?

I couldn't sleep. I thought of all the possibilities. I thought of everything that could go wrong. I was scared. What if something happened to him, and he never knew he had a baby coming? What if I had to raise our child on my own? I cried long into the night. My body felt exhausted, and as the sun rose, Linc never showed. I knew something had gone terribly wrong.

Chapter Twenty-One

"Hey." I was so caught up in my memories, I didn't hear the door open. It wasn't until he said 'hey' that I noticed he was there.

"You've been crying." he said, setting whatever giant piece of equipment was in his hands down by the door, and he moved to me.

Had I? I wiped the back of my hand across my face, and it came away damp. I guess I had been crying.

"Sorry, I didn't realize I was. How was it out there?"

"Well, for starters, I can't believe that you were out on that road. It's a nightmare. Trees are down. It's practically a river flowing down the street. What were you thinking?" He seemed agitated, and I didn't care for his tone.

"I was thinking that I needed to get to you and tell you about your mom," I snapped back.

He moved closer to me, and I could see his clothes were muddy and wet the nearer he moved to the fireplace.

"I'm sorry. It's just fucked outside, and to think that something could've happened to you and I wouldn't have known about it until it was too late has me on edge. Now, why were you crying?"

I shook my head, not wanting to get into it.

Linc tilted his head, and I could see those dark eyes of his trying to figure me out.

"Are you sad about Ma? She's strong. She'll recover, you know."

I shook my head then immediately corrected myself, "I mean I am, but I was just getting lost in my memories, that's all. This isn't easy for me, being here with you."

He nodded his head, and I knew it wasn't easy for him either.

He sighed, "I found a generator. I have to get the fuel from the back, then hopefully I can restore some power in here."

"Okay."

He left, going back outside, and, my guess was, around the back of the cabin. He was gone for maybe another ten minutes when he came back, grabbed the big machine by the door, and brought that back outside. While he was gone, I tried to pull myself together more. I didn't like how emotionally exhausted I felt thinking about the night he left me. I placed my palms to my eyes, and I tried to reduce the puffiness that was sure to be there from crying. I had no idea if this worked at all, but I was hopeful once the power came on that I wouldn't look like a total wreck.

A couple more minutes passed by, then a light over the kitchen sink came on. I took those few minutes to really take the place in, realizing with my ankle that I hadn't really done that before.

The cabin with its log walls was basically a large area with a living room and a kitchen. The bedroom door was still slightly open, the bathroom, and another narrower door that I assumed was a closet. The couch I sat on was a dark brown leather that was worn at the armrests. There was a wool rug in front of the fireplace with dark blues, browns, and a very subtle pale green woven into it. The fireplace looked like it was made out of some type of river rock. I'd seen similar things, and it was usually taken from some local river, which is what I was guessing was the case here. The mantle was a large wooden beam that had to be at least eight feet long and four inches thick. The wood was polished with deep grooves and notches in it. I knew from all of the design sketches that Ellie had shown me over the years that it was custom made and not cheap. Above the fireplace, several large bucks were staring down at me. Beside that was a fish mounted to a wooden plaque. I had no idea what type of fish it was, but it must've been at least three feet long. Several eight by ten photos were hung on the wall beside that, but I would need to really look closely to examine those.

The kitchen had granite countertops with flakes of brown and gold veined throughout it. There was a large metal sink with a newer faucet. Next to that was a newer but not overly big stainless steel refrigerator. There was a small two-seater table made from a dark wood. The table had a few pieces of fruit and a couple of tomatoes stacked on top of it. The floors throughout the entire cabin were a thin planked wood that looked original to the cabin. There was some wear and tear, but they fit the space completely.

I wondered whose space this was. My guess is it's one of Trey's old football friend's hunting cabins. It has too many expensive qualities to just be a run of the mill hunting cabin.

Linc returned again, looking dirtier than before. "There's enough fuel for two days, so let's hope the power goes on before then."

"Two days! Do you think we'll be here that long?" I gasped. I could not be stuck in here with Linc for two days.

"When I said the road was a river, and that there were trees down everywhere, I was not lying. In the morning, I'll put a call in to the sheriff's office. He already knows I'm out here, seeing as my parole officer wanted him to check in on me, but I'll let him know about Ty's Rover and that you're here. Maybe they'll be able to get us out of here sooner. I don't know. He was kind of a dick and didn't like having a 'felon in his woods,' his words, not mine."

I gulped, then nodded, then got pissed for him. "He said that to you? The felon thing?"

Linc shrugged, "It's going to happen."

"Are the cops always dicks to you?"

"No, but once they know I've got a record, shit changes."

I turned away and stared back at the fire. He'd always have that follow him. I had no idea what it was like for people to have preconceived notions about me. I knew Alex, Trey, and Ty dealt with it all the time because of their skin color. It was something I struggled with, constantly feeling let down by people who didn't even realize that they said or did things that were racist as hell. I believed most people weren't that conscious of it. It was something that was passed on by parents or society. But you had the personal responsibility as a decent human to want to be better and consciously decide to think better. At some point, ignorance was a choice.

I heard a few clinks and clatters from Linc, but was trying to give myself space, even though there really wasn't any to be had. He moved past my peripheral and my mouth watered. He was in nothing but boxer briefs, and in his hands were a pile of clothes.

"Wha... What are you doing?" I stuttered. His body had always been breathtaking, a fine piece of art, but this, it was utter perfection. The extra bulk he put on in prison was on full display. Every muscle in his abdomen was defined, creating that perfect Adonis V. His arms, which were always defined, had gotten significantly bigger, but they weren't so big that veins popped out of them. They suited his tall frame. And those thighs! Jesus, but he always had nice legs. I remembered thinking that the very first night I met him, but these thighs—they were a thing of beauty with thick cords of muscles. I imagined for the briefest of seconds without boxer briefs and how his long, thick shaft would look against those beefy thighs.

Lincoln chuckled.

I stopped gawking at his magnificent body and made eye contact. Shit! I was completely busted. "Why are you laughing?" I feigned innocence.

He shook his head. I was so totally busted, then he opened the door that I assumed was a closet. Inside was a stackable washer and dryer. I watched his tight ass as he turned his back to me to throw the clothes into the top loader. Still-utter perfection.

He turned and looked at me once he finished, and I was so totally busted, again.

"Last pair of jeans. The other pair is already in there waiting for me to wash them, and since your muddy clothes are in there too, there is no rescuing them."

"So, you're going to just what? Hang around in your underwear?" I asked open-mouthed.

He smirked. Those damn dimples of his took my breath away. I needed to get a grip. I'd seen him naked so many times, but this felt different. He wasn't mine any longer, and that last night we made love was in the middle of the night, and I wasn't able to fully ogle him. It was then I noticed that there was the smallest amount of ink on his chest. I squinted my eyes to get a better look. Linc, never missing anything, saw me and turned toward the bedroom.

"I do have an extra shirt I can throw on if that will make you more comfortable."

Not wanting to admit how affected I was by his body, I replied, "Why wouldn't I be comfortable? This couch is awesome."

He shook his head again as he disappeared into the bedroom. He so totally knew I was full of it. Whatever.

He came out wearing a t-shirt I'd bought for him as a joke. It was tight on him, and I knew from the one time I'd begged him to try it on that it fit him completely different now. The shirt read, I'M WITH THE HOT

ITALIAN, then in smaller print, if you stare at her again, it's her fiery temper you'll have to deal with.

I thought it was hysterical. Linc thought I was being a goof.

I wondered why he kept it, and why he had it on now.

"Nice shirt."

"You like it? This incredibly sexy, half-Italian, half-Spanish woman got it for me."

"Oh, yeah? I bet she was hysterical," I said, playing along.

Linc came to me, lifted my foot, and sat down on the edge of the couch, putting my foot back down in his lap. Without his jeans on and just the boxer briefs, I could feel his skin against my own, and it affected me. I was certain that it always would.

"She was hysterical. She was also incredibly intelligent. One of the smartest women I knew. She was incredibly sexy. She was sexy when she got all sex-kitten for me, but she was even sexier when she'd first wake up in the morning and her hair would be wild. That was my favorite. Half asleep, sexy hair, well-rested because I fucked her silly the night before, and then she'd wake up, and she was wild. For me. For my cock. She was fucking fire, so the shirt fit her."

My heart was beating so much faster now. His words, which at first were meant to be playful, turned into flirty and seductive. He mastered seduction.

Trying to lighten the mood, I asked, "She sounds like she was something pretty awesome. Did she ever take anyone down with that fiery temper, though?" I grinned, hoping he knew I was trying to lighten the mood.

"Only me," was his reply, and God, that stung.

He began unwrapping my ankle.

"What are you doing?"

"Now that we have better lighting, I want to get a better look at it. I don't think it's broken, but I want to look at it again."

He was careful as he lifted my foot and slowly unraveled the cloth. I winced slightly with how it moved. "Shit, sorry. Are you in a ton of pain?"

"Keep going. I've had far worse pain, so this is nothing."

I could see his questioning glance when I said I'd had worse. I immediately regretted saying that. First, it made me think of the baby we lost and how there was no pain worse than when you miscarried. I could feel it tearing away, and I knew I was losing it. Second, I didn't want to get into that kind of pain with him. I didn't want to relive it.

"Lols?" he questioned, stilling his hand at the bottom of my foot.

"Nothing. Forget I said anything."

"Don't do that. Not now. You're still my best friend. Don't shut me out like that."

I couldn't go there. I gave the slightest shake of my head and pursed my lips. "How's it look?" I asked, referring to my ankle.

He sighed, not liking how I ignored his question. "It's swollen. The color isn't great, either. I'm going to get more ice, okay." He gently set my foot down and returned a few minutes later with a bag of ice wrapped in a dishcloth, then gently picked my feet up again to sit back down. He held the ice to my ankle, and I again winced with the cold impact.

"I'm sorry," he said.

"It's okay."

"No, it's not. Did it hurt?" Fuck, he wasn't talking about my ankle. How did he always read me so well?

"It was the worst pain of my life. I was losing you and then her. It felt like everything was tearing. It hurt so bad." I closed my eyes, willing myself not to cry.

"It was a girl?"

"I don't really know. It was too early for me to actually know, but I think of her that way sometimes."

"Fuck!" He ran his free hand through his hair. "I'm sorry. I should've been there. I'm sorry." Emotion clogged his throat. So often I'd thought of this as my baby. I was alone in all of it. Alone in my pregnancy and alone in my miscarriage. I hadn't taken the time to think about what kind of pain Linc would be in. He lost a child too, and although it wasn't torn from his womb, I knew he was feeling the pain.

"A daughter. Fuck, do you know how often I've dreamed of what our kids would look like? I wonder if she would've had your hazel eyes or my brown eyes. I wonder if she would've had your lips?"

"My lips? Our daughter would've had yours. Yours are perfect. My upper lip is bigger than my bottom. Not yours, though, yours are perfect."

"I'll beg to differ with you on that one. I'd want her to look just like you. I'd want her to have your smile."

I smiled at him, feeling a strange peace talking about her with him. Maybe I was denying myself by not talking about her.

"Of course, I'd want her to have my temper," he deadpanned.

"Hey!" I bent forward and smacked him on his arm.

"I'm just teasing. There isn't a single quality about you that I wouldn't have wanted her to have. She would've been amazing."

"Yeah," I sighed, "She would've."

"WHAT TIME IS IT ANYWAY?" I asked as Linc got up to put the wet rag and melting ice into the sink.

"It's just past midnight."

"That's it? This feels like the longest day of my life."

"Well, falling asleep when it's daytime but dark outside probably confused your body. How've you been sleeping?"

I sighed. After talking openly about what our baby would've been like, it seemed like walls that had been built were slowly crumbling down. "It's been hard to fall asleep, but once I'm asleep, it's hard to wake me."

"So pretty much like it's always been except you don't have me there to work you out before you go to bed."

I resented those words a little, even though they were obviously very true, so I squinted my eyes at him. He was at the sink, though, so he couldn't see me.

He walked back toward me, and I still gawked at those meaty thighs and how they made my mouth water. What was it with me and his legs? Never in my life have I checked out another man's legs. Then again, Linc has only ever been it for me.

I briefly thought of my failed date with Jet. He was super sweet, but if I was honest, he didn't do it for me. Not like how Lincoln had.

Lincoln tapped my forehead. "What's going on in that pretty little head of yours?"

Well, I wasn't going to tell him I'd been comparing how much more attractive he was than Jet. It wasn't even a comparison. That thought kind of made me mad. I mean, would there ever be anyone who could physically hold that same candle? I knew I would never love the same way again, but I didn't know if I truly wanted to be celibate forever. The thought of being with anyone else made me shudder, and I answered, "Nothing."

"Right. Well, are you tired now? Do you want me to help you fall asleep?"

My eyes got wide.

"Not like that, well, it could be like that."

"I don't think I can go back to bed just yet, but if you're tired."

"I'm good," he quickly answered, standing next to the fire. Damn, but I wished he'd put some pants on.

He turned from me and leaned against the mantle. *Jesus take the wheel.* Now I had his ass to look at. "How often have you dated since I've been gone?" He asked, dejectedly.

I was finding myself less angry the longer I was around Lincoln. If this was when he first got out, I might've lied just to get a rise out of him, but felt like I was moving past the anger, so I answered honestly. "Just the one you crashed."

"I didn't crash it on purpose. That was *our* bar. Which makes me wonder, why would you meet someone there?"

"It wasn't our bar."

"Wasn't it? Where else would we go if we were meeting someone for drinks? Are you sure you didn't pick that bar because maybe you wanted me to be there?"

"I didn't expect you to be in there getting smashed."

"But you did expect me to be there?"

"It's close to my apartment."

"There are other bars that are closer."

"Maybe so, but I'm familiar with Auggies."

"I don't think that's it. With those sinful sex kitten heels, I think that maybe you were hoping I'd see you out with someone and that it would drive me insane. I think you might not have even admitted that to yourself that that's what you were doing, but you did it all the same."

I didn't do that, did I? At the time, I hadn't thought I was doing that, but maybe he was right. Maybe I unconsciously picked Auggies in hopes I would rub his nose in it. Maybe I was being cruel. Maybe I wanted him to hurt like I'd been hurting.

"I didn't know I was doing that. I didn't think about it."

"Not consciously," he confirmed.

"No, I guess not."

"How long into our relationship did you resent me for being gone? Did it start with boot camp? Iraq? When the Army stop-lossed me? When I missed your graduation? When was it, Lols? When did you start to get angry at me and not talk to me about it?" His voice held a tinge of anger, and it caught me off guard.

I didn't want to do this. I mean, we just hashed it out about our baby. Did we really need to go over every reason our marriage failed? I glared at his backside, not giving him a response.

He turned from the fire to look at me, then grabbed the chair from the kitchen table and brought it over to the couch. Maybe he needed to put space between us too.

"After all those years together, you can't tell me?"

I didn't understand where all of his anger was coming from. I was the one who was always left behind. Not him. I was the one who lost her baby, I wanted to say not him, but that wasn't the truth, was it? He lost his baby too, and I let years pass, not letting him in on that.

I blew out a large puff of air, "Fine. You want to do this, then we can do it."

"Yes, I fucking think it's about damn time I learn all the ways my wife secretly resented me."

Oh, now I was pissed. He had no right to come at me that way. None.

"Oh, yeah. All the ways I resented you, huh? How about all the times you chose to leave? I wasn't mad when you left for boot camp, disappointed maybe because we wouldn't be together. Disappointed because I was in love and was alone in high school. Jealous of my friends whose boyfriends were able to take them to prom, and not their boyfriend's brothers. I love them, I do. But Trey was already making it big at Florida State. People knew him. My prom became a fan moment for him. It sucked."

"So, you're pissed because you weren't the center of attention at prom how many years ago?"

That just pissed me off more! "No, ass, it pissed me off that there was always a stand-in and not you. I know the Army was your job. I was still scared that something would happen to you, and, sure, it did suck going through so many things with you gone, but I loved you. So, I had to deal. Yes, I hated that when you were supposed to come home from Iraq, the Army made you stay, but I had no control over that, and neither did you. I didn't blame you, but it sucked too. I missed you, and I was alone. Do you know how often my friends would go out and invite me as a fifth wheel? I hated that, but whatever, I chose that for myself because I loved you. Did it fucking suck graduating from college, and you weren't there? Yes, that fucking sucked too. Then grad school. I thought I'd get you back. I kept waiting.

"Sure, there were times you were home, and it was just enough to keep me hooked. There was always a promise of us finally being together, and when you asked me to marry you, I thought for sure you were going to make our life about us. But that was on leave, and I planned it all by myself."

"I thought you enjoyed planning our wedding?"

"I liked that I knew it would lead me to you. But I didn't have the support I wish I had. Then we got married, and I got to spend two weeks with you, then you were gone again. I know, I could've moved to the base then, but you promised you wouldn't re-enlist, and I thought it would be best to get my career started.

"Meanwhile, my Mom and Dad hated seeing me alone all the time. They'd come to me and question if this life was really what I wanted. No one understood how I could do it. How could I put my life on hold for someone? So, I didn't. At the time, I thought starting my career was me moving forward, but maybe it wasn't. I was just doing what I should've been doing and trying to be happy, even though half of my fucking soul wasn't with me.

"Then you were finally out of the Army. You and Ty had a good thing going with work. You were building the security firm, and it was amazing. Money was good. We were finally together. We were happy. Or so I thought, but then you always went to Alex when he called. And you chose, again, to go to Trey when I know that Ty and Marlene both offered. That is when I started to resent you. Everything else was just me trying to do what I could to make the best of a shit situation."

"A shit situation?"

"Yes, Linc! Being without my husband was a shit situation."

"You could've moved on base while I was enlisted."

"And given up my dreams?"

"We could've worked that out together. Found different ways for you to achieve them, so at least we were coming home together. Why did you never try to do that, huh?"

"Don't you dare," I hissed.

"You didn't talk to me about how you were feeling. You didn't talk to me about the shit your parents or your friends were giving you. You didn't fucking talk to me."

"Why are you pissed? You're the one who left me." I seethed.

"I'm pissed because you didn't talk to me. You are my world, and you closed a part of you off to me, and that took you from me."

"No, you took you from me," I retorted.

"Bullshit. You want to act like you weren't harboring resentments. But fucking prom, really? If you opened up to me and talked to me about what you were going through, maybe you and I could've come up with some solutions together instead of you resenting me."

"I didn't resent you. I was just alone."

"And you didn't always have to be."

"Let's talk about the biggest things then. You'd leave our bed in the middle of the night whenever Alex called for help. You left to help Trey in Florida when other family members were willing to step in. And most importantly, you went to jail for nearly three years after helping Alex do something that I begged you not to do. That was so many unnecessary years of you leaving me. Freaking years! You don't get to come at me like I have no right to feel the way I do when there were times that you could've made different decisions."

I was seething. Beyond pissed. I wanted nothing more than to get up off of this couch and storm out of here, but alas, I wasn't going anywhere with this ankle. Not having a grand exit as an option, I turned away from him and stared at the door.

A minute passed, then another. Lincoln wasn't saying anything until, in a deadly calm voice, I heard, "Trey tried to kill himself."

My eyes shot open, and I looked at Lincoln, shocked by this revelation.

"After Trey was hurt, he couldn't cope, and he took a bottle of painkillers, trying to end it. His football career was over, and he didn't know who he was without it. He didn't want anyone to know. He was embarrassed and needed help. I couldn't turn my back on him."

My mind flashed to the first few weeks after Trey's accident. He seemed so optimistic at the time.

"You could've talked to me about it. I would've kept his secret, even though it probably would've been better for everyone to know. We could've all been there for him. I could've been there for you. You were so used to doing it alone, Linc, that you didn't rely on me either. You could've talked to me."

"He made me promise," Lincoln said, and a defeated look coated his features.

"You made promises to me too, remember? Love, honor, cherish."

He put his head in his hand. "You're right. I should've confided in you. And you're right about Alex too. I just hate to think that if I wasn't there with him, he'd be dead, but we'd be together, and we'd have our baby. It's fucked up, choosing between people I love. I'm sorry, but I fucked up. I can't change it. I wish I could. I wish I could do a million things differently. I wish you were in my arms, we had our daughter with us, and this trip was a weekend getaway with our family. I wish it wasn't me trying to figure out where I went wrong and praying I don't lose the only real mom I've ever had, while my ex-wife shreds what's left of my heart."

I squeezed my eyes tight, feeling his pain. I know he felt like he was barely hanging on, and I pushed him there, but he'd pushed me too.

"I think you're right in that I should've talked to you more about how alone I was feeling. I don't know if that would've changed anything with where we are now, but maybe I got used to not having you to talk it out with, and that's on me too. I should've come to you with my feelings. I just wanted to be strong for you too. You had so much on your plate." I wasn't angry anymore. I was just trying to acknowledge where I could've been responsible.

A few more minutes passed with nothing but silence and the sound of the firewood crackling between us. "Why'd you come, Lola?"

Chapter Twenty-Two

"Why did I come?" I repeated. Was he crazy?

"Yeah, why are you here?"

"I couldn't let something happen to Marlene without you knowing."

"Why? You haven't spoken to her. You haven't spoken to Trey either. Or me. Why would it matter to you?"

"Honestly?" I asked, flabbergasted.

"Yeah."

I looked at him incredulously.

He continued, "Do you know how many men work for Ty and me?" Well, that was news to me that he worked with Ty again. I guess I just sort of figured that Ty would've dissolved their partnership when he went to jail.

"I didn't know that."

"You know Ty could make a phone call and make anything happen. My brothers should've stopped you and should've had someone else come."

That felt like a punch to the gut. "I would've come anyway."

"Why?"

"Why?" I repeated.

"I'm speaking English here."

Now, he was just pissing me off again. "Because I fucking love you, you idiot. You've been my heart since I was fifteen. Do you think I could let you find out you might lose your mom from anyone else but me?"

I swiped the back of my hand across my face. Tears had leaked with the admission that I loved him. Speaking those words out loud felt like they literally sliced my chest open. The pain in admitting my love for him almost felt debilitating. I watched his eyes flash as he heard my words, then soften as he witnessed how much pain admitting those words caused.

For some reason, my mind flashed to that first time we said I love you and how it came so easily for us then. Now it was painful, and I never would've thought all of those years ago loving him would hurt this much, but it did. God, did it ever.

"What are you doing?" I asked Lincoln as he got up and went to the dryer.

"Getting my jeans. It looks like it stopped raining. We could use some more firewood, and the supplies are running low."

He could tell how much pain our heavy conversation was causing me, so this was his way of letting it go.

I couldn't help but watch him as he pulled one leg on and then the other. The way his muscles moved as he bent was a sight to see.

Once he had jeans on, he moved to the bedroom and grabbed a hooded sweatshirt. I turned my head away. I was too exhausted, but even the most mundane things he did had a way of pulling my attention. I heard the door shut, and I sighed. This was all so very overwhelming. What *was* I doing here? Did I really think that I was strong enough to handle this? I was stuck between loving him and letting him go, and I wasn't sure how fair that was to either of us.

I stared at the fire, thinking I was exhausted—emotionally and physically. I also kept thinking about Marlene. I prayed that I could apologize for shutting her out and that she would understand why I did. The doctors seemed optimistic, so that was good. Maybe when I got back, I could help her more and rebuild that relationship. It wasn't her fault that Lincoln and I weren't together any longer.

I also thought about what he told me about Trey. Trey who got a scholarship to Florida for football. Trey, who got drafted into the NFL. Trey, who got hurt on the field and lost the use of his legs, and Trey, who was so devastated that he tried to kill himself? God, how did I not know this? He seemed so fine, so adjusted. Would it have made a difference if I knew then that was why Linc left for so long?

Trey was always so strong and so dependable. He was like this giant cuddle bear to me. The NFL was his dream, and we were all so proud of him. Hearing what he went through and understanding why he chose Linc to get him through made sense. Alex was, well, Alex, and Ty had lost his mom to suicide. I don't think anyone else could've helped get him to where he was now.

I had to let that go. I had to forgive him for that. Do I wish I would've known why and saved myself years of resentments and heartaches? Yes. But I love Trey, he's my brother, and he's Lincoln's brother. I had to be grateful that Lincoln was able to pull him out. I wish I'd known, though. Maybe I could now empathize with Lincoln on why he made the decisions he did, but that didn't mean I agreed with them.

I found myself yawning as I went over everything in my head. Eventually, I must've drifted off because the next time I blinked my eyes open, I could see early rays of light shining through the windows. The next thing I noticed as my mind became alert was the smell of bacon. I sat up a little. I was still on the couch, and there was a blanket thrown over me. Lincoln was in the kitchen in front of the stove. His back was to me as he stood with a fork in his hand. I could see him taking bacon from the frying pan, one slice at a time. As if sensing I was awake, he turned and smiled.

"Morning," I offered with a smile.

"Good morning. I made coffee. You want some?"

"Mmm. You're a godsend."

I watched as he took a few more pieces of bacon from the stove and then moved the pan to a different burner. I used to love when he would wake up earlier than me breakfast would be waiting for me. He'd run to the diner before I was awake. It was always my second favorite way to wake up. It wasn't hard to guess what my first was. He moved to a cupboard, grabbed a coffee mug, and filled it.

"There's not any of that girly creamer that you like, but will milk and sugar do?"

"Anything will do."

"The day my Lola drinks her coffee black is the day hell freezes over," he said cheekily.

"Whatever," I mumbled. Then it hit me, he said my Lola. I shook that thought away. I'm sure it was an accident.

He handed me the cup, and I took a sip, savoring it. "Thank you. This is so good." Then I immediately felt my bladder. I moved the blanket to look at my ankle that was re-wrapped. Linc must've done that while I was asleep.

He watched me do this and asked, "Does it hurt?"

I moved it a small amount and replied, "Not as much today as it did yesterday, but it's still tender. Do you think you can help me to the bathroom?"

He grabbed my mug from me and set it on a side table. "Of course." Then, just like that, he scooped me up and was carrying me in his arms to the bathroom. He set me down in front of the toilet where I stood on one foot. "Do you want to hold on to me, or do you have it?"

I smiled, "I think I can manage."

He nodded and left me to take care of business. Once I was finished, I leaned my weight against the tub to help myself up, then I moved to the sink. I found some toothpaste in the medicine cabinet and a toothbrush still in its packaging. I quickly brushed and while doing so, I gasped at my reflection in the mirror. Apparently, my bath last night didn't get all the dirt out of my hair. I could still see some mud along my scalp. After coffee, I would see if Linc thought the generator could handle the water heater heating enough water for another bath. My eyes were puffy, and I knew it must've been from all the crying I'd done yesterday. I splashed some cold water on my face, then tried to smooth my hair. It was all over the place, but I shrugged because what else could I do.

I opened the door, and Linc was standing there waiting for me. In another second, he swept me into his arms and carried to the small table in the kitchen. He had cleaned off the table, and he set out two plates with bacon and eggs. It looked delicious, and the way that bacon smelled had my stomach rumbling. My coffee cup was also right next to my plate. After Linc brought me to the bathroom, he must've immediately grabbed it up and set our plates out.

He sat down across from me, and I could tell he was waiting for me to dig in. I took my first bite of bacon, and I kid you not, it was the best bacon I'd ever had. There were rich smoky flavors followed by sweet, and it was cooked perfectly.

"This is delicious!" I grabbed my fork and aimed it at him before taking a bite of the eggs. "When did you learn how to cook?"

"Prison," he answered on a shrug as if it embarrassed him.

"You were a cook in prison?" I asked and took a bite of the fluffy scrambled eggs.

"I worked out in jail, and I occasionally had kitchen duty. There was this big-ass dude named Cedrick. I liked him. He reminded me of Alex and Trey, Alex's cooking skills but Trey's size and heart. He taught me a lot in the kitchen. You know, with you and Ma, I never needed to cook, but I actually didn't mind doing it once I learned."

His time in prison fascinated me. It was the only time in his life I didn't know much about, so I couldn't help but ask him more about it while we ate. "How often were you in the kitchen?"

"Maybe four times a week."

"Besides Cedrick, was there anyone else that you made friends with?"

"It's not my first day of kindergarten, babe," he smiled between bites.

"I know, it's just I feel a little better about you being in there, knowing that you weren't all alone."

He gave me a smile like he thought that was cute, then took another bite before saying, "There was a guy named Jax that I got along with. Both of us had to do that balancing act on which group to avoid and which one to keep close. You know that saying about keeping your friends close and your enemies closer. In there, it was all a balancing act."

I took a few bites while I silently replayed every bad prison scene I ever watched in HBO's Oz.

"I see those eyes of yours dancing. What's going through your head?"

"Oz," I responded.

He sighed, "Prison is no joke, but that shit was a day-in and day-out drama. Things could get messed up in there, but it wasn't always *that* bad."

I took another bite of bacon and decided to change the subject. "This bacon is so good."

"There was a butcher a few miles from here that a friend told me about. I stocked up before getting here. I just hope the power restores before we run out of fuel for the generator."

"Speaking of that, I noticed my hair is still pretty gross. Do you think the generator will be able to handle the hot water tank if I take another bath?"

"We can try. The worst that will happen is we flip a breaker."

"Thanks, that'd be good. Are my clothes clean too?"

"Yeah. I did the load on cold, though, so it might stain a little."

I shrugged, "It is what it is."

We finished breakfast by making small talk. I had to admit that I enjoyed the light banter. Yesterday was so heavy that I needed it. I made a grab for Linc's plate to stack on top of mine. Clearing the table was something that came second nature to me.

He placed his hand on top of mine, "Leave it. I'll get it. First, I want to look at your ankle." He moved his hand, scooted his seat closer to me, then bent and lifted my foot into his lap. The way his hands felt on my legs had that all-too-familiar intimacy. My body wanted to react to his touch. I could feel it starting, but I did my best to shut it down. He carefully unwrapped it. I could immediately see that it wasn't as swollen, but it was a lot more colorful. There were some dark greens, purples, and yellows on it.

"Can you move it?"

I moved it forward, it hurt, but I could do it, then I moved my foot from side to side. Again, it was painful, but at least it moved.

"I think a bath is exactly what you need. Heat first and then ice. Stay here."

"Not going anywhere, Captain." The words just slipped out. I didn't mean to say them. Captain was his rank when he left the Army. His eyes flashed, and I knew there was too much behind that. I knew he was proud of his military career and that there had to be a level of shame at having been a captain and now a felon. It was also something I'd occasionally call him if I was really close to coming, and he was holding back.

He moved about the small space, and I could see him turning off a few lamps. I was curious what he was doing, so I watched in fascination as he grabbed some pots, filled them with water, and put them on the stove. Then he grabbed a large pot, filled it with water, and brought it over to the fireplace. It barely fit, but he was able to angle the pot inside.

"What are you doing?"

"I'm boiling water. I think you're right. There's a good chance you won't have enough hot water, so I figured I'd boil some and get your bath started. That way, if it pops the breaker, I can add hot water to it."

"Thanks."

That was incredibly thoughtful. He'd been nothing but caring since I arrived here.

"Oh, I forgot to tell you. I called to check on Marlene again while you were still sleeping. They said she's conscious, and the doctors have been testing her motor functions. Her speech is impaired, and it seems she's having some difficulty with paralysis on half of her body. But she's alive, and it looks like she's through the worst of it. The plan is that they'll keep her for observation, then move her to a nursing home for care. Trey and Ty are already trying to figure out where the best place for her to go is."

"Wow, that's great news! Did you talk to her?"

"They held the phone to her ear. I told her I loved her and that you and I were stuck in the mud and that we'd make it there soon."

"Stuck in the mud, huh?"

"It's a wreck out there. At least the rain stopped, but there is no way, even if I get my truck out of the drive, that I'll be able to turn down that road. I'll check on the Range Rover today too."

I looked outside, "Do you think it's done raining?" The sun looked like it was intermittently passing between clouds.

"No clue, without service, it's hard to tell what the weather is going to do."

"Do you think we'll be stuck here tonight too?"

"I won't know until I see his Range Rover today, but my guess is yes. Even if I can get a car out of the mud, your ankle is an issue. I don't want you to get hurt while we try to leave, and what if we get in a vehicle and end up coming to another washed-out road? I won't risk anything happening to you."

THE BREAKER FLIPPED mid-fill-up, so I was extremely grateful for Linc's idea to heat water on the stove. I wasn't prepared for Linc to add water into the tub while I was in it—naked. Yes, he had helped me last night, but today was different.

The look he gave me was my undoing every single time. The way his pupils seemed to get larger and nearly appeared black, along with the smallest narrowing of his eyes at the corners, added to the intensity. He quickly looked away, and I knew he was trying to give me some privacy, but the look was there. I'd seen it.

He sat down on the lid of the toilet seat behind the tub. "This water's not too hot. I'll help you wash your hair."

Everything was different in the daylight when he could see the rising and falling of my chest, and I knew he would see the way my body reacted to him. I should've asked him to leave and told him I could do it, but I didn't do that. I stayed silent with my knees pulled to my chest and hoped I didn't give too much away. He poured warm water over my hair, and I tilted my head slightly back as he did. This happened several times as he poured water on my hair, then snapped opened the shampoo bottle and squirted it onto his hand. He gently massaged it through my dark hair. All the while, he was quiet.

I wanted to say something to break the quiet, but at the same time, I didn't. I wasn't sure that I could trust my voice not to give away my feelings.

His fingers worked through my thick tendrils, and he poured water on my hair, rinsing it. I tilted my head back further for him to get the shampoo out and heard his intake of breath, then felt a single finger trace down the side of my neck, hitting my collarbone. As if it didn't happen, his hand was gone, and he was standing. "I'll give you a few minutes to finish up. Will you call for me when you're ready?"

I swallowed back the lump in my throat and squeaked out, "Sure."

Lincoln left the bathroom, and I dunked myself under the water and held myself there for a few seconds. This caring, attentive, sexy-as-hell man was the same man I'd always been in love with. I came up for air.

This was the high. This was that feeling he always hooked me in with. I knew the lows; I reminded myself.

Why did it suddenly feel like I was trying to convince myself?

"I HAVE GOOD NEWS AND bad news," Lincoln said after coming in from outside.

I was sitting on the sofa, my hair was beginning to dry. Linc had given me another oversized flannel to wear. I asked about my clothes, and he said that he thought I'd be more comfortable this way, and he thought the jeans would just be difficult over my ankle. He gave me my clean underwear and a pair of clean boxer briefs that I wore as shorts. Truthfully, I didn't mind. He was right. It was incredibly comfortable.

I quirked an eyebrow, "What is it?"

"Good news is that the sun is out, and it seems to have warmed up some. The bad news is I'm not sure if I can get the generator restarted. So, we need to keep the food in the fridge cold as long as we can."

"I'm sorry. I should've just been fine with dirty hair. I could've forgone the bath."

"Who knows how long it would've lasted. Don't beat yourself up."

I nodded in response. "Hey, do you want to sit outside while the sun is out?"

I shrugged.

Linc approached, grabbed a blanket, and scooped me up. This carrying around thing was becoming ridiculous. I could bear a little weight on my ankle. I tried while I was in the bathroom, and it seemed like the swelling had gone down a little. It still hurt, but I didn't think I broke it.

He walked us outside, and it surprised me that there was a small porch with a few rocking chairs. I definitely hadn't noticed this when I got here. He set me down in one and covered me with the blanket, then sat down beside me. The sun felt warm, but not too hot that I couldn't sit here and feel comfortable for a while.

The driveway was muddy. Behind a large shed was a newer pickup truck, black with an extended cab, that I noticed for the first time.

I tilted my head and asked, "New truck?"

"It's one of the company's. Ty really expanded things while I was gone. It's weird, a few of these guys working for us have no clue who I am. Ty and I got so much of the business up and running, ya know? It almost feels like it's not ours anymore."

"Have you done much work?"

"No, but I will. Once we get back and see to Ma, I'll start trying to see to life again. I think this situation—as messed up as it is—that brought you here, has been good in a way. You know what I mean?"

I nodded and continued to take in everything around me. Besides a bunch of really tall trees, this cabin was completely secluded. I could hear birds overhead and the leaves swaying on the breeze, but nothing else.

There was something to be said about sitting in silence with someone. There was no need to talk. We just took in the quiet and enjoyed it. After a while of just sitting there, Linc got up to go inside. I didn't question him, but a few minutes later, he returned with a few mugs in his hand, and he handed me a cup of coffee.

"How'd you make coffee? Is the power back on?"

"No, I used a French press over the fire."

"You have skills I didn't know about," I teased.

He smiled in return, and we sat and sipped the coffee in silence until a cloud covered the sun, and Linc noticed me pulling the blanket up and around my shoulders.

"It's getting cooler again. Let me bring you inside. I should throw some wood on the fire and try to figure out something for us for dinner."

It couldn't be getting close to dinner already. Could it?

"All right, thanks for the coffee. I can carry the cups."

"Leave 'em. Mine's empty, and I know yours must almost be gone too. I'll get them later."

He brought me inside, and I sat on the couch while he moved around and added fuel to the fire. I watched as he pulled butcher paper from the fridge. "How's steaks and potatoes?"

"That sounds delicious."

Linc cooked our food over the fire, and it surprised me at how efficient he was doing everything. We ate, then afterward, he took me to the restroom when I needed to go. He cleaned up while I was in there and pretty much took care of anything I needed. We filled the night with light talk. We joked around a little and fell into an easy groove. When the sun disappeared into the sky, Linc made sure a few candles were lit as well as plenty of wood on the fireplace.

At some point, Linc found a deck of Uno cards, and we sat and played for a while. It felt odd to admit it to myself, but I was having fun. Which really shocked me. Not that I couldn't have fun with Lincoln, but never in my wildest dreams when I was driving out here to tell him about Marlene did I foresee Lincoln and I sitting around all day playing cards, eating, and joking around.

After a few hands, I yawned, and Linc asked, "Do you want me to bring you to the bedroom to lie down?"

"Sure. Thanks."

I wondered if he would come and lay down next to me. I wasn't sure that I would mind if he did. It felt so comfortable, and the ease in which we fell back into just hanging out should've surprised me, but in all honesty, it didn't. It never took us long to fall back to where we needed to be when he came home on leave. This was different, though. There was an intimacy, but there also wasn't. When he laid me down in bed, and I thought about the day, I felt the simplicity of us. Today was the start of a healing process.

I wasn't sure when I fell asleep, only that I was alone when I did. Sometime in the middle of the night, I swore I felt his arm around me, but when I woke in the morning, I was alone.

Chapter Twenty-Three

I woke up to the smell of fresh coffee in a cup on the nightstand. I sat up and took stock of the room. The sun was barely filtering through the window, so it must've been early. I moved my ankle, even though it was still wrapped up, to see how it moved, and surprisingly it didn't hurt as bad.

I grabbed the coffee and took a sip. Let's face it, coffee was my lifeline. I listened to the cabin and couldn't hear a sound.

"Linc," I called out, but there was no reply.

I stretched, drank some more coffee, waited a bit to see if Lincoln came back, then decided my bladder couldn't wait any longer, I needed to use the restroom. I climbed out of bed, put my weight on my good foot, and used the bed to steady myself. I tried a little weight on my ankle, and it sucked, but it wasn't horrible. I was able to hop and bear some weight to get me to the bathroom. It took me a little time, and when I finally got there, I had to go way more than I did twenty minutes ago. Thank you very much, Folgers.

I brushed my teeth and washed my face. My hair was everywhere, so whatever, then I somehow made my way to the couch. I felt pretty good about my ability to move around when I noticed a small light on in the kitchen, either Linc got the generator back up and working, or the power had been restored. I decided since moving hadn't been all that hard that I would see about making breakfast.

Inside the fridge, I found there was no more bacon, but there were eggs, lunchmeat, cheese, mushrooms, and peppers. It looked like I was making omelets. I brought the ingredients, somewhat clumsily, to the table and sat down to cut up some mushrooms and peppers. Luckily, there was a knife and cutting board nearby that I could grab.

The door opened, and I looked up. Lincoln came in carrying some wood. He had on jeans and a navy long-sleeved Henley. He carried several logs.

"What are you doing?" he asked, somewhat irritated.

"Making breakfast," I replied with a look that said: 'what does it look like I'm doing?'

I watched as he kicked the door shut behind him and brought the wood to the fireplace and stacked it. He brushed off a few wood chips, then made it to me.

"How'd you get over here?"

"I think my ankle is getting a little better. I was able to bear a little weight, and I used the furniture to get me over here."

He eyed what I was doing, let out a small breath, then grabbed a frying pan from the cupboard. "I'm sorry. I didn't mean to snap. I wanted to make it back before you were out of bed."

I let my defenses down, "Don't worry about it."

He grabbed himself a cup and poured himself a coffee.

"Is the power back on, or did you get the generator working?"

"Power came back on after you fell asleep last night."

"Yeah, and the road outside of this drive is still a mess, but I made it to the Range Rover and walked further down. It looks like the other roads aren't as bad. I didn't have the keys, so I couldn't drive it, but after breakfast, I'm going to go back down and see if I can get us out of here."

"How long have you been up?"

"I told you, I'm not sleeping that great. But I got a few more hours in than usual."

I felt bad. Here he was taking care of me, on barely any sleep, and somehow I felt like I was to blame. Maybe that wasn't fair of me, and I was being hard on myself. I wanted to make things easier on Lincoln. I suppose years of loving someone would do that.

"Why don't you try to sleep a little more after breakfast?"

"I'll never be able to get to sleep."

My next words were out of my mouth before I could stop them, "I'll help. I'll rub your temples and neck."

Linc closed his eyes and inhaled a deep breath. Then opened them and looked pained as he said, "That's okay. I'd like to try to get us back today."

I felt rejection sear through me, which made no sense since his mom was sick. Of course, he would want to get back to her. It was strange. I didn't even understand my feelings fully, but a part of me was disappointed. Maybe it was because yesterday was so comfortable and I missed that. I missed how easy we could be.

Lincoln turned on the stove to heat the pan. "I'll cook. Will you stay seated and put that foot up for me?"

"It's really not that bad today."

"Humor me then."

"All right, Linc."

Lincoln moved about the kitchen, and he took over my omelet making job. I let him because it seemed like he got some type of satisfaction by taking care of me. Maybe it settled his mind somehow? I wasn't sure.

While he cooked, he surprised me by asking about Griffin. "Tell me about your boss."

"Well, I already told you that we've recently become friends. We went out one night to this gay bar. Oh, my God. I've never seen anything like what was happening on stage."

Linc laughed as I replayed the wrestling scene.

"So, he never tried to put a move on you or anything?"

"Nope, but I wouldn't be surprised if he and Ellie have hooked up."

He nodded his head. "How about the guy you were out with?"

He didn't seem angry as he asked me about Griffin. "You mean Jet?"

"If that's the guy's name. Then yes, Jet," He said his name bitterly.

"I met him on the train. He was nice. He's in the same line of work as me, and we started talking a little. At first, I told him I wasn't at a place where I would date, but he sent me flowers, often, and I eventually said yes to drinks. That night I saw you out was the first time we were out."

He nodded. I know we'd mentioned this already, but it seemed like he needed to understand it all better. "Griffin actually helped me understand that I wasn't that into Jet. I was forcing it, and I think I was doing it because I want to be okay, ya know? I want to be happy again."

Linc nodded and turned his back to me, then plated up an omelet. I couldn't tell how that made him feel, and I didn't like feeling so disconnected from his feelings. Maybe that wasn't fair of me, but regardless, I became uneasy because of it.

We ate our breakfast, and unlike yesterday, I didn't feel comfortable at all. Something had changed with Lincoln from yesterday to today. I hated that I didn't feel like I could ask him about it, and something about his demeanor made me apprehensive.

Once we finished eating, Lincoln grabbed our plates and immediately washed them. He grabbed a hand towel, dried the dishes, and asked, "Can I take a look at your ankle?"

"Sure," I croaked out, swallowing my discomfort.

He sat down and placed my ankle in his lap, then slowly unwrapped it. "You're right. It's not as swollen. That's good."

I winced a little as he inspected it, but tried to hide my reaction as he began to re-wrap it.

"Before I go back out, do you want me to help you to the couch?"

"Sure." I began to stand, thinking he would help me walk, but was again swept off my feet and deposited on the couch.

It happened so fast, I barely blinked before he seemed to move away from me. He searched my purse and found the keys for Ty's Range Rover, then he was gone.

I sat there, stunned at the way Lincoln's attitude seemed to one-eighty. He wasn't rude. It was just off. I couldn't quite put my finger on it. Since we had power again, I found my phone and charged it. I didn't think I'd have power, but sitting there for a while, I was bored. Once my phone was powered on, I looked through my old messages and photos and finally settled on a sudoku game I had saved on the phone.

Eventually, after what seemed like hours, Lincoln returned. "How'd it go?" I asked immediately.

"It looks good. I'm going to start to pack up, then I'll piggyback you to the Rover. I see you've been moving around again."

"I couldn't exactly sit here for hours with nothing to do. I was fine."

"Right, so you want to change in the bathroom or bedroom?"

God, his curt tone was pissing me off.

"Bedroom. But what's with this attitude?"

"I don't want you to get hurt while I'm not here. I hate that you're hurt, and I hate that I haven't been able to get you the help you need. I also want to get back to Ma, and I guess I stayed up way too late with too much on my mind, so I'm sorry if I seem short. I guess it's just all hitting me."

My defenses dropped, and I reached my hand out for his and squeezed his fingers. I was trying to offer support, but Linc didn't squeeze my hand back. Instead, he let my hand fall away as he stooped down to pick me up. He then grabbed my clothes that sat folded by the washing machine and brought me to the bedroom.

His voice was intentionally soft when he asked, "Do you need help, or can you manage it?"

"I got it." And maybe it was wrong, but a part of me wished I needed him to help me, that he demanded I need him. Something was changing. Maybe it was forgiveness. Maybe it was his nearness. But somehow, after the last few days, I began finding myself wanting his touch. I felt less conflicted. I was opening up to the possibility of us again. However, Linc's sudden behavior made me draw back and second-guess myself.

He set me down and closed the door after himself. Changing was actually harder than I would've liked to admit. There was more than a little pain during all of my squirming around to get my jeans up and over my ankle. Once I was dressed, I waited for Linc to come and collect me, but after too much time passed, I got out of bed to see what the holdup was.

When I opened the bedroom door, he was at the sink with my muddy shoes. I'd totally forgotten about my shoes.

He noticed me in the doorway and turned off the water, dropping my destroyed sneakers in the trash can. "I'm trying to save these, but they're pretty much done for."

I shrugged because I could see he was right. He cradled me against him and gently deposited me on the couch, then went to the bedroom and brought back a thick pair of wool socks for my feet. "I should've thought about your shoes ahead of time. Now they're just a mess."

"It's fine. I don't know if I would've been able to put it on over my ankle anyway."

"The swelling looks a little better today, but when we get back to Chicago, I'm taking you to the ER."

"I don't think that's necessary. I'll just call my doctor and set something up."

He shot me a look that said over his dead body was I going to wait, and that look made me change my mind. He was right. I shouldn't wait.

"We'll do it your way," I said, changing my mind.

"Thank you. Are you ready for this?"

I bit my lip thinking about that road and how bad it was when I got here. "I'm ready when you are."

"Do you have everything? Your cell phone?"

I reached behind me and grabbed the phone off the side table where I left it. "I'm ready as I'll ever be. So how are we doing this?"

"You'll be on my back?"

"Pardon?"

"Piggybacking it."

"I know you're strong and all, but that's quite a way to carry me."

"I found a route through the trees that won't take that long."

I gave Linc a look that said, 'If you say so,' and I scooted a leg on one side of him. He grabbed my thighs, pulled me closer, and ordered, "Put your arms around my neck, and if you get tired or need to change positions, just let me know."

I slipped my arms around his neck, and he carefully stood as if he was making sure I had a good grip. "Lock your legs around me. You got this."

I held on to him, laughing a little at how silly I felt. As he opened the door and brought us outside, I no longer felt afraid. Being wrapped around Lincoln and having my body pressed so close to his, I felt aroused, and that terrified me even more than our upcoming journey.

He closed the door behind us, then locked it. He walked to his truck, put the keys in the glove compartment, clicked the locks on the truck, and then moved to the shed and put the truck's keys in an old coffee tin filled with nails.

I watched in fascination as he did all of this. He must've really thought it out ahead of time. We moved through the woods, and I briefly looked back to the cabin and felt a sudden loss. While we were there, it was just the two of us, and now, I had no idea what would happen when we got back.

Lincoln moved with precision through the woods, and he moved branches out of the way, being careful so they wouldn't sling back and hit me. He stepped over a log, and my body would shift on his, and I couldn't help my reaction to him. Suddenly, I understood how he felt while I was in the tub. This was pure torture.

"Are you doing okay, or do you need a break?"

"Fine," I squeaked out. Dammit, my voice was giving me away.

He paused, looked around, found a large tree that had fallen over and brought us to it, then angled back, so my butt was to the log, and said, "Here, take a break."

I watched as he moved to put space between us. Space I was no longer sure I wanted. My chest was rising and falling, and I struggled to keep my hormones under wraps. He looked up to the sky, took a deep breath, and closed his eyes as if asking for patience. Then he waited a beat as if he made up his mind on something and got closer to me. He braced his palms against each side of the tree, caging me in. "Your mouth says one thing, but your body is screaming another. Do you think I can't feel the quiver between your legs and your breasts pressed into my back—those nipples hard as a fucking rock—and I know it's not the weather? Careful what you ask for, Lols, I might give it to you."

I stared into the dark depths of his eyes, and I didn't blink or look away. My body was too wired. All of my feelings about where we were went out the window. My body took over and screamed, 'challenge accepted.'

"Fuck," I whispered, my voice barely audible as it was carried away on the wind.

"Oh, I intend to."

Chapter Twenty-Four

He was on me. His hand held a rough grip on my hair, and he kissed me. It was hard and unrelenting. My mouth opened up for him, and I wanted to press my body against his, but with his hand in my hair and the slight tug backward, I was at his mercy. He broke our kiss, pulled back more on my hair, exposing my neck and began kissing along the length of it. It drove me wild. I bucked my hips forward, not getting anywhere near him.

"I need to feel you," I pleaded, balancing myself with one hand on the tree and reaching out and bringing the other hand up and under his shirt. His skin was warm, and I ran my fingers over the sculpted ridges. I inched my hand higher, loving the feel of his smooth pecs. I wanted to run my tongue along his chest and taste every inch of him. I felt starved.

He let my hair go and pulled my shirt up over my head, exposing me to the elements.

"You're so fucking sexy," Linc grumbled, then bent low, taking my nipple into his mouth. He flicked the bud with his tongue and sucked, making me moan out. My nipples had never felt this sensitive, and I could feel myself becoming wetter.

"I want you so bad," I pleaded. My hand reached down for his buckle. I needed to slip my hand inside his jeans and feel his cock. My back arched as he took in my other nipple. "That feels so good."

"You're so responsive. You like that?" he asked, flattening his tongue against my nipple, then flicking it and drawing it in.

"Yes," I breathed.

He let my nipple go and leaned away from me as I pulled the leather through the loop and worked on opening the button. My hand fell away as he took his shirt off, exposing his mouth-watering body, and laid it flat on the log. I knew he did this to protect my skin.

"Turn around, Lols."

I looked at him questioningly.

"I don't want to mess with your ankle and those jeans. Turn around. Bend over the tree for me, yeah?"

I was panting and going crazy with need. "Yeah," I breathed out and did as he instructed and turned around. My good foot barely touched the ground when I felt him adjust me. "I don't want the tree to cut you up either."

"I'm good, Linc," I breathed.

He put a hand under my belly and lifted my hips. At the same time, his other hand pulled down my jeans to just below my ass.

He rubbed my rounded cheek, then moved his hand to the other side and rubbed that one too. "If we weren't against a tree right now, I'd have my face buried between your legs." He caressed my ass, getting closer and closer to where I wanted him to touch. I could feel my lips part as he moved across my skin, and I knew he was taking his time, drawing this out. He bent forward, and I felt his jeans against my ass, so I knew he hadn't freed himself yet. His chest pressed against my back, and my sensitive nipples dug against his shirt.

"Baby," I pleaded.

He kissed along my jaw and moved to my ear, then my neck, peppering kisses along the way. "Let me savor this."

He moved his body away again, and I felt his fingers run up between my folds. "Soaked," he growled.

"For you, Linc. Only for you. I need you, Baby."

He moved his hand away without slipping his fingers in, and I wanted to beg him to finger me. I needed something.

I needed him.

Then I felt it. His thick, long shaft slid up and down my wetness. He teased me without pushing in. With my feet dangling, I had no leverage to push back into him; I was at his mercy.

"My dick glides so nicely against this sweet pussy." He pushed his dick forward, and it slipped through my folds and hit my clit, making me moan.

"Lincoln," I begged again.

"Let me fuck you how I want to fuck you. Be patient, Honey."

"Fuck patience."

He chuckled, "I'd rather fuck you." And then he pushed inside of me, and the fullness made me scream out, what I wasn't even sure—it was just all the goodness—the fullness. I'd never felt so turned on in my entire life. He pulled back and pushed forward again, and it happened like that. Just that quickly. I came. I did it hard, and I did it fast.

"Jesus," I heard him pant behind me. "You gripping my dick after two thrusts; best thing I've ever felt."

He bent forward and grabbed my hair again, and I just knew he was going to fuck me hard. "Are you doing okay?" He asked, evidently concerned about how comfortable this tree was.

"Never better," I whimpered as he gently pushed in and out.

"Good."

He thrust deep and hard, and he did it relentlessly at the same time he pulled my hair back. Part of me wished I could face him, and another part of me craved the sexiness he was giving me. "Yes, Linc!" I called out again as I could feel it starting to happen. His hand wrapped around my hair, and he pulled back on it, making me cry out. I always loved it when he yanked my hair and rode me. There was power in taking what he had to give, and I wanted it. I wanted all of it.

He thrust in and out, then asked, "Fuck, Baby. You there? I'm about there."

"Take me there," I begged.

He went wild. So wild he placed his hand under my hip because I would've surely scraped myself. I ended up bracing myself on my arms, and I took him. I took every delicious thrust as he took us there. I climaxed so hard, I almost missed the beauty of Linc filling me up and releasing himself. The way he grunted and cussed as he was overcome with pleasure made me melt into him as I took his last few thrusts.

He pulled free, tucked himself in, and was immediately pulling up my pants. He turned me around, cradling me in his arms, as he grabbed my shirt and handed it to me. He leaned us against the tree as we both redressed.

"Are you okay? Did that hurt you?"

"Well, let's just say I'm glad you're carrying me because I'm not sure I could walk after that," I teased.

He smirked, then grabbed each side of my face and gently kissed me. "I love you," he whispered, and that look on his face from before we left returned. I didn't know what to make of it, but it worried me. It felt like walls were being rebuilt right before my eyes, and I had no clue why they were building.

"I'll just carrying you now. If you're sore, I don't think it'll be easy for you on my back." He cradled me to him, and I didn't protest. I went over everything that just happened—how good I felt in his arms—when he was buried inside of me—when it was just the two of us in the cabin. I wanted to forgive him. I felt myself letting him back in and wasn't fighting it, but the problem was, it suddenly felt like he was. All of this conflicted with the fact that he just fucked my brains out on a tree.

I was so lost in my thoughts that I didn't notice we made it to the Range Rover. He unlocked the doors and was depositing me in the seat. He was about to pull away to close the door, but I grabbed his arm and asked, "Are you okay?" He gave me a tight-lipped smile, and I knew that he wasn't.

The road was too narrow to turn around, so Linc drove in reverse. I was a decent driver, but I wasn't sure how I would've navigated the road. He did it with such ease. "Lols, belt," he ordered. I rolled my eyes, then did what he said. *He could be so bossy!*

We made it to a wider road, and he could finally turn us around. I found my sheet of paper from my trip here. "I wrote down the directions in case I lost cell service if you want to see them."

"Thanks," he responded and grabbed the directions.

We drove on in silence for quite some time, and it felt deafening. I was getting ticked, and the way my emotions were ping-ponging back and forth was quickly getting old.

Lincoln tried the radio, and after hitting the scan button for a while, he finally found an alternative rock channel that he settled on. Kid Rock came on, and then another song by him followed the first. I wasn't a fan unless he was singing that duet with Sheryl Crow.

I turned off the radio. Linc turned it back on. I shot him a glare and turned it off again. "What is going on? You just fucked my brains out, and now you're cold? What is happening in that head of yours?" I snapped.

He sighed, and I couldn't tell if he was going to give me more, then he didn't—not for at least another ten minutes, of which I spent glaring at him because I couldn't understand what was happening behind those eyes.

He sighed again, then began, "I thought it would give us closure. This whole time together has felt like closure, like we were getting to be at a place that was going to leave us as friends. Then the way you were pressed up against me, I couldn't help it. I just needed one last taste of you. I needed to feel you one more time, and I'm pissed that it's over—that I won't have it again. But you're right. Maybe we need to move on. To find some comfort in life. I know I'll never have what you just gave me, but I'm glad you gave me that one last time. I'm sorry I'm being a prick, but it was just more than I could handle. I was in the woods in the middle of nowhere trying to get over you, and there you were, right there, driving me fucking insane again. And I know it's not right, I know I should just be pissed at myself for all my fuck ups, but part of me is pissed at you."

My eyes got big, shocked at all the emotion coming from him.

"I know I fucked up. I did. But Lols, you didn't tell me we lost a child. You didn't give me that. You didn't let me grieve. And you left me there, without a word from you. You threw us away, and I don't want to be pissed at you. Talking things out and spending time with you, I thought I was getting closure, but then the way you felt, I just couldn't take it, and now it's there, burned into my brain, the reminder of what we had, but what we won't have again. And I have to be okay with that. We have to be okay with that. I don't want what we've been to ever be ugly. I want what happened to my Ma to feel like we got something out of it, that both of us can feel a little more peace."

I watched him, saw the sadness behind his eyes, saw the way he gripped the steering wheel, and I knew he couldn't handle more. I wasn't sure that I could either. I didn't want to cause him any more pain. I realized I'd been thinking about my feelings, but not so much about his, and this was hurting him. Hurting him was the last thing I wanted to do.

"Okay, Linc." I gave in. I didn't argue with him. I didn't fight. I let it be. He eventually turned the radio back on, and I didn't turn it off. We drove like that, barely speaking, and my heart felt like it was in my throat the entire time.

Chapter Twenty-Five

We made it to the hospital. It wasn't complete silence. Once we had a signal, Linc called his brothers to check in on Marlene, and I called Griffin and Ellie. Ellie had already talked with Ty, and she had also, thankfully, been in touch with Griffin.

Linc grabbed a wheelchair for me from the valet which I thought was overkill, then he waited with me until they checked me in. "I'm going to go upstairs and check on Ma. Will you be okay?"

"Of course I will. I'll text you when I'm done being checked out. I want to see her too, okay."

He nodded, bent, kissed the top of my head, then left me in the sparse waiting room. I was eventually called back and wheeled into a room, where I changed into a lovely blue and white cotton gown and explained over and over again to different people what happened. My patience was getting frayed. Finally, a doctor came in, moved it, saw how blue and green it was, and declared I needed x-rays. I could've told him that!

I waited, for lord knew how long, for someone to transport me. I was beginning to second-guess why I was in the emergency room and why I didn't just wait and call my doctor. Finally, a very nice, very large man who reminded me of Trey showed up. "Are you ready for a ride?" He joked.

"I'm so ready," I sighed.

"Sorry for the hold-up. A group of geriatrics were line dancing and went down like dominos. Broken hips everywhere."

"Really?" My eyes got big, and I suddenly felt guilty for getting annoyed by the wait time.

He laughed, "Na. I have no idea why the x-ray is backed up."

I looked up at him and smiled. He wheeled me to an elevator, and once it opened, I smiled hugely. "Trey!" I shouted as we wheeled in next to him.

"You're taking forever. I was just coming to find you and make sure you were okay. Looks like you found a matching chair."

"We're just going to x-ray. Come with me."

"That's why I'm here. Looks like your, 'I'll just go and come right back' turned into more of an adventure than that."

"You have no idea."

Trey looked at the man who was transporting me, "Hey, bro, mind if I tag along?"

The guy's eyes were big, and his mouth hung slightly open. It took a few seconds to answer Trey. "Dude! You're Trey Williams."

Trey smiled; I know he missed his football fans. He ran into them a lot more in Florida, where he used to play ball. "That's me."

The elevator opened again, and we all exited.

"Man, I watched you play in college and then in the NFL. Sorry about what happened to you."

"It's all good," Trey replied.

"You mind if once we stop, we take a selfie?"

"How about my sister takes a photo of us before she goes in?"

"Would you?" he asked.

"Of course," I responded. It made me happy to see Trey happy, and I quickly thought about everything I learned while I was at the cabin. If it wasn't for Linc, Trey might've killed himself. Linc did a lot more for Trey than just helping him adjust to his life in a wheelchair. We made it to the x-ray room, and the guy pulled out his phone, unlocked the screen, and handed it to me.

"What's your name, man?" Trey asked.

"Cordell."

"Good to meet you."

I took a picture of the two of them clasping hands, then another of them side by side, and handed Cordell back his phone.

The x-ray technician wheeled me into the room and closed the door behind us. "Ouch," she said, looking at my ankle. "That looks like it hurt. I'm going to move you up on the table, but first, is there any chance you might be pregnant?"

Oh, fuck.

I blinked at the technician, "Pardon?" I was buying time while I mentally thought about when I last had my period and how long it had been since Linc and I slept together when he first got out. I had my period weeks before that, and I should've had it by now. We didn't use protection. We didn't even think about it. We didn't again today either.

"I asked if there was a chance you could be pregnant."

"Um, maybe?"

The technician was thorough as she explained that lead would cover me to protect the baby and that the risks of not having an x-ray outweighed any risks to the baby. She had me sign a consent form. "Are you sure? I lost a pregnancy before. I don't even know for sure that I'm pregnant, but still, I wouldn't want anything to happen."

"Since it's your ankle, those rays won't go anywhere near your peanut, and we'll have you covered by lead, you'll be okay. I suggest you take a test, though."

"Thanks, I will."

I was moved to the table and covered while they snapped the x-rays. My mind was on none of that. I was in a fog as she helped me down and back into my chair.

"The doctor will review your x-ray and be in to talk with you soon."

I felt shell-shocked, and when I was rolled out into the hallway to an awaiting Cordell and Trey, Trey immediately picked up on my shocked state. "What is it, Lols?"

I tried to snap out of it. I wasn't even sure if it was true. What would that mean? Linc was trying to move on. He was angry at me. A baby. God. Why didn't we think about protection? Why didn't it even come up?

I shook my head, shaking off my thoughts as I got a look from Trey that asked again if everything was all right. "Fine, sorry. The doctor will come down and talk to me. How's Marlene?"

"She's doing good, Honey. Her speech is slurred, and she'll need rehab because one side of her body isn't working so great, but you know her. Her spirit is huge. She's a fighter."

"Do you need to get back up there? I'll be okay if you do."

"It's all good. Now you want to tell me why you look like someone kicked your kitty."

"I'd be happy if someone kicked my kitty. Have you met Izzy? She's the devil," I joked. I was trying to change the subject, and it seemed to have worked, that or Trey was just giving me a pass.

Cordell was quiet as we found our way back to the ER, and I could tell he was also picking up on the change in me.

He helped me onto my hospital bed and said to Trey, "It was really cool meeting you."

"If you post that on social media, tag me."

Cordell smiled, "Cool of you."

Then it was Trey and me. "So, did you pick the short end of the stick or something?"

"What do you mean?"

"Well, out of the three of you..." I trailed off.

"I wanted to give Linc some privacy, and Ty had to handle some business since he's been neglecting it for the last few days. What happened with you and Lincoln? Did you get yourselves sorted?"

"Is that what you think was happening up there?"

"That's what we hoped. When Linc called on the satellite phone, it felt like God was intervening."

"I don't know. I think for Lincoln, it was closure." Just saying that felt like a stab in my heart.

"What was it for you?"

"Way to get to the heart of the matter," I deflected.

Just then, the doctor came in. He turned on a screen and held my x-ray up to it. "I confirmed with radiology. Looks like you have a small break here." He pointed to a small bone in my ankle. It was hard to see the place where there was a break, but I could see it on close inspection.

"I consulted with ortho. We'll fit you with a boot, and you'll follow-up with ortho in a week. How's that sound?"

"Will I need crutches?"

"The nice thing about the boot is you can walk on it, but you should try to keep it elevated."

I turned to Trey, "Can you give the doctor and me a minute?"

"Everything okay?" He questioned.

"It's all good. I just have a question for the doctor."

Trey nodded and wheeled out of the room, but not before giving me one final skeptical glance.

"Sorry about that, but I was wondering if I could take a pregnancy test while I'm here?"

"No problem at all. Once we get you fitted with the boot, I'll have a cup left in the bathroom for you to leave a sample."

"Thank you."

"MOMMA!" I BURST INTO tears and hobbled over to the bed the moment I saw Marlene.

"I'm... o...kay," she stuttered.

I grabbed both of her hands and squeezed. "I was so worried. I'm so sorry."

Lincoln stood in the corner of the room, and Trey had wheeled in behind me. I ignored them. "Do you remember what happened before the stroke?" I hiccupped out my question.

She looked at me in confusion, and I could tell she didn't. "We were on the phone and we were in an argument, then you were gone. I'm so sorry, Ma. I love you, and I'm sorry if I haven't been there for you. I'm so sorry."

I felt Linc's hand on my shoulder. "She's okay. She doesn't remember a lot of what happened, but let's try not to stress her out."

I looked at him, and his eyes pleaded for me to calm down. I knew I needed to get myself under control. It was just I felt relieved that she was awake, and I felt overwhelmed by the last few days. I took a deep breath while I squeezed her hands. Her left hand wouldn't squeeze mine back, and when I looked at her, I saw that one of her eyes was taped shut.

"Br...eathe," she rasped out.

I bent forward, kissed her forehead, and released her hand. "What's wrong with her eye?" I asked Linc.

"Because of the stroke, it won't close, so they have it taped closed right now. They will come in and lubricate it, but the hope is that it isn't permanent. What did they say about your ankle?" He looked down at the boot I was now sporting.

"There's a break," I confirmed. "I have to wear this for at least four weeks and follow-up with ortho within a week."

"Lols." The look he gave me was tender, and I knew he felt bad that it happened when I was trying to get him.

He looked to Marlene and lightened the mood, "See, Ma. You can't be mad at her. She broke her ankle bringing me to you. I would still be none the wiser carrying on in the woods if it wasn't for her." He smiled at her then said low for me, "Why don't you sit down and rest that ankle of yours."

I took a seat near a large window and asked Trey, "When will they move her to rehab?"

"Probably in the next day or so. We found a place about forty-five minutes from here. It's got a great team of doctors." His head tilted towards Marlene. "I think she needs to rest."

"Lols, why don't I call you an Uber, so you can get some rest? Ma's going to be all right, but you look tired. We'll call you if anything changes."

I swallowed back the lump in my throat. I felt like I was being dismissed. Ma's eyes drifted closed, and I could tell that there wasn't much for her I could do. "All right," I said defeatedly. Linc pulled out his phone and hit a few buttons. "It looks like it will be here in about ten minutes. I'll walk you down."

I looked between Lincoln and Trey, and for the first time in all of our life together, I felt unwanted. Maybe they needed to lean on each other, but it felt like this was Linc drawing a line in the sand. He got his closure, and he was trying to separate us. Separate me from our family, and that hurt, especially with the knowledge that there was a good chance I was pregnant with his child, again.

I kissed Trey on his cheek, and he told me he'd call me, then Lincoln and I made the short walk to the elevator. He was putting distance between us, and I could tell he was doing it with purpose.

"Will you call me if anything changes?"

"Of course, one of us will."

One of them. Not Linc.

I swallowed back the hurt that caused. I could still feel him between my legs, and for me, it was more than a goodbye. For me, it was a beggining.

We made it to the front of the hospital, and I didn't get a chance to say anything else before Linc was staring at his phone, "Here, it's this black car pulling up."

He opened the back door for me, and I got in. "I'll call you," he assured me, and just like that, I'd been dismissed.

Chapter Twenty-Six

I was in my Uber for a total of five minutes before my phone rang. It was the hospital calling. I answered right away, afraid that something happened to Marlene.

"Hello," I answered.

"Hi, is this Lola Paige?"

"This is her."

"It's Dr. Markowitz, from the ER. I was just calling to let you know your pregnancy test did, in fact, come back positive. I'd advise you to follow-up with your OB. I see in your history you had a miscarriage previously, so you may be high risk. So, make that appointment as soon as you can."

I swallowed, "Thank you. I'll do that right away."

"Congrats, Mrs. Paige."

The rest of the drive to my apartment was a blur. I was both elated and scared. I rubbed my stomach thinking I would do anything to protect this baby. I had to stay strong. I had to put the emotional turmoil I felt with Linc out of my mind, and I needed to focus on the life growing inside of me.

We'd made a baby.

All of this hurt and pain between us and something beautiful came from it.

I took the elevator to my floor, grateful that it was working. Climbing the stairs with this boot would've been beyond uncomfortable. The elevator door pinged open, and to my surprise, I saw Jet pacing in front of my door.

"What the fuck," I mumbled under my breath. How had he known where I lived and how had he gotten into my building?

"What are you doing here?" I asked angrily. Him being here crossed so many lines.

"I... I wanted to make sure you were all right. I emailed you and hadn't heard anything, and then I heard from an acquaintance of mine that you haven't been at work. I was worried."

"How did you get in here? Better yet, how did you know where I live?"

"Oh, gosh, it was nothing weird or anything. I just wanted to make sure you got home safely that night after my set, so I followed to make sure you got in okay."

"That's weird. Jet, I think you need to leave." I pulled out my phone. "Jet, you need to go now, or I'm calling the police."

"The police?" he questioned.

"Yes, this all feels stalkerish."

"I just want to see if my girlfriend was okay. Why is that stalkerish?"

"Are you high?" I asked incredulously.

Something about the look in Jet's eyes didn't sit right with me. I backed up towards the elevator, not taking my eyes off of him. I also popped the mace lid open that was on my keychain.

He took a step toward me, then another. The elevator pinged, and the door opened. I held my hand up with the mace towards him. "Jet, stay back. I don't know what you think was going on between us, but I'm not into you. Plain and simple. Now stand back."

He held his hands up, "I meant no harm. I was just worried about you."

The elevator door shut, and I immediately made a snap decision to call Ty.

"Lola."

I cut Ty off. "I just got home, and that guy Jet was at my apartment waiting for me outside of my door. I'm scared."

"Where are you now?"

"I threatened to mace him and got back on the elevator. I'm walking off of it now."

"Go outside now and walk directly to the liquor store. Walk fast but keep an eye on your back. I'm staying on the line with you but will be there in ten minutes."

I did as he said, except it was taking me a second to get used to wearing this boot. I was a little taller on one side, and so my balance was completely off. I did my best to move quickly but was more than a little freaked as I walked outside and clumsily moved to the liquor store that was a few buildings down from mine.

"I'm here," I breathed, walking into the store that mostly sold alcohol.

"Who's working? Is it the pimply dude, or is it Amir?"

I was breathing heavily. "Amir."

"Good. Hand the phone to him."

"He has a line."

"I don't care. Walk right around them and tell him he has a call."

I swallowed. I'd never heard Ty like this. He was barking orders in this no-nonsense type of way that was far different from how Ty normally behaved with me.

I walked to the side of the counter right past a few people standing in line. "Amir?" I tried to get his attention, but suddenly my voice didn't want to work. I tried again, louder this time, "Amir, there's a call for you."

Amir was a Lebanese man who owned the store for many years. He was easy-going but wouldn't put up with much. He blinked at me twice, then took the phone. The person buying a forty of Busch shot me an annoyed look then said, "I'm in line here."

I ignored them and watched Amir as he spoke to Ty. I couldn't hear Ty. I was also freaked, so I kept looking back at the door.

Amir handed me back the phone. "Follow me."

"C'mon, dude," the guy in line yelled.

I followed Amir through a door that was on the wall behind the checkout counter. "Just sit in here, and Ty will be here soon."

"Thanks," I nodded, still too shaken up about everything.

Amir left, and I put the phone to my ear. "Ty," I sighed.

"I'm here, Honey. One of my guys called Lincoln. He's on his way too."

"What? Why would you do that?"

"Not keeping this from my brother, plus, we don't know much about this guy, and there is no one better than Linc to find out everything there is to know about a person."

"But he's with Marlene at the hospital."

"She's stable, Honey."

"But..."

"Trey's there. It's all good. I'm pulling down the alley behind the store now. I'll be there in a minute."

I sat there feeling jittery in my stomach. That was one of the strangest encounters I'd ever had, and admittedly, I was spooked.

Amir popped his head in, "My line is taken care of. Are you okay? Can I get you anything? A drink to take the edge off?"

"No," I shook my head in a stupor, "No, I can't have alcohol."

His eyes got big, and he broke out into a smile. "Ah, I see. How about ginger ale? Maybe the bubbles will be good for your Tifl." I had no idea what a tifl was.

"I'm fine, thanks."

Ty barged into the office and immediately lifted me up and pulled me into his arms. "Honey," he breathed into my hair as he spoke. "Look at your foot. You didn't tell me you had a boot on."

"I found out today that there is a small break in my ankle."

"Shit, Lols."

"You want to tell me exactly what happened, or do you want to wait for Linc?"

"I really wish you didn't call him. He's going to freak, and we've had a really hard day."

"No matter what is going on with the two of you, there is no way I couldn't call him. I love you, Lols, but we're brothers. I can't keep shit like this from him."

I nodded. That wasn't fair of me to expect Ty to keep anything from Linc. They were both business partners and brothers, and asking that of him wasn't right.

I felt Ty's hand on my own, and I realized he was prying my fingers apart. I looked down and noticed I was still gripping the mace.

"You can let this go now. No one will get near you. You're safe."

I let out a deep breath I was holding. I needed to calm down. I had a baby in my belly that I needed to consider, and working myself up wasn't helping. I closed my eyes and took a few more deep breaths. I was safe. My baby was safe. My baby that I'd yet to tell Lincoln about.

After how upset he was at the cabin about losing our baby, I wanted to make sure everything was all right first. I wanted to see my OB and then tell him. This was just a lot all hitting me at once.

I opened my eyes, "I'll tell you everything when Lincoln gets here."

Ty's phone rang, and I sat back down as he answered.

"Linc," he answered. "She's safe. I'm with her at the liquor store. I'll stay with her while you do a sweep. Call me when it's done."

He disconnected, and I focused on breathing and not freaking out.

"How's your ankle feel? That couldn't have been fun hustling over here on that thing?"

"It's all right. It just feels heavy, and like my balance is off. Plus, it's bruised still."

"Lincoln said you fell getting to him."

"I did. The road leading to the cabin was like a river, but I was already out of the car, so I didn't feel like I had a ton of options but to try to cross it."

"You could've waited in the car and turned back once the rain slowed. You could've found a nearby motel or gas station and waited it out until it was safe."

"But..."

"No buts, Lola. It was dangerous out there, and you ran right into a storm. Straight to Lincoln. I don't know what happened with you two out there, but I think it says something about the state of play that you were willing to brave that storm and go after him."

"We talked a lot while we were there," I paused for a second, "When we left, Lincoln said he was glad he got closure." I closed my eyes, feeling how painful those words were.

"Just saying, how *closed* do you think the two of you are since he's racing to your apartment right now to make sure you're safe?"

"I think he just feels obligated."

"You're kidding me, right?"

"As soon as I saw Mom in the hospital, he pretty much dismissed me. It was like he couldn't wait to get me in an Uber."

"Maybe..." he trailed off when his phone rang. "Hold on." He answered the phone, there was a pause, then I heard, "We'll be there in a minute," followed by him disconnecting. "Your apartment is clear."

"I have the keys. How'd he get in?"

Ty looked at me incredulously. "You know we all have that skill, right?"

I put my hands up and waved that entire line of thought away. Ty put out his hand to help me up, and we left the small office. Ty shook hands with Amir on our way out.

Amir smiled broadly at me, "Congratulations."

I gave him the slightest shake of my head, and my eyes pleaded with him to be quiet. Ty squeezed my hand questioningly, but I ignored him. "Thanks, Amir."

As we made the short walk back to my apartment, Ty asked, "What was that?"

"What was what?"

"You know what I'm talking about."

"No, I don't."

"I'm calling bullshit."

He opened the door to the apartment building, and I instinctually froze, afraid that Jet would be lurking nearby somewhere. Ty read my change in body language and dropped his line of questioning.

"I got you, Honey. You're safe."

We took the elevator up, and Ty gave a quick knock on my door, then moved inside, and I followed behind him. Everything looked normal, except one thing was out of place.

Lincoln.

He stood against the kitchen wall holding a purring Iz, and his eyes were trained on me. "No one was here when I got here. What happened, Lola?"

Chapter Twenty-Seven

To say I felt uncomfortable was an understatement. Lincoln had put me in a cab only an hour before, and here he was coming to my rescue. I felt Ty's hand at the small of my back. "Go on, tell us."

I rehashed the entire ordeal and watched Linc's fist tighten when I explained how Jet referred to me as his girlfriend and how I pulled my mace out.

"Then you called Ty, not me?" Linc growled.

I blew out an annoyed breath, "Two things, Linc. One, I have no idea what your phone number is. And two, you were spending time with Marlene."

"You saw for yourself that she's okay, and what do you mean you don't have my number? It's the same number I've had for years."

I squinted my eyes at him. "Why would you pay for a phone for years that you couldn't use?"

His voice seemed agitated, "So that when I was out, people I cared about could get a hold of me."

"But you called me using Ty's phone."

"That's because I didn't think you would answer my call."

"All right, kids," Ty interrupted. "Let's get back on track. What do you know about Jet?"

I dug through my purse and pulled out his business card, "Here, he gave me this on the train the first time I met him."

Lincoln put Izzy down, grabbed the card from me, examined it, and then handed it to Ty.

"What else?" Lincoln growled.

I told them about running into him with Ellie, the persistent flowers, and how I declined his advances several times until I finally said yes.

"That's a little bit of overkill, no?" Ty stated.

"That it is. I was drinking when I saw you at Auggies, but I got a good ID on him." Linc pulled out his phone and hit a few buttons. "Ray, I need a full background on Jet Ferguson. His last known place of employment is Sound Machine. No, I want to know everything about him. I want his habits. I want to know his every movement. Yes, full workup. Call me in ten, with the pre-liminary." There was a pause while he listened to what Ray had to say, then I heard, "Possible stalker on Lola," another pause and then, "Yeah, all hands on deck," and he disconnected.

I began to shake. This entire ordeal just threw me.

Lincoln, of course, noticed. "You're crashing, Lols."

"It's been a day."

"Why don't you lay down on the couch and put your foot up. That way you're getting some of the weight off. I'll get you a cup of coffee."

"No, no coffee."

Linc looked at me strangely, and I suppose I never turned down coffee. But I couldn't have caffeine any longer, and until my OB did an ultrasound, I didn't want to tell Lincoln. I saw how crushed it made him hearing he lost a child. I couldn't do that to him again. My hopes were up, and I didn't want to get his up and have something go wrong.

"Since when do you ever say no to coffee?" Ty asked.

"Since my nerves are already frayed. Coffee will make me jittery."

"I'm brewing a pot," Linc said, moving to my kitchen and opening the cupboard. "Lols, think about other exchanges you had with him. Was there anything else that was odd or off?"

"No, nothing. He's worked at a bunch of places in the same industry as me. It seems like he knows his stuff. He's friendly and outgoing. He has a small indie band. We talked on the train a few times. I ran into him with Ellie at a bar, and we had drinks that night. That's it. Oh, and we've emailed back and forth. I emailed him to tell him it wasn't going to work out with us."

"Let me see the email," Linc said after pressing start on the coffee pot.

"Sweetie, where's your laptop?" Ty asked.

"It's on the nightstand charging."

"I'll grab it." Ty moved to the bedroom to get it.

"When did you email him?"

I swallowed because a lump was forming in my throat. I didn't want to rehash this, but I suppose I had to. "I emailed him the day after Auggies."

Linc nodded; his lips were pressed tight together, and I couldn't get a read on what he was thinking.

Ty handed me my laptop, and I powered it on and quickly opened my email. I blinked. I hadn't checked my email since all of this happened; however, I had so many emails from Jet.

Linc stood over my shoulder, "Open the oldest one first."

I did and was surprised by Jet's response.

Lola,

Don't do this. We've barely had a chance to begin. Your ex is your ex for a reason. I believe things happen for a reason, and there is a reason we were on that train together. Don't give up on us. Let me see you. I know I can change your mind.

Jet

Lola,

I called your office, and they said you were on leave. Are you okay? Where are you? We should talk. Are you with him? You're with him, aren't you?

Jet

Lola,

I couldn't believe it when you said yes to going out with me. You're so pretty. I couldn't believe my luck. But I'm worried about you. Your ex was in prison. I don't think you should be around someone who was in jail. It's not the best thing for you. You're emotional and not thinking clearly. Where are you? I've been by your place, and your mail has been piling up. Will you answer me? Has he done something to you? Your phone is going straight to voicemail. I'm getting worried about you.

Jet

Lincoln's phone rang, "I'm putting you on speaker. Lola and Ty are here."

"Hey," Ray greeted.

"Hey, Ray," I replied.

"What do you have?"

"Not a whole lot. I'll email you his address. It looks like he moves every year or so. He's worked for a lot of places, the longest being a two-year stint.

He has decent credit, pays his bills on time. His record seems clean, but I found a complaint from a woman, Misty Rodgers. She retracted her statement, and nothing further was reported. Other than that, he's pretty golden."

"I want Misty tracked down to question her. Find out what really happened. This guy isn't right. I'm reading a chain of emails he sent to Lola that are more and more bazaar. I'm going to pay him a visit, but I need someone on Lola at all times. Ty, you're with me. Ray, get a phone number for Misty."

I looked at the time and noticed that it was approaching dinner time. "Why don't I call Ellie and have her come and hang out."

"What's Ellie going to do if he shows up?"

"All right. How about I call Ellie and Griffin? You do what you do, and I can find out from them if anything else weird happened that we should know about. Ellie's been here to feed Iz, so maybe she'll know."

"Ray, I'll call back if I need a man here. Lols, I'll call Griffin," Lincoln declared, hung up his call with Ray, then grabbed my phone, hit some buttons, and was standing there like he'd done this a million times before, then he was calling Griffin.

I couldn't hear Griffin answer but heard Lincoln say, "No, you've got Lincoln Paige. Lola's fine, but when she got to her place, that Jet guy was waiting for her and freaked her the hell out. I'm going to pay him a visit, but I want someone here with her until I get back. I can have one of my men here if you can't, but she's kind of shaken up, and it sounds like she wants a friend here. Can you get here?" There was a pause, then I heard, "See you in fifteen."

Lincoln handed me the phone, and I was still blinking at him, shocked that he just called Griffin and all that was happening. "I'm going to call Ellie too," I said, shaking myself out of my stupor. I dialed Ellie, and she picked up immediately, explained what was happening, and she told me she would be right over. Shortly after, there was a knock at the door. I moved to get up to answer it, and Lincoln shot me a glare that said, 'I better stay put.' I did what he said and laid there while he checked my peephole, then opened the door for Ellie and Griffin. Ellie rushed in, past Lincoln, and moved directly to me.

"My god, girly! Are you okay? What happened?" She grabbed me in a tight hug, and it was hard for me to see the exchange between Griffin and Lincoln because Ellie was Ellie.

"I'm fine," I said as she released me.

"What did you do to your ankle? And Jet? Who would've thought he was a creep? I didn't get that vibe at all. Are you sure you're all right?"

She threw question after question at me, and Griffin came over and gave me a hug, then turned to Ellie, "I'm sure we'll get the rundown in a few minutes once Ty and Lincoln leave."

"Look at my best friend, though. She's never broken a bone in her life. Me, I've broken several, so I know how badly they stink, but Lola's never had anything like that happen to her."

"It's a small bone in my ankle. I only have to wear this for four to six weeks. It's not that big of a deal."

"Are you ready?" Ty said to Lincoln.

"Yeah," he responded, then turned to Griffin. "You get a knock on the door, you check the peephole. You don't just open it. Anything weird happens, even if it's a feeling you call me. I'm calling you now from my phone." Linc pulled his phone out from his pocket, and he must've memorized Griffin's phone number because he dialed it without looking back at my phone. "Lola, keep your phone near you. Don't erase any of those emails. Give me your password, and I'll have the boys scour them."

Oh shit. LINCOLN1025 was on rotation. It was a force of habit to use the same password in a rotation; that way, I wouldn't forget. LINCOLN1025 was up, and I suddenly felt dumb for keeping it. He watched me for a minute, trying to decipher what was going on behind my eyes.

"I'll text you it." There, I could change it as soon as he left.

He kept standing there. "Are you going to do it today? That way, I can send it to Ray before I get in my car."

I sighed, grabbed my phone, found Lincoln in my contacts, and sent him the embarrassing text. His phone dinged. He glanced at it, then back at me, and I watched in fascination as his eyes warmed, and those beautiful dark brown eyes crinkled slightly around the corner.

He didn't say anything to the room to draw any more attention to me about the password, but I know it gave away too much. That after all of this time, I hadn't really let him go. Then again, maybe he just thought it was the same for years. No, he knew me better than that.

"I'll call. Don't leave her alone. If something comes up and you have to leave, call me so I can get a man on her." He again was barking orders at Griffin.

"I got this," Griffin confirmed.

Ty walked over and kissed my forehead. I expected Lincoln to do something similar, but he didn't. He nodded his head at me, then moved it in a 'Let's Go' type of way to Ty, and they left. He just left!

I blew out a large puff of air and stared incredulously at the door. Ellie sat down at the bottom of the couch, and Griffin blurted, "Girl, your ex puts alpha male at a whole other level. Hot damn, but the tension there."

"Right," Ellie agreed. "I've seen some intensity from Lincoln over the years, but that was a lot."

"Do you need anything before I sit down and you spill everything?"

"How about a glass of water?"

"I would want something a little stronger than that if I were you," Griffin suggested.

"Nope, water's good," I squeaked out.

Griffin poured me a glass of water and handed it to me. "All right, spill," he said, taking a seat.

"Wait, first, how did you guys get here at the same time?"

"Ellie's cab was dropping her at the same time I was walking up."

"It didn't buzz you?" I asked, thinking that it was odd that they showed up together and even more odd that I didn't have to buzz them in.

"It was propped open," Ellie admitted.

"It wasn't when Ty and I got back. My neighbors are dumb," I declared. "Why even have a buzzer on a door if they're just going to let whoever in?"

"Do you want me to call your management?" Griffin offered.

"No. It's late. I'm sure if Ty or Lincoln saw that on their way out, they would have closed it, and knowing Linc the way I do, my guess is he'll be having words with management."

Ellie nodded her head, silently agreeing that was what Lincoln would do.

I took another sip of water, then asked, "Where do you want me to begin?"

"YOU'RE PREGNANT!" ELLIE exclaimed. I just finished telling them everything, and I mean everything.

"I'm scared out of my mind."

"Honey," Ellie said gently.

Griffin stood and ran his hand through his salt and pepper hair. "That day we all had lunch, I was going to say something to you, but I stopped myself. I see that maybe I shouldn't have held back."

I thought back to our exchange that day when we got back and remembered the awkward way Griffin had said 'nevermind' to whatever it was he was about to say.

"Don't hold back now," I said.

"I don't know you that well, but for the few years we've worked together, up until recently, you've kept yourself locked up tight. You dress to perfection every day. You're one of the first in and one of the last to go. It hasn't been until Lincoln was released that you even seemed to take a breath. I mean this with all the care in the world, and getting to know you, I think you are a spectacular woman, but it is clear as day that your heart is with that man. It seems obvious that you're at war within yourself. Before I even met him, I knew you were in love with him. I knew you were hurt and lost, and I was trying to be supportive, but it's pretty obvious. And do you know what is even more obvious than that? It's watching you both in the same room. How you two look at each other, there's so much pain and want, it's almost painful to watch. Now, you're pregnant with the man you love's baby, and you didn't tell him right away?" He shook his head, "I don't get it."

I looked at Ellie because Griffin's speech made me want to cry. There were so many truths behind everything he was saying.

"What if something happens to this baby too? What if I lose it and he has to go through that pain?"

Ellie's gaze was soft as she patted my hand, then said, "Then you go through it together. Griffin's right. You've been tearing yourself in two. I thought that you needed to move on, but it's clear as day that neither of you wants that."

"Lincoln said he got closure. You saw how he left and didn't glance back. He's moving on."

"He's surviving," Griffin declared.

I wiped a tear from the corner of my eye. I hated that truth, but Griffin was right; saying he got closure was his way of surviving. If I wanted this life with Linc, all I had to do was reach out and take it. I'd already begun to forgive him at the cabin, and I thought about what would happen if I just let go of it all. If I was honest, yesterday with the two of us just hanging out, I was more content than I had been in a long time.

"I'm scared," I admitted again.

"Be brave," Griffin said, "And trust that he'll take care of you."

I nodded, taking in everything they had to say. I needed to trust in Lincoln. It was hard because I'd felt let down by him, and that messed with my trust, but I knew he loved me, and maybe I needed to just trust in that.

Ellie, sensing I needed a break from the heaviness of the conversation, said, "Let's see these insane emails from your stalker that are making Lincoln lose his mind."

I opened the emails, grateful for the weird distraction, and we read every email that Jet sent.

"He's a whack-job. I'm going to talk with Lincoln when he gets back and see if he wants me to call Jet's boss. I know him well."

I nodded. I'd leave all of that up to Lincoln. It was then my stomach rumbled, and I realized I hadn't eaten in a while.

"Do you have anything to eat in there?" Ellie asked, pointing to the kitchen.

"I probably should've gone shopping a week ago."

"I got this," Griffin said, pulling out his phone. "Hello, Antonio. You too. It's been too long. Indeed, a favor. Dinner for five. I need it delivered too. I know it's a dinner rush. I wouldn't call if it wasn't important." He smiled, and I could tell that there was some type of intimacy between Antonio and Griffin. "Thank you. Make sure your man uses the buzzer. The last name is Paige."

"A man with connections," Ellie said playfully, and I wasn't sure yet if there was anything between Ellie and Griffin. I'd gotten that impression a few times, but I hadn't had a chance to ask her about it.

We chatted, and they went over various conversations with me that I'd had with Jet to see if anything else seemed off. I mean, maybe we were blowing this out of proportion, and he was just not getting over the fact that I wasn't that into him? I wasn't sure. I mean, it's not like he really did anything but act oddly.

Our food came, and savory Italian spices filled the air as Griffin peeled the tin foil back on the takeout dishes. "It's served family-style. There's chicken marsala, meatballs, cavatelli, and stuffed peppers. It's the best in Chicago. No lie. Just wait until you taste it."

He scooped a little bit of everything on a plate for me, and Ellie made a plate up for herself. "When do you think these boys will be back?" Ellie asked, putting a meatball on her plate.

"I have no clue." Griffin handed me my plate, and I took a bite of the cavatelli. My eyes got big, "Holy shit, this is delicious!"

Ellie took a bite of the cavatelli before while she was in the process of serving up her plate. "Wow. It's so good. Griffin, you might have to carry me home later."

He chuckled, "I'll tell Antonio."

"That I have to be carried home?" She flirted.

"No. *That,* Sweet Thing, I'll be doing."

Wow, wow, wow. Something was going on between the two of them. I watched them through the most delicious meal I may have ever eaten. I wanted to ask Ellie what, if anything, was going on between the two of them, but I didn't want to ask her in front of Griffin. I knew he was bi-sexual, and that Ellie was pretty open sexually. She had lots of random hook-ups, and I didn't judge, although I hoped one day she could find her way to some type of happiness, and it wouldn't be just one and done. It was relatively quiet while we ate. The food was just that good that everyone simply savored it. Ellie grabbed my plate and brought it to the kitchen to rinse it. "I could get used to this—you two waiting on me," I joked.

Griffin followed Ellie into the kitchen, and I didn't miss his hand on the small of her back. I was focused on the two of them that I wasn't paying attention to the sound of the front door unlocking. Griffin's eyes darted to the door, and his body stiffened, then his shoulders relaxed as Lincoln and Ty returned.

"Did you find him?" Griffin asked.

"Yeah," Lincoln said, looking pissed off.

"What happened?" I questioned.

Ty walked into the kitchen and looked at the food. "Is this Mia Bella's?" Ty asked, grabbing a plate.

"Yes, the chef and I are friends," Griffin said.

Lincoln sat down at the foot of the couch. "Why don't you eat too? It's been a long day. I'm sure you need to eat."

"After," he grunted, and I could tell he was more than a little agitated.

Ty leaned against the wall and began to eat. Apparently, *after* only applied to Lincoln.

"He acted shocked that we were there. He said he didn't mean to frighten you, just that he had a friend mention that you hadn't been in, and he was worried. He said he was shocked when you ran off the way you did, and he meant no harm. He said he would stop contacting you and apologized if it scared you."

"Did you believe him?" I asked.

"Not at all. In prison, I met some real pieces of work who think they're smarter than everyone. In reality, they're just sick fucks, and I can't put my finger on exactly what it was about him, but I didn't trust him at all."

"I got the same read on him."

"Wow, when I met him with Lols, I didn't get that at all. And I'm a fairly good read on people," Ellie added.

"I know his boss. Do you want me to call him?" Griffin asked.

"Not now. Not yet, at least. Maybe tomorrow you can see if you can confirm that he is at work, that would help? I want one of ours to get inside his place." Lincoln said.

"You're going to break and enter?" I asked incredulously.

"Not me personally. But one of our guys is extremely talented."

"Why not just call the police?" I asked.

Ty answered my question, "And say what? That a guy you went out with came by to make sure you were all right? And when we confronted him, he said he would back off?"

I saw his point.

Lincoln let out a deep sigh, "I don't trust this guy. I'm staying on your couch, and I'll take you to work. You don't go anywhere on your own right now. If you need to leave the office, you call me ahead of time and one of my men will escort you. I'm not taking any chances. Something about this guy feels very off to me."

I nodded, "I get it."

"I'll have a word with our receptionist. If we get any calls that seem off or seem like they're questioning Lola's whereabouts, I'll make sure you know. I'll be in touch in the morning," Griffin told Lincoln, then yawned. "I think I need to call it a night, though. Ellie, do you want me to drop you off?"

"Sure," she replied quickly. Too quickly.

I squinted my eyes at her, and she mouthed 'later.'

Griffin walked to me and squeezed my shoulder. "Try and get some rest, and good luck."

Ellie moved to the door. "I'll call you tomorrow," she said, then gave Ty a hug and smiled warmly at Lincoln.

They left, and it was just Ty and Lincoln. "Linc, you should get some of this. It's delicious."

Linc nodded, got up, moved to the kitchen, and got himself some food. Ty came to me, leaned down and hugged me, then whispered, "It's going to be all right."

I think he thought I was freaked out about Jet, but I was also freaked out about the conversation I knew I needed to have with Lincoln.

"I know," I smiled warmly. However, I wasn't sure exactly how everything would go.

"I'm taking off too," Ty told Lincoln.

"I'll call you," Linc said without looking up from what he was doing in the kitchen. Then it was just the two of us.

Chapter Twenty-Eight

"Where do you keep the extra blankets so I can make up the couch?"

"In my closet on the top shelf."

I'd been stalling. Linc had finished his dinner, and we sat in a kind of awkward silence. I knew I needed to talk to him, but I wasn't exactly sure where to start. I didn't know why this had been so difficult for me either? I mean, we'd been together since we were kids. We'd had sex earlier that day. There should be no reason at all that I couldn't talk to him.

Lincoln came back from my closet, carrying a blanket and pillow. "Are you going to go to bed now?" He asked. "It's been a long day, and I'm wiped."

Going to bed would've been the easier thing for me to do. And it really felt like Linc was trying to put space between us, but really, hadn't we had enough of that? Griffin and Ellie were right, Lincoln was trying to survive, and I was doing a fine job lying to myself about where we were. It was time I forgave him, and it was time to make us right. I was scared, but I had to trust that he would take care of me, take care of us.

"Lincoln?"

He raised his brows at the way I said his name, like he knew a question would follow, and I should continue.

"We need to talk."

He sighed again, and I knew today had been emotionally hard on him, "Lols." The way he said my name made me think that he was done talking, but I had to do this.

"It's important."

He took his shoes off, turned off a few lights in the apartment, then resumed his seat at the end of the couch.

"Okay, what is it?"

"I don't know where to start," I bit my lip nervously.

He gave me another look that said I just needed to get on with it.

"At the cabin, hearing everything you had to say and spending time with you, I was beginning to forgive you and let things go. I liked yesterday and how comfortable we were. Then, when we were leaving and," I blushed, remembering how he fucked me so very thoroughly. "And well, you know, then you said you got closure, and you shut me out. And I was beginning to want us to move on from everything too, but not closure." I was babbling, and I knew it was because I was nervous, because the next thing I had to say was huge. "At the hospital when they sent me for x-rays, they asked me if there was a chance I could be pregnant. A few weeks ago, when we were together, we didn't use anything, and I didn't even think about it, because it was us and it was heavy, but then, I don't know. When she asked, I did the calculations, and I should've had my period. Then I asked the ER doctor to do a test, and he called me after I left the hospital to tell me my test was positive. He also said that I needed to make an OB appointment right away since I'd previously miscarried and that I could be high risk and I'm so scared. All I know is that you and I might get a second chance to be parents, but I want more than that. I want us to have it all—you and me, and the future we promised each other." I began to silently cry, and I wasn't entirely sure why. Perhaps it was an emotional overload. "I love you, and I'm sorry I didn't give you…"

"Stop," Lincoln demanded.

My heart was beating incredibly fast in my chest, and I had no idea what he was going to say. "Linc?" my voice broke, completely unsure.

"You're telling me you're pregnant, and you want us back?" His dark, soulful eyes seared into me. There was longing and hope all mixed with pain, blending together, and creating something beautiful.

"That's what I'm saying. And there's more."

"Go on," he swallowed.

I swung my legs off the couch and stood, then I moved to my desk. I opened the drawer, grabbed the divorce papers, and then brought them back over to Linc and handed them to him. He unfolded them, and I knew exactly what he saw.

"You never signed them."

"No. I tried. I just couldn't seem to do it. I kept thinking I needed to, but then my heart would ache, and I couldn't."

"You're my wife."

"I'm your wife." A sob tore free from me as I confirmed that we were still married. Lincoln grabbed my hand and pulled me down on top of his lap. He framed my face with both hands, and he stared into my eyes.

"I promise you, I'll never leave you again. I never want you to hurt in silence again. I want us to be open, and I'll do everything I can to make sure you and our baby never question that you're first in my life. I love you so fucking much."

"What if something happens to this pregnancy too? What if I lose it?" I voiced my biggest fear since I'd found out earlier that I was pregnant.

"Then we deal with that together. You never deal with anything on your own again."

I nodded and squeaked out, "Yes."

Lincoln kissed me, and it was everything. It was all the longing and desperation that we both felt. His lips were soft at first, gently nipping, then our tongues touched, and he sucked my lip into his mouth.

"I love you," I said in between kisses.

He peppered kisses all over my face, then he was hugging me, just holding me against him so tightly, I felt as if he was soaking me in. Soaking us in.

"I want to take you to bed and make love to you, but I want to make sure everything is okay first. God, I fucked you so hard earlier, what if it wasn't all right for you to take it like that?"

I wanted that too, but I completely got where he was coming from.

"Come on." Next thing I knew, I was up and in Lincoln's arms. He carried me into the bedroom, sat me on the side of the bed, and then undid the straps on my boot. "Let's get you out of this thing. I might think it's best that we wait for a doctor to give us the all-clear, but I still need to feel your skin against mine."

I readily agreed and whipped my shirt over my head. He just got the plastic part of the boot off, so I grabbed at his shirt. I wanted him naked just as much as he wanted me. We rid him of his shirt, and I ran my fingers along his smooth, hard pecs and licked my lips.

"I'm going to bite that lip," he grinned.

I did it again, teasing him.

"Jesus, I'm going to be hard all night, laying next to you."

I reached for his jeans and popped the top button while he pulled down the long sock underneath the boot.

"You don't think I won't be just as turned on lying next to you all night?"

"Take off your bra. I want to see my wife's breasts."

I closed my eyes hearing him call me wife, opened them and reached behind myself to pop the clasp on my bra. I slid the straps down, ever so slowly, one at a time, until my breasts were free.

"Lols," he groaned. "Lie back. Let me get you out of these jeans."

"Gladly, but first, why don't you take yours off?"

He smirked then, without delay, took his jeans off. I could see his thick bulge straining against his black boxer briefs. I wanted to reach out and stroke him through the thin cotton but heard, "Lay back."

I did as Lincoln ordered and laid back on the bed. He leaned over me, undid my button, slowly lifted my hips, and pulled my underwear and jeans down. He paused and went even slower around my ankles, and I loved that he was so gentle with the boot.

"Scoot to the top of the bed. I'm going to grab those pillows I brought out to the living room. You should try to keep that elevated while we sleep."

"How can you be thinking about sleeping right now?"

"Trust me, I want you. I've only ever wanted you. I want to be inside of you as your husband, not a broken man who's lost everything. I need to take care of you, though. I need to feel you in my arms, and maybe for once, in the last three forsaken years, I'll sleep."

I hated that for him. He was so tortured by everything that happened. I did as he asked and scooted up the bed while he grabbed the pillows from the living room. He returned, propped them under my ankle, then went back out and grabbed the blanket. I watched as he peeled his boxer briefs down and climbed in bed next to me. His erection sprang free, but suddenly I didn't feel like this was sexual. It was a base need for our souls to connect in a way we'd been depriving ourselves of.

He curled next to me. His hand held mine as he wrapped his body around mine. I could feel his length hard against my side, but it wasn't about that. Not at that moment. It was about our connection. It was about finding the other in the dark and holding on.

We were quiet for some time, and I would've thought Lincoln fell asleep, but his grip on my hand was still tight.

"We can get past everything. You know that, right?" He whispered, and I knew it would take time for him to have faith that I forgave him.

"I can't promise you that I won't be insecure sometimes about us. I know you, and you'll have a mind to that. I can trust that you'll do everything you can to take away that worry."

"I promise you, I will," his voice was filled with conviction. "I promise you, I'll never let you doubt where we are again or my love for you. And God willing, this life we created together is safe and healthy. I'll protect her with my life, and she'll know how much I love her and how much I love you."

I kissed Lincoln. It was soft and sweet. We both gently kissed one another. Our eyes were open, and it was like our kisses were a vow to one another. In the darkness, after we finally moved to just holding each other, we both had something we hadn't had in a very long time—peace.

Chapter Twenty-Nine

I awoke to Lincoln's mouth at my neck. He kissed me softly. "Wake up, beautiful." I nuzzled into his warmth.

"I don't want to get up yet."

"You have work, right?"

I groaned. I had work, and Griffin was an amazing boss, but I just missed plenty of work, and I really needed to get up and get my butt in the office.

"I'll start coffee," Lincoln moved to get out of bed, but I curled my body around him.

"I want to feel you for just a few more minutes," I mumbled.

My fingers brushed against his length, and he groaned. "I've been hard for the last six hours. You touch me, Baby, I'm going to explode."

My nipples reacted instantly, and I needed to touch him. I needed to taste him. I kissed his jaw, then moved my kisses further down his neck and then across his chest.

"Lols," he breathed.

"Let me taste you, Honey."

He moved the hair from my face. "You're so fucking sexy in the morning. It's my favorite when you wake up, your hair is all unruly, and you get this sleepy just fuck me already look."

"Mms," I mumbled, then moved lower so that his hard length was right there. I didn't wait. I didn't even use my hands. I just wrapped my lips around him and sucked. I bobbed my head for several pumps, then placed a hand under his balls and gently rolled them while using my other hand to pump his cock.

"Baby, that mouth of yours. Fuck," he hissed.

His hand fisted in my hair, and he was at his breaking point. I loved it when I made him wild, and this was the part that just did it for me. He thrust his hips forward and began to fuck my mouth. I slackened my jaw as much as possible, and when he hit the back of my throat, I swear I almost came. My nipples tightened, and I could feel the wetness between my legs.

"I'm going to come. You ready for me, Baby?"

I moaned in response as his hard shaft pumped in and out.

He groaned loudly, then he was coming, and I was swallowing.

Tasting him.

When he was finished, I circled my tongue over his shaft one last time and looked up at him. "Morning," I said, now much more awake.

He looked down at me with sated eyes, then grabbed me under my armpits and lifted me, so I was on top of him. "That was…" he paused, looking for the right word.

I bit my lip, knowing how it drove him wild. "I better be able to get into the OB today because I might be dying a little." He ran his finger through my folds, making me groan.

"Soaked."

"Mm hmm," I confirmed, really wanting him to touch me more.

"Promise, once we get the all-clear, I'll take care of you."

"I know. I'm just a little turned on here."

He kissed me lightly. "Promise. Now you want me to shower with you or get breakfast ready, so you have it when you get out?"

"If you shower with me, I'll probably die from needing an orgasm, so you're on breakfast.

He chuckled, moved me off of him, got up, walked to the bathroom to turn on the water so it would warm for me, then picked up Izzy, who was circling his feet. "Are you hungry, pretty girl?" he cooed.

I smiled to myself and got up to shower. While I washed, I thought about what a difference a day made. I remembered how lost I felt leaving the hospital yesterday and how, even though everything with Jet was bizarre and frightening, it brought my friends here who helped me work through my feelings with Lincoln. And now I had him back, and all the feelings that I had, as valid as they were, felt insignificant. We were going to be all right. We hopefully were going to be parents. I couldn't believe it. I rubbed my loofah over my stomach and prayed, "Please be okay, Baby."

"HE SEEMS LIKE A GOOD guy," Linc said as we got into the elevator, ready to head up to my office. Lincoln had just spoken to Richard. He explained I may or may not have a stalker. I was hoping not. Maybe it was all being blown out of proportion.

"He is a great guy. His wife and him just had a huge baby. I hope ours is a healthy weight, but not that big," I smiled, liking talking about our future baby.

"I'm going to talk to Griffin." He looked at his watch then back to me as we exited the elevator. "It's quarter till nine. Will you call the OB once nine hits, and I'll be in to see you before I go?"

"Sure thing, Captain," I grinned, then gave him a quick kiss. The receptionist who had been with the company for some time mouthed, 'Lincoln's back.'

He caught her saying this, grinned, then said, "Yes, I am. Listen, do you have a second?" he asked her, and I knew he was going to grill her about phone calls for me and giving out any information.

I walked to my office and got a few looks. It may have been the boot I was wearing, but I had a feeling it was more. Several people knew Lincoln, but I didn't think that was it. Since I gave Lincoln head this morning, I didn't have time to straighten my hair. I left it wild. He liked it, and it was easier. I also wore a light blue top with black pinstripe slacks. I never wore pants or colors. I suppose I'd been in a routine of sorts since Lincoln had been gone and today was day one of feeling a little normal.

I powered on my computer and got to work. Once the clock struck nine, I waited on hold for my OB. They didn't want to see me for weeks. Weeks!

I told them that I could be high risk, and they promised Dr. Brandenburger would call me soon. I worked for fifteen minutes and was relieved when my phone rang.

"Dr. Brandenburger!" I nearly shouted into the phone, "I'm so relieved to hear from you. I broke my ankle and took a pregnancy test at the hospital, but I need to confirm that the baby is okay since I lost my last pregnancy," I said all of that before she even got a word in edgewise.

"Hello, to you too, Lola," she laughed.

"Sorry. I'm just really anxious and scared that something could go wrong."

"That's understandable. I have a full schedule today, but considering I've known you most of your life, and I know how hard the loss was for you, I can fit you in on my lunch break. That's if no one has a baby. How's one-fifteen? Will that work for you?"

"Oh, my God, yes. It will work. Thank you. Thank you. Thank you," I repeated several times, grateful that she was going to take me today.

"I'll see you in a few hours," she said disconnecting.

It was at that very second that Lincoln walked in. "Was she able to get you in today?"

"One-fifteen."

"Good. I talked to Griffin. Your receptionist doesn't remember any calls asking about you. But it is a small industry, and it could've been an employee he spoke with. Don't leave. I'm going to stop by Ty's to shower and get some clothes, then I'm going to stop by and see Ma. Richard has my number, and I sent him a picture of Jet."

"How did you get a picture of Jet?"

"Babe." he looked at me like, 'How do you think?'

I waved my hand at him in a 'whatever' kind of way. "Come kiss me before you go."

He walked to where I was sitting at my desk and gave me a kiss to knock my socks off. I briefly heard someone walking past gasp, then I smiled at Lincoln, "I'll see you in a few hours."

"I TAKE IT EVERYTHING went well?" Griffin placed a bagel down in front of me.

I shot up from my chair and hugged Griffin. "It went so good. I'm still scared, but it was good, and we're going to see my OB today around lunch, so I'll need to take a half-day. Is that okay?"

Griffin smiled at me, "Of course it is. See, now you're evening out my numbers on 'the coolest place to work.' HR will be so happy."

I laughed. "With how much time I've missed, they'll be over the moon. I'll bring my laptop home and catch up on things. I'm pretty far behind."

"Nonsense. You and that hunk of a man have more important things to do."

"But..."

"No, buts. And it's nice to see you let go a little." He grabbed a crazy curl of my hair and quickly let it go, then left my office. I worked hard for the rest of the morning until Lincoln showed up a little after noon.

"You ready?"

"Yes, let me power down." I shut my computer off. Lincoln walked to me, kissed me, then asked, "Did everything go all right?"

"Yes. I'm going to use the restroom, and I'll be ready."

I did my thing, and we walked hand in hand from the building, then made our way to the parking garage and drove thirty minutes to my doctor's office.

The waiting room was empty. I figured since it was lunchtime, that was why. At one-fifteen, Dr. Brandenburger popped her head out from the back. "Good, I was hoping the door was you. All the girls are on lunch right now, so I'll have them get your insurance info and any co-pay you may have when we're done. Are you dad?" she asked Lincoln as we followed her down a corridor, passing by several closed exam rooms.

"I am. I'm Lola's husband, Lincoln."

"Nice to meet you." She gave Lincoln a warm smile then said to me as we entered an exam room, "I'll have you undress and change into the fabulous paper gown. You can leave your bra on. Undies off. Take the boot off too, so we can get a good weight on you. How did you do that anyway?"

"It's a long story," I shrugged, "But the break is small, so I shouldn't have to wear this for very long."

"Good. I'll give you a few minutes to change. Just open the door when you're ready."

She left the room, and I took off my top. Lincoln helped me with my boot and pants, and I put on that god-awful paper gown.

"This is so surreal. If you had told me yesterday morning that this is where we would be, I'd never have believed you," Lincoln said, opening the door.

"We'll do an internal ultrasound. This means I'll put the wand inside of you, and then we'll be able to see what's going on."

"I remember."

Lincoln squeezed my hand, knowing that must've been hard for me.

I sat on the table and placed my feet in the stirrups. She put a condom type thing on top of the wand then lubricated it. There was an ultrasound machine next to the bed. "Are you ready?"

I nodded, and Lincoln held my hand while she inserted the wand.

A hazy image appeared on the screen, and then there it was: a tiny little bean with the smallest heartbeat. She hit a button on the machine, and a thumping heartbeat filled the room. "That's your baby's heartbeat. Everything looks good."

Lincoln squeezed my hand, "I love you so fucking much."

He wiped my face, and it wasn't until he did that I realized I was crying.

"Everything is really okay?" I asked the doctor again.

"Your baby looks perfect. I'll print you some pictures, and we'll get you scheduled to come in once a month. Limit caffeine to one cup a day. No smoking or drinking and let's get you started on a prenatal. There are plenty over the counter, but sometimes insurance will cover it if I write a script. You can see what the cost is and decide from there. Since you had a miscarriage before, I do want to see you take one with higher folic acid. But since you've only had one miscarriage, that shouldn't increase your risk much. In fact, many women miscarry and never even know it. They just think that they had their period. If you experience any cramping or bleeding, call me, but don't freak out. Sometimes a small amount of bleeding is normal in the first trimester."

"Can we have sex like normal?" Lincoln asked.

"Yes, your wife's womb will protect that baby. You don't have to worry. You can have intercourse until the end, and when she is ready to deliver, sexual intercourse can actually help speed up the delivery process."

Lincoln gave me a look filled with promise, devotion, and so much love. We sat there watching for a few minutes while our little bean bounced around the screen. I looked up at Lincoln and saw tears shimmering in his eyes. "I'm so happy, Baby. Thank you." He bent and gave me a gentle kiss. "Thank you, Doc."

"Congratulations. Now, I have a kit we give to first-time moms that will go over some basic things like the dos and don'ts of pregnancy. It will also tell you what to expect during each phase. Since you're in the early stages of your first trimester, you'll probably be tired more frequently, and you can expect to have to use the restroom more regularly."

"You really think everything will be all right?" Lincoln asked again.

"It's understandable that you're nervous. Just remember that women have been having babies, since forever, and the female body is pretty amazing with everything it can do." She printed off a few pictures and handed them to us, then told us I could dress and that I should make my next appointment on the way out.

We drove back home, both of us beaming at each other. "Ellie and Griffin know I'm pregnant. Can we wait to tell my parents and Marlene? Not long, I just want to give it a little time until we're sure that everything is good."

"Understandable, but I have to tell my brothers. If they found out that Griffin and Ellie knew, but they didn't, they'd never let that go."

"Sounds like a plan."

I pulled out my phone and put it on speaker. "Let's tell them right now."

"I told Ty we worked things out last night when I saw him earlier, so let's call him first and then Trey."

I couldn't help my excitement as I hit call on Ty's name.

"Everything all right, Lols?"

"Yes. Hey, actually, I'm in the car with Lincoln, and you're on speaker."

"Things are going good then?" he asked, chuckling.

"We got something we want to share with you," Lincoln said.

"I got some news too, I need to brief you on. I was just going to call you."

"Fuck. That bad?"

"Jet didn't show up at work today. Griffin reported that Jet's boss said he's been sketchy with attendance. I also got a lead on that woman who filed a report against him."

"Good. We'll follow-up on that tomorrow. Right now, Lola and I have something to tell you."

"So remember when I saw Lincoln when he first got out? Well, we slept together, and you're going to be an uncle. Surprise!"

There was a long moment of silence, then, "No, shit? That's amazing. Happy for you both."

"I'm going to call Trey next, but don't say anything to anyone yet. We want to wait until she's further along."

"That's the best fucking news." I could hear the grin in Ty's voice as he spoke.

"We'll talk tomorrow," Lincoln told Ty.

"Sounds good. Love you guys."

"Love you," we both said in unison and hung up.

We glanced at each other with huge grins. "I'll call Trey," he said after a few minutes of us staring back and forth at one another.

He told his phone to call Trey, then put it to his ear. "Hey, Brother. Are you still at the hospital? Can you step out into the hall for a minute? Yeah, everything is good... real good. I just want to talk to you about something, and I don't want you to talk about it in front of Ma." There was a pause which I presumed was Trey wheeling out into the hall. "A few weeks back, Lola and I slept together. It all felt like a goodbye at the time, and then when we were at the cabin, we talked a lot about everything. She knows what happened with you and why I stayed so long. We worked through that. You can let that burden go. It's not on you."

I squeezed Lincoln's hand; I had no idea he was going to talk about all of this, but maybe it was what he needed to give to Trey before he gave him our news.

"I know that was what you were dealing with at the time, but she's my wife, and I shouldn't have shut her out. That's on me. It is, Brother." There was a long pause, and I knew Trey was responding. "We worked through it. I thought we were gaining closure, but last night I found out we were working more towards forgiveness than goodbye," another pause, then, "Yes, it means what you think it means, and get this, she never filed." Lincoln's face broke out in a grin, and I knew whatever it was Trey said was good and that he was happy for us. "There's more, but I'm going to connect you to the car's Bluetooth. Lola's here, and we have something we need to tell you."

Lincoln hit a button on his phone, then we heard 'Bluetooth connected.'

"Hi Trey," I said.

"Hey, Honey. Glad you decided to take his ass back," he joked.

"You know yesterday when we went for x-rays? Well, you see, they asked me a question, and I wasn't sure, but then the doctor called me." I was babbling and just decided to spill, "I'm pregnant."

"Ah, fuck really! That's awesome. Congratulations. Great fucking news. I'm gonna be an uncle! I can't wait to spoil my niece or nephew." I heard the genuine excitement in his voice, and I was so lost in all the goodness, I didn't realize Lincoln was parking in front of my apartment building. "Damn, bro, you're going to make an awesome ass dad."

"Thanks. We're keeping it just between us for now until she is further along."

"Everything okay with the baby?"

"Yes, we just left the OB. I'll send pictures of our little peanut," I said.

"Baby's good. Strong heartbeat too. Just want to make sure before we tell her mom and dad and Ma."

"That might be the kind of news that's good for her recovery," Trey pointed out.

"Lola and I, we'll talk about it."

"Sounds good, Brother," Trey said.

"We're in front of her apartment. We'll talk later, yeah?"

"Before you go, I was going to call you. They're moving Ma tomorrow. She's doing good."

"That's good. I'll come see her in the morning before they transfer her. Are you going to stick around for a little while, or will you be flying back to Florida?"

"Shit. With a brand-new baby coming into our family, I might have to think about whether I can bear these Chicago winters again. Heck, I'm thinking I may need to call a real estate agent."

"I know an amazing interior designer who can help you with the inside of any place you buy." I was talking about Ellie, and he knew it.

He chuckled. "She'll be the first person I call when I find a place. I'll let you guys go, real happy for you."

"Bye," I said at the same time Lincoln said, "Later."

I WAS SITTING ON MY bed. Nervous butterflies fluttered in my belly. Lincoln was in the bathroom, and I just changed into a black lace teddy that was tight around my breasts and flowed from there, stopping just above my cheek line. I'd bought it for Lincoln before everything happened, but he never got a chance to see it.

We'd been back at the apartment for only a short time. Lincoln insisted that I eat as soon as we got back. I had a feeling he was going to be a bossy dad-to-be. The entire time we were both smiling at each other goofily, and it almost felt like we were those teenagers who first fell in love all over again.

The bathroom door opened, and Lincoln walked out bare-chested. Damn, my husband was sexy. His dark eyes heated as he took me in, and I scooted further back on the bed, anticipating him coming closer.

"You're a fucking dream, Lols."

I smirked at him, feeling brazen, "Why don't you come show me what your dreams are like, Captain?"

"Gladly," He pounced, and before I knew it, he was at the bed, grabbing my ankles and pulling me down the length of it. I squealed as he did this. "I'm going to return the favor from this morning," he licked his lips, and I swear I felt that right between my legs. He had the sexiest fullest lips and the things he could do when he worked my clit with that tongue of his.

He reached down, lifted my legs, and ever so gently, slid my panties down my legs, then began to kiss. He started at my bruised ankle, kissing it gently, then moved the kisses along the inside of my leg until he got higher and higher. I could feel his hot breath against my clit, but he didn't go there, not yet. He was building the anticipation, and it made me fucking wild. He kissed next to my clit, but didn't touch it, and I groaned because I wanted him to. He then lifted my nightie higher and placed soft kisses on my stomach. He moved higher and higher with soft sensual kisses, then he moved to one of my breasts and pulled the lace down, exposing my taut nipple. He sucked it into his mouth, flicking the hard bud with his teeth.

I moaned.

"Damn, Baby, your nipples were always sensitive, but now, I bet I could make you come with just my tongue on your tits."

"Mmhmm," I agreed as he moved to my other nipple, licking that one through the lace. My hands were in his short hair, and I felt myself pulling his head up. I needed to feel his lips on mine. He easily complied and kissed me. What a kiss it was!

It was soft at first, but then our passion and lust took over, and it was greedy and demanding, filled with promises of what we had to come.

Once our mouths broke apart, Lincoln kissed my neck, then my ear, and whispered into it, "Can't wait to sink into you, knowing that everything we ever wanted is right at our fingertips." As he said fingertips, I felt his finger slide through my folds then enter me, making me cry out, "Yes."

He lightly pushed his finger in and out, not giving me enough of what I needed. Then with his free hand, he grabbed my jaw and turned my face towards his. "I'm so in love with you, Lols. It's never changed. You're the love of my life, and today, you've made me happier than I could possibly put into words, so I'm going to show you."

Then he moved down my body again, and he showed me. He kept on showing me throughout the night.

Chapter Thirty
Six months later

"That's it. The last of the boxes," Lincoln said, walking back into our apartment. It was moving day. We would no longer live in the city. Instead, we were going to have nearly a forty-minute commute to work every day. I still hadn't made up my mind on whether I would return to work once the baby was born. I loved my job, but I'd wanted to be a mother for as long as I could remember. The closer my due date got, the more I found myself questioning if returning to work was what I really wanted.

The last six months were a dream. It was as if everything I'd ever hoped and wanted for Lincoln and I had all started to come to fruition. Lincoln had been in touch with my Mom and Dad more, and we started to rebuild that relationship. I think it will take them a while to get completely on board with Lincoln, but the fact that they have a grandbaby on the way has definitely changed things. Marlene got out of rehab about four months ago. Trey bought a sprawling mansion with an in-law suite, and after lots of persuading, she moved in there. We hadn't heard anything else from Jet. In fact, it was like he disappeared altogether. I was more than okay with that!

Ellie and Griffin, who I learned occasionally slept together but weren't really a thing, threw me an intimate baby shower last weekend.

We also visited Alex. That was one of the hardest things for me to do. I needed to forgive him. He was still my brother-in-law, and I loved him. Tears glistened in his eyes when he saw me, and I really wished I was allowed to hug him.

"Just one last thing," I said, reaching up on my closet shelf and feeling around for *Our Beginning*. It wasn't there. "Linc," I called. "Have you seen our book?"

Lincoln walked into the closet behind me and peered at the shelf, "It must've gotten packed away." I looked at the closet skeptically. I didn't pack the book on purpose because I wanted to carry it. I didn't want anything to happen to it during the move.

"I didn't pack it, did you?"

"I've packed so many boxes that I'm really not sure."

I didn't like that answer, but I had to hope that it was in a box. "Are you ready?" he asked me.

"Let me just do one final walkthrough to make sure I have everything."

I walked through the kitchen and opened the cupboards, then made my way into the bathroom, double-checking that it was empty there too. "It's all clear."

"Are you ready, Mrs. Paige?" He slid his arms around me from behind and circled my enormous belly. "What about you, Baby Paige? Are you ready?" I entwined my fingers with his. "Take us home, Linc," I said, giving his fingers a squeeze.

"Gladly."

We made the drive to our new house, and anxious butterflies rolled through my belly as we pulled up. We were on a cul-de-sac in a brick colonial that was meant for us to grow into. I thought it was too big at first, but Lincoln talked me into it. There were also a few other young families on the street, which I really liked. I hoped as our family grew, there would be neighborhood kids for them to play with.

We hired movers to take the majority of stuff. We had some of our more valuable things with us in Lincoln's SUV, so a lot was going on when we pulled up. There was a big moving truck with a group of men walking back and forth, carrying things into the house. Ty met them here and was dictating where things should go.

We got out of the SUV, well Lincoln got out, and then he came over and made sure I got out of the SUV okay. I had to admit; it was trickier with this basketball belly.

We walked up the small walkway, and before I knew it, Lincoln swooped me up into his arms. That couldn't have been as easy as it was six months ago. "What are you doing?" I slapped his arm playfully. "Carrying you over the threshold. But close your eyes, okay? I have a surprise. It's from me, Ty, Trey,

Ellie, heck, even your dad was here helping." I bit my lip nervously, nodded, then closed my eyes as Lincoln carried me inside.

"Can I open them now?"

He set me back down on my feet, holding me steady, "Now, Baby. Open your eyes."

I blinked, then blinked again, and tears filled my eyes, "What? How?" I asked, taking it all in. My living room was completely done in creams and beiges. There was a brand new cream sectional with a white farmhouse style square coffee table in front of it. A large chunky knitted tan blanket was over the side of the couch. There were matching farmhouse style end tables with new lights. There was a new rug that looked full and comfy with whites and creams mixed together. I could see our baby learning to crawl on that comfy rug. The fireplace was also white-washed, and there was a new beam on the mantle where pictures of Lincoln and I in black and white were up. Over the mantle was a large black and white of our wedding day on one side, and on the other side, there was a handmade wooden farmhouse style sign that read:

I love you more than words
I love you more than touches
I'll love you till the end of time

It was so beautifully touching. It was then I noticed on my coffee table sat Our Beginning. Next to that, there was a new book. I picked it up, unsure of what it was because it looked similar to *Our Beginning,* and on the cover, it read *No More Goodbyes.*

I opened it, and there was a new letter from Lincoln.

Dear Lola,

Today marks a brand-new journey for us. We're in a new house, surrounded by our friends and family. We're starting a family together, and soon our son or daughter will be here. I wanted to start our new life together with a brand-new picture. This book will be us forever. There won't be any goodbyes because it's you and me and soon to be our baby, and then, hopefully, more after that. To start this day, there is one thing I'd ask of you: will you marry me all over again? I want to renew our vows and start this new journey with us as strong as we can be. Our friends and family are in our backyard, waiting for us. Ellie is waiting for you upstairs to put on a dress. Marry me again?

I love you more than words

I love you more than touches
I'll love you till the end of time
No more Goodbyes
Marry Me
Again
Lincoln

I was crying and couldn't believe what was happening. I looked around and could see that there was more to my new house. It looked like it was out of a magazine. Everything was new, but beyond that, I could just make out a tent in our backyard.

"This is real?"

"Yes, Baby. Ellie's upstairs. What do you say? Will you renew your vows to me today and marry me all over again?"

"Yeah, Captain. I'll marry you all over again."

He kissed me, and it was intimate, but it was quick. "Go on up."

I walked up the stairs and had to pause. Everything was decorated. It was all light and airy. There was a console table and a mirror at the top of the stairs, and across from that, the baby's room was open. My dad was in there, and he was tightening a screw on a shelf.

"Daddy," I cried.

"Just finishing up some last-minute touches before I walk you down the aisle again. Don't you have a wedding to get ready for?"

I was standing in shock, and that was because I had the most beautiful nursery I'd ever seen. It was all creams and neutrals like the rest of the house, which was good since we were waiting to find out what we were having. The space was amazing, but even more so was seeing my dad standing there. He was dressed in black dress pants and a white dress shirt, but he had his tools nearby, and I knew this was because there were now beautiful built-ins that weren't here before, and they screamed of my Daddy's handiwork.

"Daddy, these are beautiful," I said, walking over to the built-ins framing the window. They were painted a soft white, and there was a window seat in between them with a grey and white chevron patterned cushion. There was also a shelf underneath the window seat filled with books. I pictured sitting here and reading to my baby, or the two of us curled up here together with a good book.

"Ellie put everything together. I just did the grunt work."

"Dad, it's amazing. I love it. Thank you."

Dad came close to me and gave me a kiss on my cheek. "I love you. I know it seems like your mom and I have been distant, but we just wanted the best for you, and we wanted you to be happy. I can see that your husband loves you, and he's doing everything he can to give my little girl the life she deserves. And that's all that any parent really could ask for."

I started to cry again. This was a lot—stupid hormones. I hugged my dad and thanked him again.

"You better get ready fast. There are hors d'oeuvres and drinks being passed around out there. Your momma and Marlene cooked. So you know it's good. You should've seen those two in my kitchen."

"Marlene came over to your house to cook?" My eyes got big. I'd never seen them spend time together, just the two of them. So much was changing and in such a positive way.

"She did. Now, go! Get ready."

I left the nursery and walked into my bedroom, which had a pile of boxes on one side.

"There you are!" Ellie exclaimed. "You were taking forever. So, what do you think? We were going to decorate in here too, but Lincoln said your bed was the shit and that he wanted to keep that. Those poor moving guys, half the stuff on the truck, I'm having them donate. Sorry, hope you weren't attached to your old sofa."

"Oh, my God. You sneak. I can't believe you did all this. I haven't even had a chance to go through all of downstairs, but it's amazing. You put the quotes from our letters on the wall. That is so pretty. You just threw me a shower, and you were doing all of this behind the scenes. It's too much, it's so pretty. Everything is amazing."

Ellie, never one for taking praise, waved her hand, "It was my pleasure. Now we have to get you in a dress and get some makeup on you. No more crying either."

I wiped my eyes. "That's going to be pretty hard not to do."

"You didn't open any of the spare bedrooms. Once you do, you won't love me as much, considering there are boxes to the ceiling."

"Boxes won't make me love you less. This is really amazing. I just saw my dad in the nursery."

"Girl, those shelves he did... I know he is retired, but I might just have to pull him out of retirement to work for me on the side. It's beautiful."

"It really is."

"I measured your belly at the baby shower, so your dress should fit."

"That's why you made us play that stupid game?"

"How else was I going to get your size, now strip."

I laughed, then started to undress. I had no problem getting naked in front of Ellie. She was the closest thing I had to a sister, and we long ago pushed past any of those barriers. Besides, while I took off my clothes, she took a white satin gown from a garment bag. It was nowhere near as fancy as my first wedding dress, but I loved it and couldn't wait to see what it looked like on.

"I bought you new pretties to put on underneath too." She tossed me a Saks bag, and I opened it and let out a small gasp. The lace cheeky panties and strapless white lace bra were absolutely stunning. I quickly put those on, well as quickly as a seven-and-a-half-month pregnant chick could move, then I was ready for the dress.

"Hold on to me for balance, and I'll help pull it up," Ellie offered.

I did as she told me to, and I was immediately in love with the dress. It hugged my curves but showed off my belly in a way that made me feel both sexy and beautiful. My shoulders were exposed, and there was a three-quarter length sleeve. I walked to the mirror. "You know me so well. It's amazing."

"Nope, this dress was all your husband. I just made sure it would fit. It looks amazing on you. Here, you're going to need shoes. Hope you can handle a heel for a little while." She handed me a box that said Prada, and inside was a sleek white pair of heels. "These are gorgeous." I put them on and had about one second to admire the dress before Ellie was sitting me down at a brand-new vanity.

"We don't have a ton of time, so how about we just put some product in your curls and work with what we have, and then we can do your makeup."

"Sounds like a plan."

I was quicker than I thought possible. There was a knock on the door, and my Dad was there. "Look at you, pretty girl. You're going to make that man fall in love with you all over again."

"I don't know if that's possible for him to love her any more than he does," Ellie joked. "I'm going to go tell them we're ready. See you in a few. You really do look beautiful."

"Thank you, Ellie, for everything."

She left the room, and it was just my dad and me again.

"Are you ready to do this?"

"I sure am." I looped my arm in my dad's and smiled as we walked past the nursery, down the stairs, and out the back door to my awaiting husband.

I stepped outside, and Mazzy Star's *Fade Into You* began playing. There were maybe twenty-five people here, but I had a hard time focusing on any single one of them. All I saw was my husband. Lincoln stood there, wearing a dark navy suit that fit him perfectly. If the waddle wasn't alive and real, I'd have broken out into a run to him. My Dad seemed so proud, and even though he'd given me away to Lincoln already once, somehow, this felt more profound. It felt like he was truly happy for me.

We reached the end, and Linc's smile was gigantic. That little dimple made me swoon every single time his face lit up. My dad kissed me, and it was then I noticed my mom sitting next to Marlene. They were holding hands, and they must've bonded. I loved that. It's taken years, but finally, it felt like my family was together. I quickly noticed Ty and Trey right next to them as well. Trey winked at me, and I turned my attention to my husband.

Fade Into You continued to play in the background, but the volume seemed lower. Lincoln finally spoke, "You're the most..."

"The most?"

"The most. My everything," this was whispered for my ears only. Then he spoke to everyone in the room. "When Lola turned sixteen, we danced to this song in Ma's backyard. I gave her a promise ring that day. I knew from the very beginning that she was it for me. But somewhere along that road, I failed to take the care she needed."

I squeezed his hand because this was a painful subject, one we've spent a lot of time working through, and I'd accepted that it wasn't completely on him either. I should've talked to him about how I was feeling. At some point in our relationship, I shut him out, trying to protect him from my feelings instead of leaning on him and working through my feelings.

Lincoln continued, "I'll never make that mistake again. Thank you, everyone, for being here. It was important for me today to renew my vows to Lola, but also, I want all of you to know that I'll cherish what we have, and I'll protect it every single day of my life."

"I love you," I mouthed.

Ty stood from the audience and walked up to us. I looked at him questioningly. "I have some vows for you two to repeat."

"Before we get to that part, I have something I'd like to add."

"By all means," Ty said.

"Hi, everyone," I said nervously to our friends and family.

I got a few chuckles at my nervous energy. A few waves and a few people said, "Hi, Lola."

"This is all a surprise to me and a little overwhelming. My house. It's amazing." I looked to Ellie, my dad, Ty, Trey, and finally Lincoln. "Thank you for all of this. Thank you. It means a lot that we're about to renew our vows, that you would think of that and do all of this. It means so much to have all of you here. I've loved Lincoln since I was fifteen. We've been through a lot together, and one thing I've always known to be true was that you would never intentionally hurt me. You've taught me so much, about myself, about forgiveness, and soon we're going to kick this parenting thing's butt." I smiled. We were both super excited. "Fighting against the pull of you was the hardest thing I've ever done. I know it caused us both pain, but I love who we are today. I love who you are. I can't wait to spend forever with you, Lincoln Paige. I love you more than words."

"I love you more than touches," Lincoln vowed.

"I love you forever."

"Till the end of time," he responded.

I stared into his eyes, then I didn't hesitate another second, I kissed him.

"Shoot, I guess you didn't need me," Ty joked.

Our kiss went on for several seconds, then Lincoln broke it.

"We better say the rest of our vows, even though that was good enough for me," he winked.

"All right. Repeat after me..."

THE REST OF THE EVENING was a beautiful whirlwind. Lincoln and I said our vows. We talked and laughed with our families. I danced with my dad. I'd danced with him at our first wedding too, but everything felt different. I felt acceptance from my family in a way I'd never had before.

I got a better tour of my house, which was pretty much amazing. I hadn't had a chance to take everything in before, but it looked like a magazine farmhouse, something you would see on HGTV. I was in love. With it all. My house, my husband, my baby in my belly, and my life that was laid out before me.

Once everyone left, Lincoln carried me upstairs. I wish I could say we had this night of wild and crazy sex, but the truth was, I was exhausted. He helped me out of my dress, laid behind me on the bed, and rubbed my aching lower back. It wasn't this gigantic romantic night, but it was what I needed, and I knew I could trust Lincoln to take care of my needs. Before falling asleep, I heard Linc whisper, "Forever." I smiled as I drifted off.

Chapter Thirty-One

I grabbed my keys from my purse, balancing all of my shopping bags in my hand as I waddled through the parking garage. I was leaving the mall after a last-minute baby shopping spree. I couldn't help but shop. It wasn't easy buying a bunch of neutral tone clothes, so I bought some boy's clothes and some girl's. I was going to keep the receipt and just return whatever we didn't need. They were just all so cute! I was thinking about this frilly baby dress when I beeped the locks on the SUV. I placed the bags in the back of the car, hit the button to close the trunk when suddenly I felt a sharp sting at the back of my neck, and everything went dark.

I awoke groggily. "Where am I?" I mumbled, unsure of what happened. I searched my memories and recalled the prick at the back of my neck. I attempted to feel my neck and had an 'Oh shit' moment. My wrists were handcuffed together. Now that I was coming to, I realized I was in a basement. Between my arms, there was a large metal pole that I was handcuffed around. Fuck, fuck, fuckity, fuck. I began to freak out.

But then I thought about Lincoln and how many times he tried to go over with me what I should do in a bad situation, and the first thing was to stay calm. He ingrained in me that panicking was the biggest mistake people could make.

I felt a sharp pain in my abdomen, and I whimpered uncontrollably.

"Ah, sleeping beauty's, awake." I heard and froze. I knew that voice.

Jet.

"What... what am I doing here?" I asked on a shaky breath.

"You're getting close to having our baby. I couldn't let you live that lie with that animal anymore. It's time you come home."

What. The. Fuck.

He was out of his damn mind. I had to play this right. I was shaking and scared, but I knew I needed to keep it together.

"Jet, you're not thinking clearly." It was then I felt that tight pain in my stomach again. I breathed deep and squeezed my eyes shut as the pain rippled through me. It was dark in here, and once I opened my eyes again, I could just make out Jet pacing back and forth watching me. What I saw shocked the hell out of me. There were pictures of me and Lincoln everywhere, walking into the office, renewing our vows, shopping at the grocery store.

There were tons of solo pictures as well. It was beyond obsessive. The rest of the room horrified me even more because a crib was set up next to a bed. Over the crib was a mobile that was made up of pictures of me. This was so fucked up. I needed to get the fuck out of here. I pulled at the handcuffs. I'd never get free.

"How long have I been here?" I asked, wondering if enough time had passed that Lincoln would be worried about me and start to look? He ignored my question and fixated on me, saying he wasn't thinking clearly.

"I'm thinking more clearly than I have in a long time. You and I got along so well. And a baby is on the way. We'll make such good parents, not like that criminal that you've been spending time with. I know he forced you to marry him the other day. What kind of man forces a woman..."

He was so fucking insane.

I continued to look around to see if there was anything that could help me figure this all out. I noticed a glass block window. I knew that it was the kind that helped you see out, but that you couldn't see in. Still, it told me it was dark outside. I went shopping around one and was at the mall for two hours, so I knew enough time would have passed that Lincoln would be going out of his mind.

"You'll see Lola. I have it all set up for the baby. We can be happy. Life will be good. Look at how nice I made it for us."

"Listen to me, Jet. You have to let me go. I can't have a baby here. It's not safe."

I didn't want to make him mad, so I stayed quiet, trying to calm my nerves because I was pretty sure that was a contraction. It was then I remembered I had on an Apple watch. Why he didn't take that from me, I had no idea. I could only guess that he just believed it to be a regular watch. I deep breathed, trying to calm my nerves as much as possible. Freaking out would only make my contractions worse. I tried to move my legs so they hid my arms. It was dark, and the light from the watch would alert him. As soon as I moved my legs, though, another contraction ripped through me. I had to try to message now.

Maybe if I could keep Jet talking, I could distract him while I called for help. "Jet, how did you get all of these pictures?"

"Oh, it wasn't easy. That criminal had you on lock down. I had to be quiet about it. I had to hide. Do you know how many times he's had men stalking you?"

He continued to talk, but I scrunched my hand behind my legs and pressed the side button, and slid the emergency bar over, hoping like hell, 911 connected.

I put it on silent so as to not alert Jet. He continued to rattle on, and I felt another contraction. "Jet," I said, becoming more worried with the severity of the pain. "I think whatever you gave me started contractions. You better unchain me. I'm pretty sure I'm in labor."

"Yeah, right. You have more time before the baby is born for us to get reacquainted. You'll be fine, and you'll deliver here. Everything should be okay. Women have been having babies for a long time."

"I don't think you understand." Another contraction rippled through me. I practiced breathing again, and he walked over to me. For the first time, I was able to get a good look at him. Gone was the put together hipster I'd met. This version of Jet was a disheveled mess. His hair was grown out and unruly around his face. It looked like he hadn't shaved in who knew how long, but that wasn't the most disturbing part. What disturbed me the most was this crazed Charles Manson look he had in his eyes.

"Oh, I understand." He grabbed me by the hair, pulling it tight at the scalp. "You think I'm dumb and will believe anything you say."

"No, that's not it all. Feel my belly. You can feel when I contract. I'm not lying. I need help. Please untie me."

I moved, hoping he would reach for my stomach, but another contraction rolled through me, making me jerk my head back, causing me a ton of pain. I began my breathing techniques again, but it felt pointless. "Oh, god. It hurts. Untie me. I'm going to have this baby. Please," I begged. "I need a hospital."

He released my head, then looked down in shock as my jeans became soaked. "Holy shit. Our baby is coming."

"It's not our fucking baby, you psychopath!" I roared. I couldn't fucking help it, that last contraction came on really strong, and I was pretty sure my water broke. There was no more trying to play it cool. I was beyond freaked out.

"Please. My baby is coming. Please, I can't let anything happen to her. Just let me go," I begged as another contraction rolled through me.

"No, this isn't how it's supposed to go!" He shouted back at me, looking lost and manic at the same time.

"Fuck!" I yelled. "It's early. It shouldn't be this early, please Jet. Take me to the hospital." I was crying and mumbling hysterically. "I'm sorry if somehow you felt led on. I love my husband. We were going through something, but I need him, and I need our baby to be okay. Please help me."

As if being awoken by a stupor, Jet looked down at me as if the situation was finally dawning on him. He reached in his pocket and grabbed the key.

"Yes, that's it, Jet. Unlock my cuffs, let me go. This baby is coming." Another contraction tore through me, and I wished I had it in me to fight, but the baby was coming, and it was coming soon. I was shaking and crying. It must've all been hitting me at once because it felt like I was going into shock.

For a second, I thought I heard a noise outside, but I wasn't sure because suddenly Jet was undoing my cuffs. "Don't worry. We'll cut the baby out of you."

Say what!

"No. Jet, no. You don't need to cut me. I just need to go to the hospital. I won't tell them about you. Please, just let me go," I begged.

One second Jet was there in front of me, and the next he was being slammed into. Lincoln was there, hitting him repeatedly. It looked like he was going to kill Jet as he landed blow after blow. "That's my family!" Lincoln roared.

Another contraction tore through me. "Lincoln," I shouted. "I need you."

Lincoln left Jet bloodied on the ground and came to my side. "I'm in labor. The baby is coming and quick."

Lincoln pulled me into his arms. "It's going to be all right." He pulled out his cell phone. "I've got her. We need an ambulance now. We're at that freak's address."

A contraction more painful than any before hit me hard. "They're coming quicker, Lincoln. The baby's coming."

"Fuck! Hang on, Lola. Ty, I need to be patched into the ER. Can you do that?"

It was then I heard Jet moan on the ground. "Lincoln, he's coming to. His handcuffs," I gritted out. "Use them." Then another contraction rolled through me. Lincoln saw the cuffs, his face got red, and I could tell he was holding himself back from killing Jet. He moved away from me and hand-cuffed Jet to the same damn pole that I had been.

He was still talking into the phone, and I heard him say, "This is Lincoln Paige, an ambulance is on its way to get to us, but my wife is about to have a baby. Her contractions are coming hard and fast. From the looks of things, her water already broke. Can I carry her upstairs? We're in a basement."

"Lincoln," I pleaded, "My pants, we need them off."

"Fuck, Baby, I'm carrying you upstairs. I can't let you deliver with this fucking psycho watching." It was then I noticed Jet was awake and staring at us through his quickly swelling eye.

"She's mine. Do you hear me? Mine."

I saw the look in Lincoln's eyes. I knew he was so close to going back to Jet and hitting him again.

"Ignore him. I need you."

"Let's go," Lincoln said.

I tried to do that Lamaze class breathing to help. "Okay. Fuck," I screamed as he lifted me in the air. He carried me as fast as he possibly could up the stairs, and pain wracked through my body with each jarring step.

He opened the door, and we were in a kitchen. I could hear sirens faintly in the background, and I hoped they were coming for us, except another contraction tore through me, and I knew that this was it. I had to push.

"Lincoln now. I can't wait."

Lincoln laid me down on the floor, peeling my pants off as well as my underwear. "You got this, Baby," he said to me, then spoke into the phone. "She's early. Going into her 29th week. It's too soon." I heard the panic in his voice, and I prayed that the ambulance got here soon. "It's coming!" I roared as I felt the overwhelming urge to push.

He put his phone on speaker and set it down. "The baby's coming. I can see it."

A voice filled the air. "They should be there in two minutes."

"Another contraction is coming, I can tell," Lincoln said to the woman on the phone. "Lola, Honey. It's okay. Push if you need to. I'm here, and help will be here in a minute. You're doing good. You're so brave."

I pushed even though I knew it was too early.

"That's it. The baby's head's out."

I pushed more and felt a huge amount of pressure release, then heard Lincoln say, "You did it, babe. She's here. We have a daughter. Doc, there's a lot of blood. Is there supposed to be this much blood?"

I blinked, looking at my daughter, who wasn't making any noise, and my world went black.

LINCOLN LAID NEXT TO me in my hospital bed and held me while I cried. "You're okay, Honey. You're safe. The police have him in custody. He was so sick. There were so many photos, and yours were just the ones on display. The police said they found evidence of at least three other women he stalked, and it seemed like each time he got more and more brazen."

"If you didn't have that TrackMe app, I hate to think of what could've happened."

"But I got there. I made it to you."

"But our baby."

"Shh, it's all going to be all right." He kissed me on the top of my head while I took a few more minutes to compose myself. I could tell he was beyond exhausted by the dark bags under his eyes. This all had to be scary for him too.

The door opened, and the nurse walked in. "Are you ready for your ride?"

I wiped my eyes, and Lincoln kissed me again, this time by my temple, then stood, leaving me alone on the bed as the nurse removed my blood pressure cuff. "Can you help with her fluids?" She asked Lincoln, and I knew she wanted him to follow us with the pole that carried my IV bag. We were waiting on toxicology still because whatever cocktail he injected me with wasn't something that came up right away, and it caused me to go into early labor. My body wasn't ready for labor, and I immediately started hemorrhaging following the birth. I needed immediate transfusions. It had scared the hell out of Lincoln, and I knew he was beyond panicked. I was moving past all of that, though, and was recovering.

We moved to my favorite part of the hospital. Well favorite for right now: the NICU. "Are you ready for some skin on skin?" She asked.

"Yes!" I couldn't wait.

Lincoln washed his hands and walked with the nurse to the incubator. "You can hold her," she said to him. "Just be careful."

The nurse disconnected monitors from our baby, and Lincoln gently reached in and picked her up. "You're so strong, my beautiful warrior. Keep fighting. Are you ready for your Momma?" He asked, kissing our daughter on her head and handing her to me so that we could have skin-on-skin while she nursed. Since she was so premature, she only weighed about three pounds. She was a tiny little thing, but he was right. She was a little warrior. She was so strong and brave. She was only on a ventilator the first day she was here. I wasn't awake for that, and I was glad I didn't have to see that. Just watching her in that incubator made my heart squeeze.

The doctors couldn't believe how strong she was and how developed her lungs seemed already at just twenty-nine weeks.

I unwrapped her and opened my gown. She squirmed her little body until she found my nipple. She was too young to truly nurse, so we supplemented with a small tube that went into her mouth, and I had to pump to keep up my supply. She'd only been at this a few days, but I knew when she could take the real thing, she would be a little pro. Lincoln tucked a blanket around her while she nursed, then took a seat at the end of the bed and watched us.

"I can't believe I could've lost this if I'd gotten there just a little later..."

My eyes pleaded with him not to go there, and I had a feeling it would take a long time to get over how stressful my delivery was, and everything Jet had done. Lincoln, being Lincoln, already held some unwarranted guilt. I knew he thought that he should've still had someone watching me, but after so much time with nothing from Jet, it seemed silly.

Linc's eyes softened as he lifted his phone and snapped a picture. "I look insane. What are you doing?" I knew my hair was crazy wild, and that I had dark bags under my eyes. They were starting to get a little better, but who could sleep in a hospital? Especially after the ordeal we'd been through.

"You two look beautiful, and staring at you, I guess I just had to capture how perfect you both are. Because, despite what we went through, I'm so lucky to have you both right here."

My heart melted. "I love you."

"Are we going to finally name her?" he asked, directing his gaze to the Baby Girl Paige sign on her incubator.

"I like Avery. She looks like an Avery."

"She's a little furball is what she is," he joked because her body was covered in Lanugo, which is a hair that coats the baby's body in the womb but usually is gone before birth if the baby is carried to term.

"Avery Harry Paige doesn't have a good ring to it," I joked.

"What about Avery Valerie Paige? Valerie means strong, brave, and fierce," he suggested.

"I like that, Linc. What do you say, Avery? Do you like the sound of that?" I asked my suckling baby. Her suck seemed to pull just a little harder on my nipple, and I declared, "I think she likes it, Captain."

She moved away from my nipple, and I took the tiny tube from her mouth. I would need to begin to pump my milk as soon as it was fully in. I wasn't looking forward to it, but I knew at least I'd have a nice back-up supply stored.

"Your turn," I said, knowing he enjoyed the skin-on-skin contact with her just as much as I did.

He pulled off his shirt, then carefully grabbed Avery, and he placed her on his bare chest, then put a blanket over the two of them. His eyes were warm as he stared down at our little sleeping miracle. I couldn't help it. I grabbed my phone that was tucked next to me and took a photo. I knew what he meant about it being perfect.

"I think my photo and yours will need to go into our new book," I suggested. "You look so happy."

"I am. You know, if you'd have asked me a year ago, I never would've thought that this kind of happiness was possible."

"I know what you mean."

And I did. A year ago, I felt like my days would always be a little incomplete and that I would have to just deal with it. I thought that I'd have to live my life with a part of my heart missing, but how wrong I'd been. Staring at my husband, holding our newborn baby, filled me with so much gratitude and love. I knew that no matter what kind of obstacles life threw at us, we would get through it because we had each other.

Epilogue

"Who's the best auntie in the whole wide world?" Ellie cooed, then blew a raspberry on Avery's belly, causing her to giggle.

"Momma, Elwee!" My daughter squealed, making me laugh. Today was her second birthday, and I always laughed at how she said Ellie's name.

"Don't look to your mom for help. I'm gonna get you!" Ellie blew out another raspberry, and I swear my daughter snort-giggled.

"Oh, my God!" Did she just snort?" Trey asked from across the room.

"I think she did!" I responded, smiling at the image of Trey holding our three-month-old son, Andrew Ryker Paige. Naming him was much easier as we named him after Linc's brother that he lost. He came out with a head of dark hair, and right away, I knew he had Linc's full pouty lips.

The doorbell rang. "I got it," Linc said, walking into the living room from the kitchen.

He opened the door, and in walked my Mom, Dad, and Marlene. Ever since we renewed our vows, my Mom and Marlene had become increasingly close. "Hi," I stood, greeting everyone.

Marlene practically shooed me off as she bee-lined for Andrew. "Give me my grandson," She said to Ty. You would never know that she had a stroke a few years ago with the way she moved.

"How about you give your son a hug hello first," Lincoln chuckled.

"Fine," she laughed.

"Suddenly the house is filled with grandbabies, and I'm chopped liver."

"Boo-hoo," Ty said, walking in the front door. His hands were full of presents and balloons. "Ty, Ty!" Avery squealed, forgetting all about Ellie. My mom and dad hugged us, and my dad asked where he could set his gifts down.

"I wish the weather held out for us. You can just set it down on the dining room table." We would've been outside, but it started raining a few hours ago.

"Thanks, Honey," My dad said, bending forward and giving me a kiss on my cheek.

The doorbell rang again, and this time, I walked over and answered the door.

"Griffin. Hi. I'm so glad you could make it. Who's your friend?"

Griffin smiled warmly at me. I stopped working after Avery was born. I just couldn't seem to care about it like I used to. One day I might go back, but I found I liked my time home with my babies. It filled me with more joy than I'd ever felt crunching numbers.

"This is Michael, trying the boyfriend thing on for size. Michael, this is Lola."

"He makes it sound like I'm a pair of jeans," Michael said, extending his hand.

I shook his hand, then they followed me inside. Griffin bent and gave Ellie a hug who was still sitting on the floor, giving Ty a side-eye since Avery just ditched her for him.

Ellie and Griffin had become amazing friends, and although they were both tight-lipped about what exactly they were to each other, I knew that the most important thing they shared was a deep-rooted friendship.

A buzzer went off in the kitchen; our appetizers needed to come out. "I'll get it," Lincoln and I said at the same time.

We walked into the kitchen, and Lincoln grabbed a beer from the fridge while I took out the bubbling spinach artichoke dip.

I set it down on top of the stove and shrieked as Lincoln grabbed me from behind. "You look good in these jeans," he growled into my ear, nipping my neck. I bit my lip, feeling his hard body pressed against my backside.

"You're insatiable, Linc," I said, closing my eyes. He kissed my neck again, and I could've moaned, but our entire family was in the other room. "Linc, everyone is out there."

"Keyword. Out there. Not in here." He kissed my neck again when Ty walked in carrying Avery.

"Break it up, you two. This little lady is asking for juice."

"No juice, Sweetheart. You had a little apple juice this morning," Linc told Avery, releasing me. She stuck out her full bottom lip, and her dark curls bounced around her shoulders.

"Maybe if you ask really nicely, your Daddy will change his mind since it's your birthday," Ty suggested.

"Daddy pwease?" Avery begged. Lincoln took her from Ty's arms, and she went willingly. There was one person my daughter loved more than Ty, and that was her daddy.

"All right, sweet girl. How about a little bit of apple juice?"

Avery gave Lincoln her big doe eyes and nodded her head. She had him wrapped around her finger, and I didn't blame him one bit. Since she was a preemie, she was smaller than a lot of girls her size, but that didn't stop her. She had this fierce little personality. Just then, I heard wailing from the other room, and I left to check out why Andrew was crying.

"Looks like it's feeding time," Marlene said, handing me my, now, fussy baby.

"You just ate an hour ago," I scolded.

"Here, Honey. Take my seat. I'll help Marlene in the kitchen to get the rest of the apps out." My mom said, getting up from a chair. I sat down with my baby boy, who stopped crying and grinned up at me like he knew exactly what he was about to get. I situated us so that my breast wasn't completely on display, and my greedy son quickly latched on. I had no qualms about nursing in public, and I tended to think people who did were out of their minds. Why try to hide the most naturally beautiful thing in the world? With that being said, I wasn't one to plop my boob out either. I could feed him whenever and wherever, though, and I loved that I could nurse.

Lincoln walked in the room holding Avery, who had a sippy cup upside down while she vigorously sucked at the juice. She let it go with a loud pop, then reached for a nearby balloon. Lincoln's eyes landed on me, and there was an appreciation that passed between us. I could see nothing but warmth and love on his features as he looked at me nursing our son. "I love you," I mouthed.

"More than words," he mouthed back, making me smile. I looked at him holding our daughter, who batted at a large pink balloon, then I looked around the room and saw all of our loved ones. A few years ago, I never dreamed that I would be this happy, that Lincoln and I would have two beautiful babies, and we would be surrounded by all of our loved ones under one roof.

My eyes then trailed over to our books that adorned our coffee table. *Our Beginning* was in our bedroom for the two of us, but I didn't open it that often. I found that I didn't look back the way I used to. We had so much more to look forward to.

Our table now held new books filled with pictures and moments beginning with the day we renewed our vows, to so many moments with our two children and all of these people we cared about so much. I would forever be grateful that Lincoln and I found our way back to each other, and that we didn't have a last goodbye. We had a new beginning, one that just kept getting better. I no longer doubted where I fit into our relationship. I no longer had doubts about anything, really, and that was because together, Lincoln and I made it work. It took time, and it took effort, but in the end, it was paying off with the best kind of reward.

The End
The Last Goodbye

Acknowledgments

Thank you for reading. There are so many books that are released each and every day and the fact that you've taken the time to read mine means the world. If you are so inclined to leave a review, that would be much appreciated.

Louisa Brandenburger, thank you for being my cheerleader and always there to support me. You were a Godsend to the blog, and I love that you know everyone's reading tastes. I'm going to invite myself to PA when this is all over! Chrissy Weston, thank you! I love that I can always ask you to beta, and you come through every time! I'm grateful for Renee and your support. Emily Kidman, you'll always be a book person who has made a world of difference to me. Nicole Mesco Reid, thank you for always being there when I have any kind of random book question to run by you. Thank you to the rest of the girls in The Blushing Babes Reading room, Sandy, Stephanie, Christina, Tera, Kerry, and Dawn. Many of our lives have taken twists and turns over the years, but you're my book people :). Thank you, my beautiful sisters. I love you. I value your opinion and your support. Jessica, Shana, and Misty, I love you. You keep me sane or crazy, lol.

Thank you to my family. Love you. Abby's Awesome Allies, you rock! Thank you, Give Me Books. Thank you, Kyleigh Poultney, for editing. Last, but certainly not least, Hang Le, you rock! You always create the most beautiful covers!

CHECK OUT THE PLAYLIST on Spotify by clicking here[1].

---

1. https://open.spotify.com/playlist/62SZsyyx4mEIrlXseHRdRg

About Abby McCarthy

Website
http://abbymccarthyauthor.com/

Twitter
abbyemccarthy[1]

Facebook
Facebook http://www.facebook.com/abbymccarthyauthor

Abby McCarthy is reader and a lover of words. She is a blogger turned author and released her first novel in May of 2014. She is a mother of three, a wife and a dog person. She has always written, sometimes poetry, sometimes just to vent about failed relationships, however in parenthood she has found her voice to help keep her sanity. Words have flowed from her, and with the support of amazing friends in the Indie community she has decided to pursue her dream of writing! She loves to write and read romance, because isn't that something we all yearn for? Whether it be flowers and hand holding or just the right tug on your hair. Isn't that what life is about? The human connection?

---

1. http://www.twitter.com/abbyemccarthy

Other books by Abby McCarthy

The Bleeding Scars MC

Cut Wide Open[1]
Explosive[2]

Standalones

Tainted by Crazy[3]
Current[4]
Series
The Wrecked Series
Wreck You[5]
Fight You[6]
Hurt You[7]
Stronger Than This[8]

---

1. http://www.audible.com/offers/30free?asin=B073G1XWQ6

2. https://amzn.to/2P7VS18

3. http://amzn.to/2i7Ldn7

4. http://amzn.to/1Oqt7W8

5. http://amzn.to/1JQU3wN

6. http://amzn.to/1FgJPFZ

7. http://amzn.to/1HGHi8D

8. https://amzn.to/2HrrmxE